One of the most popular s-f authors ever, and one of the great yarnspinners in any genre, Jack Williamson has surpassed himself with this new novel. A complex and breathtakingly adventurous story, THE MOON CHILDREN is also a deeply thoughtful exploration of man's potential for finding a place in the Universe.

Combining the fascination of Wyndham's THE MIDWICH CUCKOOS with the awesome insights of Clarke's CHILDHOOD'S END—Jack Williamson has produced a riveting future adventure tale that is ultimately unlike anything you have ever read.

The Moon Children

Jack Williamson

A BERKLEY MEDALLION BOOK
published by
BERKLEY PUBLISHING CORPORATION

*A slightly different serialized version of this book appeared
in Galaxy magazine in 1971 (copyright 1971
by VDP Publishing Corporation).*

G. P. Putnam's Sons
200 Madison Ave.
New York City, N.Y. 10016

Library of Congress Catalog Card Number: 73-186646

SBN 425-02432-6

*BERKLEY MEDALLION BOOKS are published by
Berkley Publishing Corporation
200 Madison Avenue
New York, N.Y. 10016*

BERKLEY MEDALLION BOOKS ® TM 757,375

Printed in the United States of America

Berkley Medallion Edition, October, 1973

Contents

		Page
One:	HEREDITY	7
Two:	DIVERSITY	42
Three:	INIQUITY	76
Four:	PERPLEXITY	110
Five:	FATALITY	144
Six:	FUTURITY	180

1

Heredity

On that epic day when man first touched the moon, we —my brother Tom and I—lay on the floor of our two-room flat over our father's shop in Newark, drinking in the drama of it through our old black-and-white TV.

"One small step for man, one giant leap for mankind. . . ."

Those electric words of Armstrong's still shiver in my memory. The worn brown carpet smelled of our father's strong Turkish tobacco and our mother's lavender body powder, and those stale scents are still mingled in my mind with the unforgettable throb of wild pride that caught my throat when his searching boot found the moon.

"Now they've got themselves the gelt." Tom's raw envy nearly spoiled the moment for me. "And here I am, still stuck in Hotzenplotz!"

The history of the moon children begins with that instant, even though they weren't even born for many years. I wish chance had selected a better historian, because their story seems too big for me to tell. Looking at the task, I think of Swift's Gulliver.

Gulliver has always been my favorite literary character. I never understood all the higher criticism of Swift as a theological satirist, but I always felt close to Gulliver—a very plain, ordinary human being, reasonable and honest, involved through no fault of his own in affairs that were too much for him.

The lives of the moon children are a vaster adventure than anything Swift invented for Gulliver, and telling it well calls for more style and wit than I possess. Perhaps my brother Tom should have been the narrator. He was involved as deeply as I, and he had humor and imagination. I recall our father saying that he was the natural poet of the family, and I was only the schlemiel.

"Please, Gamal!" Mother came plaintively to my defense. "You're hurting Kim and teaching Tom too many of your own slick tricks. Better a schlemiel than a gonef!"

"Your own son a thief already? Hoo-ha!"

He gave her a black-eyed blink of wounded innocence and told a Yiddish joke that I didn't understand, though Tom snickered knowingly. Mother stared back indignantly, and suddenly decided to send me down to the delicatessen to buy boiled ham hocks for our dinner. Father snarled bitterly at that, but she said ham hocks were cheap.

In spite of such bickering, Tom knew how to make up with me. We were generally friends. After the moon landing, when we knew the *Eagle* was safe in space again, I remember how we stood up and shook hands and resolved to be astronauts.

"What chance have you got?" With a weary sigh, Mother looked up sadly from the potatoes she was peeling. "Gamal Hodian's kids?"

"What's wrong with Pop?" Tom stared at her. "He outsmarts everybody. Anyhow, like the TV says, things will be different now. Kim can be your pet schlemiel if he wants, but me, I'm grabbing my share of the planets."

"Don't call Kim that—"

"Pop does." Tom reminded her. "Me, I don't care what he is. I'm on my way to the moon."

"Better finish high school first."

"Better help your little yekl blow his nose." Tom smirked at me. "I'll do okay. Pop says I'll be another macher, just as good as him."

White-lipped, Mother bent over her potatoes again. My eyes blurred with pity for us both. She was a big, rawboned blonde. She must have been a striking girl, though her wedding pictures show her already worn and fading when she married.

Once she caught Tom and me rummaging through a lavender-scented black-lacquer box of old photographs and trinkets he had found in her dresser. Her pictures looked lovely to me, but he was snickering at her "cow-sized tits." She slapped him and snatched the box away, but later she let me see her souvenirs and told how she had run away from an unhappy home in the Arkansas hills, hoping to break into show business.

She couldn't help sobbing when she talked about it. She said her voice had been too thin and her bones too big. She tried the Nashville "Grand Old Opry" and tried Hollywood and tried New York, but her luck never broke. She was a waitress in a third-rate bar when she met Gamal Hodian.

Hodian must have been an alias, but I never knew my father's original name. He was a dark, stocky, evasive man, who spoke several languages badly, English worst of all. He was secretive about everything. Mother thought he was an Egyptian native. Tom believed he was Jewish. I once heard a business associate call him "a sneaking Armenian thief." He used to say himself that he had no country. His passport was Turkish, but probably forged.

He had wanted to name my brother Tamar and me Kemal, but Mother had him call us Tom and Kim. The Hodian name must have been assumed when he began visiting the United States, soon after World War II and long before he met my mother. He called himself an importer, and we always lived in some low-rent section, over or behind a grimy little shop that was sparsely stocked with the cheap perfumes and tarnished brassware and tattered scraps of carpet that he had imported.

There were other imports, I think, that I never learned much about. Strange customers always made him nervous, and he was away most of the time on what Mother called buying trips. One of those lasted nearly three years. Mother told us he was ill in Ankara, but Tom snorted that he was somewhere in jail.

The year I entered high school, he disappeared. He had always hated Sicilians, and Mother insisted that the Mafia

9

had murdered him. Long after, however, I found among her things a little packet of scented letters mailed in Marseilles to "M. Hobereau" at a Staten Island post office box. In a very feminine French hand, they begged him to come back to his *cherie* and their *petit enfant*. Perhaps he did.

Though he had never been a bountiful provider, times grew even harder for us then. Mother closed out the shop and began to look for a job. Some of my father's old friends put her on an uncertain dole, I think to keep her from telling what she knew about them.

Once one of them took me into a bar to talk about my future. A dark, watchful, jumpy little man who stank of garlic and cheap wine, he whispered questions and blinked in unbelief at all I didn't know about my father's connections. Mother must have been begging him to offer me some kind of job, but finally he stalked indignantly out and left me to pay for the drinks.

Mother stumbled or jumped in front of a truck, the spring I finished high school. Two fat sisters and a Baptist preacher-brother came from Little Rock for the funeral. I had cleared the empty gin bottles out of the flat, and I didn't tell them about the needle marks the coroner had found on her arms.

Tom was already on his way toward the moon by then. Older than I, stronger and darker and smarter, more like our father, he always had a keener eye for the main chance. He weeded the Yiddish expressions out of his speech and earned a college scholarship to major in space science.

I did worse. With no head for math, I got no scholarships. Mother's insurance came to six thousand dollars when all the bills were paid. I went to Las Vegas with my share, to try my luck. It was bad. The money lasted three nights.

My actual education began with that disaster. Sometimes I was hungry. The police picked me up two or three times before I learned I hadn't inherited my father's talents. I tended bar and drove taxis and sold used cars. I bought a guitar and tried crooning folk ballads, but my

10

voice turned out no better than my mother's. I wrote songs nobody sang and a novel nobody would print. I was a disc jockey and a TV reporter and even a political campaign manager—for a candidate who lost.

Tom, year by year, got closer to our old dream. He went from college into the Space Force, and finally into COSMOS—the acronym stood for Civilian Organization of Man in Outer Space. Its idealistic aim was to explore space in peace for the common good. Tom used to poke fun at the high-minded slogan, "free worlds for free men," but he lifted off for the new training base on the moon with the first class of COSMOS cadets. He had already changed his name to Thomas Hood.

He wangled an assignment to a satellite survey team. The COSMOS space engineers were then developing the seeker-type survey rocket, which carried a dozen tons of sophisticated hardware designed to chart and analyze the surface of an airless world from low orbital flight. The seeker survey was planned to cover a hundred satellites and large asteroids, beginning with test flights around Earth's moon.

"Not that I think we'll find anything," Tom sniggered. "But the moon's a cozy little mission, close to home and Robin Hudson."

Robin was the jet-set daughter of Howard Hudson, a hotel tycoon he had managed to meet. With her sullen charm and her father's fortune, she was more exciting to Tom than the moon was now, since the spacemen were passing it by.

He took me to one of her father's floating resorts, the Antilles Hudson, for a weekend with the other members of his three-man survey team. Seeker One was already in orbit around the moon, and Tom's Seeker Two crewmen were waiting for the space engineers to analyze the data tapes.

The invitation surprised me. Annoyed when I wouldn't change my own name to match his, he had begun treating me like a beggar relation. Yet I was glad enough to go, because the failure of that political adventure had left me without job or plans.

We found his teammates on a bright sundeck, high above the milky glitter of the hot Caribbean. They were quarreling about the real aims of the seeker survey.

"Security!" Erik Thorsen was a huge, red-haired Viking. He had lately shed his major's rank in the United States Space Force, because COSMOS personnel had to be civilians, but he still wore his military bearing like a uniform.

"Military security!" He banged the table with his empty beer stein. "That's all I'm looking for."

"Then you'll never find it," Yuri Marko answered. "All you'll find is your own destruction. I'm searching for something else—"

He paused when he saw us, and Tom introduced me. Marko was a tall, mild man, owlish with his black-rimmed glasses, intensely serious. He seated us courteously, and turned doggedly back to his attack.

"We're looking for life," he told Thorsen. "Nothing else is worth the cost—"

"God save us from alien life!" Thorsen waved his stein like a club. "We've got the people-boom right here, without looking for trouble on other planets."

"Trouble?" Marko's dark anxious eyes appealed to Tom and me. "Our space neighbors have never harmed us yet. I don't think they will. I hope to find higher life than we are. Something with mind enough to cross the space between the stars."

Thorsen muttered skeptically.

"That's our real goal." Marko bent intently toward him. "I believe life can spring up on the worlds of any star. The older forms should be far ahead of us. If interstellar travel is actually possible, space explorers should have touched our worlds. We should find their footprints."

"On the moon?"

"The airless worlds are the place to look," Marko nodded. "Wind and water wipe out everything. But the signs of a landing on the moon—a broken tool or an empty fuel

12

container or even a literal footprint—might last a good many million years."

"I pray to God we never meet another creature!"

Thorsen lurched to his feet and stalked away. Tom followed to soothe him. I was left with Yuri Marko. His reserved, schoolmasterish manner put me off at first, but we soon found things in common.

His parents, like my father, had been immigrants—they were Ukrainian defectors from the First Soviet. A political idealist, he had even voted for my unlucky United World candidate. I caught his contagious interest in the seeker project.

The bioforms of Mercury and Venus and Jupiter were still at that time mostly inference and mystery. Nobody had ever seriously proposed that these near neighbors in space might be advanced beyond us. Marko's hopes took hold of my imagination.

"Just suppose we're not alone." His dry Slavic accents excited me with a sense of the dimensions of the universe I had never felt before. "Imagine other minds, and greater ones. Picture an intelligent society spread across the stars —a society in which our earth would be a nameless village. Perhaps you can't quite visualize our fellow creature out in space, but at least the effort gives you a truer image of yourself."

On our last night together at the Antilles Hudson, Robin gave a party for us in her surfside apartment. The lights were dimmed, so that we could watch the waves exploding into white phosphorescence against the glass seawall. Her father was there, the ice-eyed money-king, and at last I guessed why Tom had invited me.

Howard Hudson, with the world in his web of floating hotels, had turned acquiring eyes toward space. The Orbital Hudson and the Crater Hudson were soon to open. What he wanted from us was a quick secret report on anything of commercial promise the survey might uncover. The news was to come from Tom through me, coded into some harmless personal message.

Erik Thorsen flushed with anger when he understood

13

what was up. He smashed his champagne glass against the glowing seawall and threatened to expose the plot. Silkily, Tom suggested that Thorsen had secret military ties to the Space Force that COSMOS wouldn't like. Thorsen turned pale and agreed to say nothing.

I saw Marko's hurt contempt for me.

"Listen, sir," I begged him. "Tom's taking too much for granted. He never mentioned a word of this to me. I won't touch it. Believe me, sir!"

I don't think he did.

That incident brought the party to an awkward end. Tom told me curtly that I was no longer his guest. But as things turned out, I remained at the resort after his team was gone. Marooned there, without money to pay my unexpected bill, I went to the publicity office and talked my way into a copywriting job.

Surveying the moon, as things turned out, was not the cozy little mission Tom had anticipated. Seeker One crashed behind the moon, with no survivors to report what had gone wrong. Tom and his team were called out to continue the moon survey with Seeker Two.

My brother was not alone in his surprise at what the seekers found. The moon had kept her secret well. Vaster than all Africa, she had room enough. The early astronauts and cosmonauts had seen too many empty craters of every size to expect much else. They went on, as soon as they could, to look for more exciting worlds.

The moon was very dead, but the planets were already promising the menace and allure of unknown life. When the robot probes on Mars began to scrape up samples for analysis, their telemetry indicated complex organic molecules. The first men to touch that tawny dust caught a tormenting illness that kept them in quarantine at the COSMOS base on Phobos till they died.

The blinding clouds of Venus veiled the same sort of ambiguous mystery. Unmanned probes brought back simple organisms of microscopic beta-life from the highest levels of her atmosphere, but no vehicle, manned or not, ever returned from the unseen surface beneath.

The first men to station themselves in orbit around her found new riddles, rather than answers to old ones. They saw dark dots above the clouds—larger creatures, they suspected, in an ecological pyramid based on the beta-life. They described a sudden color change that stained the blank planet with swirls of brown and yellow. They were reporting an unexplained power loss when their signals faded out.

One lone member of the first three-man team came back from Mercury. He had seen nothing alive and he lived through his year at the quarantine station on the moon, but he brought pictures of a queer crater-ringed, iron-walled tunnel from which his companions had never returned.

Though no probe had yet come back from the atmosphere of Jupiter, a COSMOS expedition had touched the four large satellites. The first craft to visit Io, nearest the planet, reported that its takeoff had been followed by a narrow beam of intermittent radiation, as if something on the planet was observing it with radar.

Against that background of ominous uncertainty, the crash of Seeker One shocked the world. The first response was a jittery fear that something unfriendly had established itself on the back of the moon. Howard Hudson made the most of that brief panic.

I was still working in the Antilles Hudson, and what I saw was a business education. Public announcements of the crash were delayed for several hours, first by the fuddled COSMOS bureaucrats on the moon and later by official censors on earth, while Hudson's private spy system coined money for him.

News of the crash came in on our astrofac circuit, disguised as a weather observation from the Orbital Hudson. It was decoded by a file clerk in our office, who couldn't help talking when space issues dived on the stock market.

Hudson had his brokers sell space industries short. Next day, when the story broke, he used the publicity office to spread a wild rumor. The creatures of Venus had learned about space from the hardware raining out of their clouds. Now they were building a military base on the moon to stop our astronauts from polluting their air.

The news that COSMOS was now transmitting from the moon gave that rumor more support than it deserved. The bottom fell out of the market, and Hudson's brokers picked up space stocks for peanuts. As office gossip had it, he cleared three billion in three days.

COSMOS tried to cool the rumors with a bulletin phrased in wooden officialese. Responsible space authorities had found no evidence of hostile action against the lost seeker from any source whatever. Neither the observers on the orbital moon platform or the crew of the seeker itself had reported anything unusual before the crash occurred. Salvage crews already at the site could find no indication of attack or sabotage. Presumably, instrumental malfunction had allowed the survey craft to drift out of its very low orbit and graze a lunar peak. The media would be instantly alerted to any new developments, but there was no reason whatever for public apprehension.

Seeker Two was standing ready to resume routine flights as soon as her crew reached the moon, the bulletin concluded. Thus far, the survey had made no newsworthy discoveries. None, in fact, were actually expected, because the moon was utterly dead. The test flights, however, had already established the value of the seeker vehicles for mapping the resources of other airless worlds.

Five minutes after that stuffy statement came over the transfac net, our office was buzzing with livelier news from the moon. It came by laser beam from the manager of the New Crater Hudson. After our laserman had relayed the message to Hudson's office, he replayed his tape for us.

". . . Listen, Mr. Hudson. Don't swallow the COSMOS line. They're covering something up. I don't know what—maybe just the fact that this thing shows them up for

16

idiots. But they're sitting on something I think you ought to know.

"It's true that Seeker One dived out of orbit for no apparent reason. She'd been flying her survey pattern, just ten kilometers high, flashing a routine report to the platform on every pass. Not a word about any trouble.

"But the story here is that the platform did observe something odd. A queer glow, down on the lunar surface. It blazed out just before the seeker passed over. Her retro-rockets fired a few seconds later. A laserman on the platform was following the seeker with a telescope and he saw it happen. He thinks the seeker was trying to land in the glow. Of course she overshot it, maybe four hundred kilometers. Came down near the moon's south pole at half her orbital velocity. The salvage craft found nothing worth picking up. Meantime, the glow had faded out.

"That's the story here, sir. We thought you'd want to know about that glow. Even though we can't say what it was. The laserman says it looked like a fluorescent effect excited by the surveyor's radar gear. The space engineers out here say radar pulses don't excite fluorescent effects. Off the record, the COSMOS wheels think that laserman was drunk. They aren't talking for the record.

"That's it, Chief."

If Howard Hudson made another fortune out of that report, I never heard about it, but my brother and his team were already on their way to Skygate, the COSMOS center on a mesa in New Mexico. By spaceplane to the earth platform, by shuttle nuke to the moon platform, by skipper craft down to Armstrong Point, the flight to the moon took a day and a half.

Up to a point, the story of Seeker Two is easy enough for me to reconstruct. I followed the official bulletins COSMOS saw fit to release and shared the private tips we received for Hudson. Later, I talked to Tom and his companions. I've even used the tapes and transcripts of the official investigation, which somehow still survive.

Seeker Two took off from Armstrong Point. In circumpolar orbit, radar-stablized at ten kilometers mean eleva-

17

tion, she picked up the survey pattern. With gravimeters and magnetometers and radiation counters and a hundred other sophisticated research instruments, she was charting a five-kilometer strip of the moon, recording every possible detail of every crater and mascon, every significant surface and subsurface feature.

In a wider orbit, four thousand kilometers out, the moon platform monitored her flight reports and kept watch for any interference. Her first transmissions were completely routine.

"All systems go. No anomalies noted."

However, as she neared that point where Seeker One had fired her retro-rockets, the watchers on the platform made a terse report to the COSMOS center at Armstrong Point.

"Platform to Moon Control! We've got something. A surface glow, apparently touched off by approach of Seeker Two. A luminous streak, maybe twenty kilometers long. Arrowhead-shaped. Brighter toward the point. Location estimated six hundred kilometers from south lunar pole."

Moon Control replied with an urgent query to Seeker Two. What was she observing?

"Lunar surface lighting up under us." Marko's taped voice sounds crisp and cool. "Bright rays spreading north from a small crater just ahead, which looks like an impact point. We've got spectrometers running on the rays. They appear to be fluorescent material scattered north from that crater. Spectral analysis not yet complete."

"Keep in orbit." Moon Control seems more alarmed than Marko is. "Monitor everything but don't leave your flight pattern—"

"Seeker Two to Moon Control." Marko's voice is quicker on the tape, but still oddly calm. "Reporting visual contact with uncharted installation ahead. Something standing on that impact point. Position estimated sixty-nine degrees south latitude, on circumpolar survey track eighty-eight. A shining tower—"

Marko's voice fades out.

18

"Seeker Two! Seeker Two!" Moon Control shouts. "Keep talking. Tell us everything."

"A vast installation!" Even Marko sounds breathless now. "I can't imagine why it wasn't seen before. The tower dome stands miles above our flight path. Dead ahead! It looks like some sort of beacon. Changing color. Red, yellow, orange. It's running through the spectrum—"

"Platform to Seeker!" A sharper voice cuts in. "We're tracking you by telescope. We see the surface phenomenon—bright streaks converging toward the impact crater now just ahead of you. But we see no tower. No obstruction. Your flight path looks clear."

For long seconds, the tape records no voice.

"Seeker Two!" Moon Control is hoarse with tension. "Seeker Two! Seeker Two!"

"Seeker Two to Moon Control." Marko's voice comes back at last, pitched lower, relieved. "We've made voice contact and identified the installation ahead. It's the base of a transgalactic mission seeking peaceful interaction with mankind. We're following instructions to land at the base on our next orbital pass."

"Don't do that!" Moon Control sounds almost frantic. "Climb clear of apparent obstruction—don't try to land! The platform sees no tower. We think you're caught in some kind of trap. Remember Seeker One. Don't touch your retro-rockets."

The tape rustles with solar static, but there is not reply.

"Moon Control to Seeker Two!" The voice rises raggedly. "Don't try to land. Repeat: don't try to land. Break off contact with surface point. Change flight pattern to avoid vicinity of survey curve eighty-eight. Acknowledge and stand by."

The tape runs on, but Seeker Two does not acknowledge.

Moon Control at the moment was Sherman Parkinson. Like Erik Thorsen, he had recently resigned a military

19

commission to make himself eligible for the civilian space organization. To judge him by his own standards, he was no doubt a brave and well-trained officer, loyal to the ancient traditions of the United States Marine Corps if not to the COSMOS ideal of a united mankind.

I saw him back on Earth two or three years later, confined to the alcoholics' ward of a veterans' hospital. The events on the moon had evidently been too much for him. Habit-driven as a dinosaur, he was not prepared to cope with anything so far beyond his own experience.

But the drinking came later. He seems to have remained sober during that crisis. The panel of special investigators saw fit, in fact, to commend him for a steadfast devotion to duty.

He was keen enough to see that Seeker Two was flying into some kind of trap, but he seems to have been taken in by Hudson's rumor of attackers from Venus. When Marko ignored his orders, Parkinson called Skygate to ask for military support.

Space was international, Skygate reminded him. As the COSMOS administrator on the moon, he was in command, but he was not to make any use of military force without the explicit unanimous prior consent of the COSMOS directorate on Earth.

Angered, Parkinson issued new orders for Seeker Two to leave the survey pattern and return at once to Armstrong Point. Even under the kiddies' picnic rules of COSMOS, he pointed out, Marko and his men could be taken off flight status for failure to obey direct orders, fined for misuse of COSMOS property, and imprisoned up to ten years for conduct endangering public safety. When such threats evoked no answer, Parkinson tried gravel-voiced appeals. Hadn't the team heard the platform's report that the transgalactic base didn't exist? Didn't they know the hazards of contact with alien biocosms? Couldn't they recall their obligations to COSMOS and mankind?

Seeker Two kept on its silent path. When it went behind the moon from the platform, cutting off laser contact,

Sherman Parkinson turned his attention to the platform itself, which still had that luminous streak in view. It was slowly fading behind the seeker, the platform reported. The raylike splash of scattered material was now barely visible, but the circle of the impact crater was still distinct.

The platform picked the seeker up when she came back across the moon's north pole, reporting that she had changed course just enough to follow the rotating moon, so that she was returning along survey curve eighty-eight toward that dying gleam.

Parkinson bombarded her with desperate questions. What kind of creatures manned that transgalactic base? How had they concealed it? What language had they used for voice contact? What data had the sensors recorded?

Seeker Two flew on with no reply.

The platform tracked her back down survey curve eighty-eight. Soon after she crossed the moon's equator, that arrow-shaped impact-splash blazed out again ahead. Presently her retro-rockets fired, lifting her on a long arc that slanted back toward the glowing crater.

The watchers on the platform followed the flare of her jets, which contracted to an incandescent point as she came down. Their instruments recorded an anomalous surge of hard radiation which peaked at the instant her jets went out.

At that point the platform lost contact, as its own orbital motion carried it behind the moon, out of laser range. Its observers reported the rayed crater still glowing on the moon's horizon as long as they could see.

Sherman Parkinson called Skygate to beg for help. Told again that COSMOS couldn't break its code of peace in space without proof of actual attack, he said profanely that he would get the proof. Ignoring all protests, he took off in an unarmed skippercraft for the site of the crash.

The sun was rising there when he arrived. Its harsh glare washed out any trace of that dying glow. The impact crater and its northward rays now looked black, his taped report states, as if a shipload of ink had struck and splashed. The skipper's counters detected no anomalous radiation, and nothing revealed any sign of a transgalactic base.

There was only Seeker Two, standing tilted among the boulders on the steep north crater rim. She showed neither damage from her reckless landing nor any trace of life. Parkinson dropped cautiously a little farther from the crater lip and made a discovery that exhausted his Marine vocabulary.

As he hoarsely reported to the moon platform, three sets of footprints left Seeker Two. They wandered north among the boulders for a distance of several hundred meters. Finally they returned. It was those returning prints that set off his most explosive diction. Magnet-cleated flight boots had made the outgoing prints, but three sets of bare feet returned.

"Relay this to Skygate." Parkinson pauses on the tape as if to clear his head and clean up his language. "We've found Seeker Two—and something the medics have to explain! Prints in the dust show that all three crew members went for a barefoot walk and somehow got back aboard."

"Better check your eyes and look again," the platform advises him. "Men don't go barefoot on the moon. Not far, anyhow. You'll have to collect some pretty solid evidence, sir, or you won't last as long as Moon Control."

Parkinson looked again. He moved the skipper twice to photograph the prints before he sealed his own moonsuit and went out with a spaceman to inspect the seeker.

The air lock had been sealed again. Hammered signals got no response. Parkinson had to knock out an emergency access plate to cycle the lock and get aboard. Marko and Hood and Thorsen lay sprawled on the deck where they must have collapsed when they got back from their unexplained excursion into the moon's deadly night.

The three men wore neither boots nor gloves nor helmets. Their faces were stained with dried blood, which must have boiled out of their lungs into the vacuum of space. Parkinson felt certain at first that they were dead.

The damage to their bodies was far less severe, however, than might have been expected. Savagely cold as that dust must have been, their feet were not frozen. The rigor of death had not set in. On a second examination, after he had increased the oxy-helium pressure, Parkinson decided that they were still breathing.

"I think they were out collecting this black dust," he reported to the platform. "The stuff that colors the crater dark. A sort of coarse grit, actually. Sprayed all around the crater. But mostly north, as if scattered by an impact from the south.

"Queer stuff!" Parkinson's voice on the tape sounds hoarse and breathless. "The particles are sharp-edged and they have a bright black shine and they all look identical. Like nothing else I ever saw.

"These men were after this queer grit. Their boots are stuffed with it. Their tool pockets are full of it. Hodian had it crammed in his mouth."

Relayed from the platform to Armstrong Point, and from there down to Skygate, Parkinson's reports elicited every shade of amusement and disbelief. He was variously advised to change his brand of whiskey, to get the fingerprints of the little green men, and to photograph everything before he touched it.

"I nearly wish we had found those invaders from Venus," he told the spacemen on the seeker with him. "We know what to do with enemies we can reach."

Sifting now through the COSMOS bulletins and the leaked reports from Hudson's spies, I can almost watch the interrogation of the seeker crew there in the hospital under Armstrong Point. Details emerge from the raspy tapes. The dull drone of the fans. The chemical sting of the air. The narrow tunnel room, drill-scarred moon rock glistening with glassy sealant. The three tired men, cocoons in white gauze, reeking of sterifoam, surrounded with medics and guards. Parkinson barking questions at them, growing redder and louder with every answer he can't accept.

Yuri Marko is questioned first.

"—a secret base." The surviving tape begins in midsentence. Marko's throat is raw and swollen from his unbelievable exposure to the lunar night, his scratchy voice hard to make out. "But the beings there aren't from Venus, sir. They aren't from any planet of our sun."

Parkinson sounds grittily skeptical. "How do you know?"

"I saw the base," Marko answers. "I talked to its people. They belong to a high culture that spreads far through the galaxy. They've been stationed on the moon a long time to watch our evolution. They're delighted that we've come far enough to qualify for contact."

"Hunh!"

"Sir, think what it means!" Marko's awed elation comes clearly through his hoarseness and pain. "They want to share their tremendous civilization with us. Our lives will never be the same—"

"There is no base," Parkinson cuts in. "The platform was watching the spot. I've just been out there. There's nothing but some odd black grit scattered around an impact crater. If you saw anything, it must have been some sort of space mirage."

For a few seconds, the tape runs silently.

"Sir, I know what's real," Marko's faint whisper insists at last. "I've tried drugs. I've had illusions. They *feel* different. No matter what anybody saw, that base is real."

"Tell about it."

"It's a structure." Marko pauses as if to think. "But everything about it reflects an unknown culture. The design, the materials, the unbelievable dimensions. Our language doesn't fit it, but I'll try to give you my impression. Imagine a tight cluster of round white columns, each a different height. The six lower columns are capped with platforms arranged in a rising spiral around the central tower. It's *tall!* Its onion-shaped dome must have been ten kilometers above our orbit. That dome changes color like a beacon, and I think the platforms are landing stages under it. Some were empty, but I saw great globe-shaped ships on two of

24

them." Marko raises his voice. "Sir, does that sound like a dream?"

"It ain't there now," Parkinson sneers. "You say you were in voice contact with—whatever you thought you saw. What language did you use?"

"Why—" Marko pauses as if astonished by his own recollection. "Ukrainian! The voice I heard wasn't human. It was a modulated electronic hum, like—like a computer simulating speech. I remember wondering if it didn't come through some kind of translating device. But it spoke the Ukrainian peasant dialect my parents used at home. That *is* remarkable!"

"Remarkable ain't the word. What happened after you landed?"

The tape whirs quietly.

"I can't recall," Marko mutters at last. "That buzzing voice coached us in. I remember firing the retro-rockets. I remember watching the lowest stage of the tower, where I thought we were going to land. I remember thinking we were coming in too low to make it. Then it all fades out."

"Because it wasn't there!"

Erik Thorsen is next on the tape. Parkinson greets him heartily as "Major," as if expecting something saner from a fellow soldier, and asks him to tell in his own words what happened to Seeker Two.

"Yes, sir, Colonel Parkinson!" Thorsen crisply returns the military courtesy. "We were all three on duty, sir. Alert for whatever got Seeker One. We were all observing that luminous patch on the surface ahead. We all saw something beyond it at the same time, sir. What I saw was a fort."

"Venusian?"

"I can't say, sir. It was enormous. Round like a turret. Buried in the moon. Camouflaged with a rocky ridge that looked like a crater rim. It rose as we got closer. Bristling with missiles like I never saw before."

"Did it fire on you?"

"No, sir. Hood was working our radio and laser gear. He picked up a voice commanding us to land beside the fort. That voice—" Thorsen hesitates. "It spoke Norwegian, sir. My own good mother's Riksmaal, that I learned at home in Stavanger."

"Norwegian?" Parkinson's startled voice has lost its warm tone of military fellowship. "Is little Norway building forts in space?"

"That's all I know, sir." Thorsen sounds angry. "I don't remember landing."

"Listen, Colonel." My brother's voice comes on the tape, husky from exposure but still shrewdly fluent. "Don't let 'em put you on. I saw what they did—and it was neither a galactic base nor a Venusian fort. They're trying to snow you, sir. To hide a million tons of gold!"

"What's this, Hood? What gold?"

"What I saw was a gold meteor," Tom says. "It hit the moon hard enough to burst. But the mass of it stands up in the middle of that crater. A blazing hill of yellow gold. More gold scattered all around. Hundred-ton nuggets of pure shining gold!"

"Did you hear any voice?"

"My father's voice." Tom pauses, as if struck with awe. "My own father's! He disappeared on earth a dozen years ago. We gave him up for dead. But here he was, calling from his own little survey rocket—speaking broken English with a funny Turko-Yiddish accent, as he did when I was a kid. He said he was all alone. He'd located that gold with electronic gear and swept the moon dust off it. He wanted us to land and witness his finder's claim, under the conventions of COSMOS. That's what we did." Tom's voice turns sharp. "And that's why these men are lying— to defraud my poor old father of that gold claim!"

"I saw no gold," Parkinson grates. "Let's go over all this again."

He keeps hammering questions at all three men as long as they can talk. When the doctors make him stop, he orders them back to their wards under guard, and calls in the engineers who had been at work on samples of that black grit. Their answers don't improve his temper.

The grit is impure carbon in crystal form, the engineers

26

report. Most of the crystals have been damaged by impact or eroded by long exposure to micrometeors, but apparently they had all once been perfect tetrahedrons, crystals of something new to science.

The intact samples measure nearly eight millimeters on edge. They are slightly radioactive and strongly magnetic. Besides the carbon content, chemical analysis shows 6 percent silicon, 3 percent gold, and nearly 2 percent thorium, with traces of lead and a few other elements. One chemist suggests that the crystals are unknown allotropes of natural carbon.

"Hogwash!" an engineer objects. "They're too much alike. Originally, they seem to have been identical in every feature, down to our limits of measurement. Nothing natural is quite that perfect. I say they're manufactured."

"Who made 'em?" Parkinson's voice demands. "What for?"

The tapes run on, revealing Parkinson's blundering efforts to answer that question. When Seeker Two has been inspected for possible damage and checked out to another team, he sends her back into orbit to resume her interrupted survey flight.

Observers eye her from the moon platform, as she returns along her chartered path to the impact crater. Engineers in skippercraft watch from posts near the crater, prepared to photograph and measure anything that brings her down again.

But nothing happens. The seeker skims low over the crater, observing neither transgalactic base nor space fort nor golden meteor. The platform watchers observe no surface glow. The engineers discover nothing to photograph or measure.

The voices of Marko and Thorsen and my brother sound stronger on the tapes when Parkinson questions them again, but they refuse to reconcile their contradictory stories. Each remains stubbornly certain of what he thinks he saw, and none of them remembers leaving the seeker to gather that black grit.

Parkinson delays his own second visit to the crater, run-

27

ning down blind alleys and filing his inconclusive reports while he waits for night to end there. The tapes record his landing, timed to meet the lunar sunrise. Now he finds something new.

Reporting to the moon platform, his voice sounds apoplectic. Somebody else hasn't waited for the sun. Sometime after Seeker Two lifted off the impact site, a cargo rocket has landed there. Magnetic gear has been used to sweep up the remaining crystal grit. A few bootprints are left in the dust, but nothing more revealing.

Parkinson spends half the long lunar day at the site, sifting the surface dust again and drilling a pattern of test holes around the crater, but all he finds is disappointment. No buried mascon, nor any trace of the impact object. Nothing to explain the crystal grit. Not even a broken tool to identify the raiders.

At the Antilles Hudson, we had been able to follow events to this point through those intercepted reports, but now our news from the moon was cut off. Hudson's leaking secrets had spread from the office to the hotel guests. An unfriendly newsman broadcast the story, adding a notion of his own that the midnight raid on the crater had been planned and led by Hudson himself.

Hudson was away when the story broke, but he called home. Half a dozen of us were instantly fired, and nobody shared any more tapes from the moon. When Hudson returned—in about the time his private spaceplane might have required for a quick return flight from the moon—he had no comment on the story, or his own absence, or anything at all. I was still marooned. After all deductions for room and food and bar chits, my discharge pay came to twenty-three dollars. I lost that at the hotel casino, trying to win my fare to the mainland. When I went back to the employment office, an unpleasant clerk suggested that I might either wash dishes or swim for it.

I said I'd swim. As I walked the decks that afternoon, uncertain what I could really do, I heard a news announcement that Robin Hudson had arrived to spend the weekend with her father. On impulse, I went up to her suite.

Surprisingly, the doorbox let me in. Robin met me with a moist kiss, but her smile went out when she learned I had no news from Tom, and she turned nasty when I asked her to help me ashore.

Perhaps I lost my own temper. I remember calling her a rich bitch. She replied that she was entirely happy to be rich, and quite content that I was a pauper. She added that Tom said I had always been a sniveling schlemiel, and they'd both had more than plenty of me.

She did listen sulkily, however, when I decided to apologize and explain my predicament. For Tom's sake, she called the flight deck and got me a seat on the Key West jet.

Back on the mainland, I took a job writing publicity for Dial-a-Mood, an emotion-conditioner designed for home installation. We were at war with a rival named Joy-Aire. The Joy-Aire people had spread rumors that our toners were loaded with addictive psychedelics. My new job was to plant counterrumors that the Joy-Aire toners had such undesirable side-effects as excessive weight gain, paralysis, and idiocy.

For some months, all I knew of the moon story came from the colorless COSMOS bulletins. The seeker survey was still in progress, with no further incident. Sherman Parkinson had been replaced at Moon Control by a former manager of the Crater Hudson. Thomas Hood and his fellow crash survivors were well enough to be returned from the moon to Skygate, for further examination at the laboratory of exobiology there.

That was all. Filled with news of the amazing bioforms seen flying above the atmosphere of Jupiter, the COSMOS releases said no more about the moon. I mailed two or three letters to Tom at Skygate, which he didn't bother to answer.

Never quite secure at Dial-a-Mood, because I lacked what our president called "conditional sincerity," I kept job applications going out. One went to Skygate. The reply offered me a special assignment to write a report on the commercial use of space science. Though the salary wasn't half what Dial-a-Mood paid, I accepted with delight, because I was so anxious to pick up the story of the moon grit and its queer effects on the crew of Seeker Two.

Skygate was their birthplace.

A delicate green had dusted the mesa before I arrived, in the wake of rain, but its more common colors were sandstone red and the yellow of wind-drifted dust. The spaceplanes came down on an asterite strip fringed with resin-scented piñon and juniper, and tiny green oases like scattered beads were strung along the Albuquerque road, but the wild ridges west were as bleak and barren as the moon.

The riddle of that crystal grit was still unsolved, so far as I could learn, but my brother and his team were apparently recovered from their crash behind the moon. Discharged from the space hospital, they had been allowed to marry. All three wives were pregnant.

My brother's wife was Robin Hudson. The match surprised me. Tom had always said no woman would get her hooks into him, and frankly I thought Robin might have done better. Perhaps she was drawn to a sort of wolfish rapacity that Tom shared with her own father, and I think she liked the notion of becoming Robin Hood.

Thorsen's bride was a nurse he had met at the hospital on the moon. Her parents were Japanese, and her dainty, sloe-eyed charm made an odd contrast to his brawny Viking power. Though her hesitant English was hard for me to understand at first, I could feel her kindly warmth and her lively comic sense. In fact, I fell in love with Suzie Thorsen.

Marko's wife became almost as dear to me. She was Dr. Carolina Carter, whom he had met at a briefing session in space labs on his way to the moon. The daughter of a black astronaut who had died in quarantine in Phobos, she had earned her own degrees in exobiology. She was a tall beauty, scholarly and gracious, but Robin refused to receive her.

She was employed in the labs when I came to Skygate, working with cultures of the microscopic beta-life the probes had brought from the upper air of Venus. She was generous with facts for my special report. She and Marko asked me to their home for dinner, and it was Marko who later offered me a permanent job, doing publicity for COSMOS.

My own faith in any united human undertaking was pretty well eroded by that time, but I was eager to stay at Skygate. I wanted more facts than anybody yet knew about those small black crystals. I wanted to know what had brought the seekers down, and why the contradictory stories of Marko and his men differed so bizarrely from the apparent facts. I took the job.

At that point I had seen nothing remarkable in the sudden decision of all three men to marry. Nothing had prepared me for the coming of the moon children, whose lives I am trying to describe.

Somewhat ironically for me, it presently developed that my actual task in the publicity section was not to tell their story, but rather to conceal it. The unfolding wonders of their lives soon began to draw too much notice. My job, it turned out, was to protect them from the painful consequences of their own surprising strangeness.

Young Nick Marko's first surprising act was his birth. Carolina had carried him less than seven months, and she was still at work in the exobiology lab, running amino acid tests on her cultures of microscopic bioforms, not an hour before he was born.

At three pounds and no ounces, Nick surprised the neonatal specialists with his tiny-scaled maturity. He breathed easily without waiting to be spanked and nursed with an uncommon eagerness.

His color was equally surprising. Born pink-and-white, neither tomato-vermilion nor with any visible touch of his

31

mother's rich pigmentation, he turned nut brown in five seconds under the lights on his father's movie camera. Ten minutes later, that instant tan was gone.

His pattern of sleep perplexed his doctors and frightened his parents. For almost a month he stayed awake day and night, learning to turn himself over and ceaselessly exploring every object he could reach. On his twenty-eighth day, Carolina found him limp and cold in his crib. Marko felt no pulse and thought he was dead.

Two physicians agreed. No test found any sign of life. Even his brain waves had ceased. But Carolina wouldn't give him up. She was with him all night, tending him as zealously as if he had been another Venusian bioform. At eighty-one degrees, his falling temperature stablized. Four hours later, it began to rise. He woke in her arms at dawn, babbling happily and ready to nurse.

That same night, Valkyrie Thorsen was born. No robust battle-maid, notwithstanding the name her father chose, she was even tinier than Nick and just as remarkably mature. Very fair at first, though Suzie Thorsen was almost as dark as Carolina, she turned briefly golden under the lights in the delivery room.

Oddly alike, Kyrie and Nick were equally precocious. They shared the same minute perfection, the same shy grace, the same happy tempers, the same traits of pleasing but nonhuman strangeness. Both had the same unearthly sort of slim, elfin, large-eyed beauty. Both were warmly perceptive, yet often untouchably aloof. Both slept only at month-long intervals, in the same deathlike way.

They even seemed somehow aware of each other before they ever met. Carolina discovered that one morning when she had driven Marko to work at the Center, where he was now head of the Life Science Section. Baby Nick was with her, slung in a harness to the car seat. He began leaping and crowing as they passed Thorsen's house on the way home.

Carolina had not meant to stop, but Nick cried out as she drove by the house and began moaning so sadly that she turned back around the block. He was yelling and wriggling again with glee when she parked in front of the house.

Inside, Kyrie had been sitting against the end of her crib, solemnly shaking a rattle in time to a dissonant blue jazz number that she had learned to request by beating out its syncopated rhythm. Before Carolina reached the door with Nick, she began tossing rattles and toys out of the crib. When Suzie let them in, Kyrie pulled herself upright to greet them, squealing with delight.

With eager screams, they persuaded the mothers to put them together in the crib. Seated face to face, one at each end, they fell abruptly silent. Wide eyes changing slowly from opal gold to midnight black, they studied each other for five endless minutes.

Nick pitched suddenly forward and got Kyrie's doll foot into his mouth. Carolina swooped to the rescue, because Nick was already cutting teeth. Kyrie howled, however, when she tried to pull Nick away. They lay for another hour in the crib, prodding and kicking and gently biting each other, sometimes laughing, sometimes so grave that Carolina was frightened again.

They clung to each other when Carolina wanted to go, until the mothers promised that they could visit again whenever they pleased. Nick seemed to understand. He crooned solemnly to Kyrie until her somber eyes turned slowly golden and then he looked quietly up at his mother, ready to leave.

They let nothing stop those promised visits. One morning, when it was Kyrie's turn to call on Nick, the mesa was buried under an unusual snowfall. Cars were stalled, and Suzie refused to go out. Kyrie whimpered so piteously, however, that Thorsen put on his skis and carried her to see Nick.

My brother's child was also surprising, but in more distressing ways. Tom was still at Skygate, in a new job as assistant director of Operation Seeker, but Robin had never liked the place. It was Sticksgate to her. She was abroad

33

most of the time, flitting between her father's floating resorts with her own jet set, until her unplanned pregnancy alarmed her.

She begged for an abortion, but Tom and her father opposed it. Howard Hudson wanted a granson, and Tom may have been still responsive to some undiscovered influence from the moon grit. She might have ignored both of them, but when her doctors heard about what they called the idiopathic births of Nick Marko and Kyrie Thorsen, they advised her for her own safety to come back to the space hospital and bear her child under expert care.

To Robin's dismay, the child wasn't born at seven months. She waited fretfully, staying in a suite at the Skygate Hudson because my brother's house had no room for her nurse and her French maid and her hypnotherapist, hating what the desert was doing to her skin.

At nine months, the child was still unborn. By then Robin was growing hysterical about more than the fun things she was missing and the freckles she was getting. She called her father and her astrologer and a guru she had met at the Bengal Hudson. They all advised her to demand a Caesarean section, but the knife terrified her.

She had passed ten months, when Nick and Kyrie came to call. It was a sunny afternoon, and Marko had taken the babies and their mothers on a tour of the complex. They had watched a spaceplane roaring off toward the earth platform, an ancient Indian building, a mountain of juniper firewood on a tiny burro, and a tall cactus blooming, all with the same silent, huge-eyed intentness, but a chance glimpse of the Skygate Hudson tower sent them into shrieking fits.

Their whooping eagerness was so insistent that Marko drove them to the hotel. Robin wouldn't see them at first. My brother came down to meet them in the lobby. With an embarrassed glance at Carolina, he said his wife was not receiving anyone.

Nick and Kyrie refused to be taken away, however, and evidently the unborn child in the tower suite somehow sensed their presence. While the mothers were still trying

34

to quiet the screaming babies, Robin's nurse burst in with a whispered message for my brother.

He asked Marko to wait, while he went back to Robin. A few minutes later he came down again. Looking pale and shaken, he announced that his wife had changed her mind. She wanted to see Nick and Kyrie. Their mothers could come if they liked.

Carolina chose to wait in the lobby, but Suzie Thorsen told me later what happened up in the suite. They found Robin sprawled on a chaise longue, under a heap of pillows and blankets that failed to conceal the bulge of her belly. The maid and the nurse and my brother were hovering over her uneasily, and her face was streaked with unbecoming tears. Suzie felt sorry for her.

Nick and Kyrie shrieked with joy to see her, but their interest was all in her swollen abdomen. They stared at it with wide and darkening eyes. They leaned eagerly toward it. They prodded wildly at it, when Robin tried to take them in her arms.

Suddenly savage, she shoved them off.

"Hideous little m-m-m-m-monsters!" Suzie mimicked her stammering rage with a quaint effect. "Horrid little b-b-b-b-bastards! They're too bright to be h-h-h-h-human. Take 'em away!"

Marko and Suzie took them away. Strangely subdued, they went without protest. Their huge eyes remained very solemn and dark. They clung to each other in a frightened way as Marko drove them home, and Nick was disconsolate when Suzie took Kyrie out of the car.

Late that night, Marko and Carolina were awakened by Nick's frantic screaming. They could find nothing wrong with him. The phone rang before they got him quiet, and Suzie told them that Kyrie was also moaning and sobbing in terror that had no visible cause.

Hoping the two might comfort each other, they rushed Nick across town to Kyrie's nursery. Sitting in the same crib, the two stared blankly at each other and howled in harmony.

When Marko thought of the third child, he called

Robin's suite. The French maid told him that she had gone to the hospital for a Caesarean delivery. Marko talked to her doctors, who were already washing up. They said they had waited as long as they dared, and they refused to delay the operation.

Nerved by a new burst of terror from Nick and Kyrie, Marko called Colonel Petrov. A nominal civilian, Maxim Petrov was the retired Sino-Soviet officer who had replaced Sherman Parkinson as head of the Space Studies Center. He had no more faith than Parkinson did in the altruistic ideals of COSMOS, but he was just as anxious to discover the power of the moon grit. When Marko pointed out that Robin's unborn child would be another guinea pig that might help him crack the mystery, Petrov called the hospital.

Huffily, Robin's surgeons agreed to wait for additional clinical tests. The tests revealed an unknown antigen in her blood and a dangerous sensitivity to the anaesthetics they had meant to use. Over Robin's profane protests, they put off the operation.

The moment she was wheeled out of the delivery room, Nick and Kyrie relaxed in their cribs and went happily to sleep, a week earlier than usual. My brother took Robin back to the Skygate Hudson under mild sedation, sobbing and seething, cursing him and his child.

She had another month to wait, swelling enormously and quarreling venomously by phone with everyone she knew, refusing to be seen by anybody except her nurses and her doctors and the puzzled staff of exobiologists and other specialists they had called in.

Carolina believed that Nick and Kyrie were aware of her delivery when at last it came. They wanted to be together and they cooed and trilled excitedly, sometimes with expectant attention, large heads lifted as if they were listening. Whatever they perceived, it did not alarm them.

Robin's delivery was normal, in fact easier than the obstetricians had expected, but her child was not. A lax, shapeless, sluglike thing, it weighed thirteen pounds. It was all body, the head grotesquely broad and flat. The limbs were undeveloped flippers, with the barest hint of human form. Short dark fur covered it all over.

The obstetricians failed to start it breathing. They found no pulse or any other sign of life. Its temperature was sinking fast. Helplessly, they surrendered it to the jostling specialists, who looked for brain waves and blood reactions and autonomic reflexes. No test revealed anything. An empty bag of unnameable flesh, the creature hung inert and monstrous in their hands.

They declared it dead.

Carolina asked to see Robin's baby. Relieved to wash their hands of the inexplicable, the doctors let her take it. She bathed it and held it in her arms all night. Its falling temperature steadied at eighty, and finally began to rise. By noon next day it was awake.

The specialists had it carried to Robin's room, urging her to nurse it, because they were afraid to risk bottle feeding. Though they had warned her the child was exceptional, she hid her eyes after one glance and shrieked until her physician ordered heavy sedation.

My brother hinted that the creature should simply be allowed to die. Merely as a biological specimen, however, it was far too valuable to be abandoned. Many of us, besides, had caught a warmer personal interest in it from Nick and Kyrie. Since neither parent wanted to see it again, Marko and Carolina took it home until the nursery was finished.

That nursery was actually a special laboratory, designed by Colonel Petrov himself for the observation of these unique guinea pigs. A low-roofed ranch-style building, it looked deceptively homelike, but there were offices and instrument rooms and a record vault as well as space for all three children and their custodians. One-way mirrors and a network of sensors were built into the walls.

Robin's baby was moved there as soon as a room was ready, a week ahead of Nick and Kyrie. To Carolina's surprise, they seemed to miss the baby painfully, even though

37

it was nearly always asleep. Allowed at last to explore their own new quarters there, they squealed with glee when they discovered that that child would be with them again. Though most of the nurses shrank from its shapeless strangeness, Nick and Kyrie clamored to be near it, their great eyes glowing as if it was beautiful to them.

By that time, Carolina had decided that it was going to be male. She named it Guy, after the way she heard the shouts with which Nick and Kyrie greeted it. Its soft flippers had begun to look more like hands and feet, and it sometimes twitched and blinked when the other babies were near, though for several months it made no sound at all.

Robin tried peyote for her jangled nerves and yoga to restore her precious figure. She returned to the Bengal Hudson with her guru, and married him before the year was up, promising a gossip columnist that she would never bear another child.

The divorce did no apparent damage to the curious tie betwen my brother and Howard Hudson. Tom left his Skygate job as soon as Colonel Petrov would release him, and I heard that he was joining Hudson in a venture to exploit the astonishing discoveries on Mercury, where the seekers had begun to chart wide craters walled with piled nodules of alloyed iridium and gold—one exobiologist made the bizarre suggestion that those rich nuggets were excreted waste from the unknown creatures that had dug those iron-walled tunnels.

In spite of those rich finds, and stranger ones reported on the moons of Jupiter, COSMOS had begun to fall apart. The rumors and suspicions that grew from the riddle of the moon grit raised new tensions between its uneasy partners. Maxim Petrov resigned, in the wake of a scandal that linked him with a Sino-Soviet spy ring. Washington threatened to cancel the lease on the mesa and reclaim all the Skygate installations. Erik Thorsen became the new director of the Center, through a precarious compromise, and was soon accused of setting up his own spy apparatus for the United States.

Naïvely, as we sat one morning over coffee in the nursery kitchen, I asked Marko what those spies were after. After all, COSMOS was neutral and international. Our research reports went out to every member. I could understand Howard Hudson's interest in the seeker surveys, but we had no iridium boulder-fields here at Skygate.

"We have something else, that might surprise you." Marko gave me an owlish blink. "Thorsen questioned me the other day, and finally warned me against his rival spies. What they want is information about the three fathers—him and Tom and me. About our sex lives."

"Why—?"

"The children are the most exciting results of space research up to now—and a deeper mystery than the nature of whatever dug those tunnels into Mercury. A lot of scientists and several governments want to know whether there'll be more."

He stirred his coffee moodily.

"Carolina wanted another," he added at last. "But the lab says my semen's sterile now. Thorsen didn't exactly say, but I think he's impotent—and distressed about it. Which leaves your brother."

I thought that over. In the divorce action, Robin's lawyers had named a hotel manicurist and a nurse in the space hospital and a typist in the records section. Had some of them been secret agents?

"Tom's gone," I said. "Maybe back in space—we don't keep in touch. But who would want another creature like his son?"

"Don't look down your nose at Guy." Marko seemed almost hurt. "Nick and Kyrie idolize him. My wife has learned to love him, too. She keeps quoting proverbs. She says you can't see the oak in the acorn."

That image of the acorn stuck in my mind, apt for all three children. The mystery of life showed special shapes in them. Delicately new, they kept unfolding unexpected strength and startling surprise.

Marko was in charge of the nursery now, with Suzie and Carolina as official assistants. They nurtured those seedling beings with love and wonder and frequent alarm. Guy Hood slept most of the time for his first few years, but Nick and Kyrie kept everybody busy recording the data Thorsen demanded.

Though they looked more human than Guy, their bodies were equally strange. All three possessed temperature regulators that baffled the biolgists. When snow fell, they wanted to play in it naked. The hottest desert sun gave them only a temporary tan. Nudists by nature, they had no use for clothing. We learned to let them go without it.

Marko tried to run intelligence tests. Even when he was awake, however, Guy Hood had no mind that anyone could measure. Though Nick and Kyrie seemed happily cooperative, their erratic responses were a puzzle until Carolina discovered that they were making a gay little game of observing their observers.

When Suzie taught Kyrie to wink her varicolored eyes, she started winking at everybody who tried to spy on her through the one-way mirrors, no matter how silently. Thorsen wanted to know how she sensed us, but nobody could discover that.

Nick discovered arithmetic before he could talk. Two months old, he began playing counting games with Carolina, pushing beads on a toy abacus to add and subtract integers up to ten. A month older, using a larger counting frame Marko made for him, he learned division and invented a system of his own for extracting roots.

Beyond that point, his mathematical intuitions became vaguely disturbing. I remember the puzzled dread I felt one day in Marko's office. We were watching a salesman demonstrate a compact new computer. Carolina came in carrying Nick, who was always as eager as anybody to see the new lab equipment.

Not six months old and not yet walking, he leaned and whined until Carolina set him on the desk in front of the computer. The amused salesman pointed out the switch and gasped when Nick started the machine. He ran it for half an hour, tiny fists tapping out his problems with a gin-

40

gerly care, bald head bobbing to bring his huge eyes within an inch of the answers.

Abruptly then, with a shy little smile that seemed to hide boredom with the machine and amused wonder at all of us, he tore the paper tape from the machine. Before Carolina could help, he slid through a chair to the floor and scurried back to rejoin Kyrie where she sat in the hall, hammering an empty pabulum tin with a teaspoon and the plastic case of Marko's slide rule, beating out an irritating rhythm that somehow stuck in my mind so that I can still recall it.

I asked the salesman not to talk about the children, but when he was gone I discussed that disquieting incident with Marko and Carolina. "Sometimes those two frighten me," Marko admitted. "I got the oddest feeling just now that Nick can think circles around our new computer."

Carolina put a warning finger on her lips, though he had closed the soundproof office door.

"What are they?" I almost shivered when I recalled the enigmatic amusement on Nick's elfish face as he crumpled that discarded tape. "What will they be when they are grown?"

"Guy's the one that worries me," Carolina whispered. "The other two are happy. Bright as they are, I understand them most of the time. But Guy's different. A different breed. I think I love him just as much—he does need love. But I can't help feeling that he was born for tragedy. I'm afraid for Guy!"

2

Diversity

Our work with the children was wonder and delight, at least for the first few years. Carolina used to say they were like the blooms of some exotic tropic bulb unfolding. With each new day, they brought us glad surprises.

Music was Kyrie's first interest, but she seemed bored with all our favorites before she learned to talk. She began beating out her own music on any resonant object she could reach, or sometimes trilling it in a keen mockingbird voice, inventing complex scales that seemed difficult and unmelodious to us.

Seven months old, Nick walked his first steps on the same morning that she uttered her first careful syllables. Gravely intent, they tutored each other all day. That afternoon they swayed hand in hand to meet Carolina, proudly cooing in unison, "Watch us—walking!"

Nick learned to read before they were two, apparently from a set of picture books about the planets. He taught Kyrie. They were not yet three when Marko found them one morning on the nursery floor, huddled over his desk dictionary.

"Now." Kyrie's bird-voice had an interrogative lilt. "Biocosm?"

She turned the pages to find the word and Nick bent over the book, his whole head sweeping the lines at a distance of two inches.

"A planetary ecology of related and compatible bioforms." He formed each word with a painful precision, mispronouncing one or two he had probably never heard. "Though all known biocosms of the solar system display certain similarities, biological materials from one biocosm are generally useless or poisonous to members of another."

"What does that mean?" Kyrie looked up at Marko. "Uncle Yuri, what *is* a biocosm?"

"A chain of life," Marko said. "Here on earth, we all belong to a single chain. Cows eat grass and we eat cows and the grass grows on animal stuff. We breathe out carbon dioxide the grass needs, and the grass breathes out oxygen for us. In our own biocosm, we are all made of similar chemicals, and we are all adjusted to one another."

Nick nodded brightly, but Kyrie was still frowning.

"We call our own world the alpha biocosm," Marko said. "Our space machines have to carry little alpha biocosms, because we can't breathe the air on any other world or eat the things that grow there. The beta-forms of Venus and the delta-forms of Jupiter can't fit into our chain. That's a problem for space explorers. Different biocosms can't easily be friends."

"Thank you, Uncle Yuri." Kyrie shook her head, still unsatisfied. "Now what about Guy? Does he belong—" She caught her breath. "Does he belong to our biocosm?"

"We don't know much about Guy." Marko hesitated uncomfortably. "We're learning all we can. We want to help him grow up and be happy."

"Please—help Guy!" Her small voice quivered. "We need you, Uncle Yuri. You and Aunt Carolina and Uncle Kim. Because my own man-father is afraid of Nick and me and he doesn't love Guy at all!"

We tried to help all three. Nick and Kyrie needed little teaching. Nick soon began consuming books with a computerlike efficiency that almost alarmed me. After music, Kyrie found and dropped a dozen other interests, as if searching for something she could not identify.

We arranged a vacation tour for Nick and Kyrie, the summer they were four. Though we had trouble with hostile crowds in several cities, they made a light-hearted game of evading both mobs and protectors. Nick learned Ukrainian from Marko's father in Lucerne and picked up spoken Japanese from Suzie's mother in Honolulu—he was disappointed when she didn't know the ideograms.

43

Though Nick seemed to be drinking in everything with big-eyed delight, Kyrie made us cut the trip short. Guy had been left at Skygate because of the spreading fear of space aliens, and Kyrie kept fretting that he was lonely. Perhaps he was. He squirmed against her like a hungry kitten when he saw her again, and mouthed a sound she said was her name.

Guy was now awake three or four hours at a time, though he slept for days on end. His furry limbs had begun to develop, but all his movements were still sluggish and uncertain. Kyrie got him to stand that summer, towering over her like a gray ogre, but another year had passed before he could walk or speak. Even then, his speech was a slurred mumble that she had to translate for the rest of us.

Somehow, Guy became a special friend of mine. Perhaps I found it easy to forgive his slow gray strangeness because he was my brother's son. He seemed to show a kind of animal affection for me, even before I could understand his voice, when he snuggled up for me to stroke his fur.

As he became aware enough to miss his parents, I suppose he tried to replace them with me. I remember a painful scene in the nursery, the summer he was five. Kyrie had been sitting on my knee. She slipped down when Guy shambled in. Perhaps he wanted her place, but he had grown too heavy to be held. He leaned over me, whining and clumsily pawing at me. A wave of his special odor struck me—a sharp, clean scent, a little like a dry barnyard.

"Little Guy wants to know what he is." I smiled when Kyrie called him that, but she was very serious. "He wants to know why he's not like Nick and me. He can't see why he has no father and no mother to love him and make him beautiful."

Robin was on the moon by then with her fourth husband, a lunaculture faddist who was converting the Crater Hudson into a low-gee rejuvenation mecca for aging billionaires. My brother had managed to disappear completely.

"You're all right, Guy." I touched his naked fur. "You do have parents. They're traveling. Your mother's on the moon, but I'm sure she often thinks of you—"

He mouthed a savage sound. Kyrie rushed to him and reached up to wrap her golden arms around him. Tears welled out of her midnight eyes.

"We do love you, little Guy." She looked helplessly at me. "He wants to know why he's something nobody—hardly anybody loves."

"Tell him the three of you are different." Though I knew Guy could understand, I found myself speaking to Kyrie instead. "Different—and very wonderful! Tell him we're working in the lab to find out why."

I was trying to look into Guy's face, but its inhuman strangeness distracted me. The eyes were wet, black lumps, yellow-rimmed, with no expression I could read. They stared without winking. Slow tears ran out of them to make blue streaks down his furry cheeks. His voice croaked dismally again.

"Little Guy, you too are wonderful." Kyrie gulped and looked at me, her enormous eyes almost accusing. "He says he's dull and ugly like a toad. He wants to know why he isn't beautiful and bright like Nick."

There was nothing I could say.

In the publicity office, we had a shifting mission. At first we tried to sell the children as the exotic and delightful wonder babies of the moon. When that program began to sour, we tried to shield them from all the fear and fury we could not prevent.

Once I showed Marko our file of hate mail. Its growing virulence sickened me. Writers called the children filthy names, accused them of kinship with the enemy biocosms on the other planets, even demanded their destruction.

"To a lot of people," I told Marko, "they're monsters. Not just Guy—though I guess he does look the part. But Nick and Kyrie too. I can't understand it. Why should anybody hate them?"

"They're vulnerable." He slowly crumpled an ugly letter. "I suppose we all look for demons outside, when we can't endure what's in ourselves. We project our hates upon them. The creatures of Mercury and Venus and Jupiter might do for demons, but they are out of reach. The children are strange and here and vulnerable."

"But they're human," I protested. "Partly, anyhow."

"Partly." Marko scowled at the paper ball. "But partly not. I suppose that explains the irrational nature of the hatred." He nodded somberly. "The horror of the old taboo against sex between beasts and men."

I often thought of that. Guy at least, with his sullen moods and shaggy fur, must have seemed as alien to people outside as the beta-life of Venus was. Though Nick and Kyrie were appealingly human most of the time, I remember disquieting bits of strangeness.

Even their play sometimes disturbed us. I remember walking into the nursery one afternoon, the summer they were four. Absorbed in the game, they ignored us. Nick knelt on the floor, very carefully erecting a tower of white plastic blocks. Kyrie was dancing around and around him on tiptoe, carrying an old golf ball over her head and buzzing in an odd way through her teeth. Guy squatted near them, following the ball with his sleepy yellow stare. I was smiling at their grave intentness, but Marko froze.

"Nick! What's all this?"

"Just a game, Dad."

Painstakingly, Nick crowned his tower with a bright orange block. Marko bent to stare. Nick glanced at Kyrie. Her buzzing changed. Dancing closer, she brought the golf ball down along a spiral path and placed it on a shelf of the tower.

"Nick—" Marko's voice was so queer and high that Kyrie gave him a wondering look. He caught his breath and tried again. "Where did you learn this game?"

"Just made it up."

"Will you tell me about it?"

"You saw it, Dad." Nick shrugged. "That's all it is."

46

"But I can't understand what I saw." Marko turned to Kyrie, almost desperately. "Can't you help me?"

"I'll try, Uncle Yuri." She nodded solemnly. "In the game, we don't belong. We're space folk, marooned on earth. We find a way to send a message to our own far people, and they send a ship to pick us up." She touched the ball. "This is the ship."

"The tower." Marko's pointing finger trembled. "What is that tower?"

Kyrie turned in a puzzled way to Nick.

"It's a tachyon terminal." He spoke the words with a careful precision. "You see, Dad, the ball is a tachyon ship. That means it goes faster than light, out in the space between stars. But here it needs a proper terminal, with a tachyon beacon to show it where to land."

"I—I see." Marko gulped, trying hard to play the game. "But how did you learn about tachyons?"

"In a book." Guy nodded vaguely toward the nursery library. "A book about ships and stars. The writer said tachyon ships would never work, because the speed of light is a barrier we could never pass. Maybe he's right. We're only playing a game. In the game we just skip around the barrier, by using a minimum-energy shift of state." He must have seen my puzzled look, because his elfin face grew graver. "You see, that converts the mass of the ship to the tachyon state, at any speed we like."

"I—I see." Marko was blinking again at the plastic tower. "Why did you build it just that way, Nick? I mean, with those seven columns and the colored block at the top."

"I don't know, Dad." Nick shrugged, with a look of bored impatience. "After all, it's just a game."

"And Guy is sick of it," Kyrie piped. "Because he doesn't dig tachyons. If you will please excuse us now, he wants to go out to the pool."

Still unable to walk alone, Guy whined eagerly. Kyrie ran to him and waited for Nick to help. Together, they hauled him upright. He tottered away between them, a gray, ungainly beast.

The toy tower was left behind. Its stacked blocks were cylinders of a common magnetic plastic, from a set Carolina had given Guy. I saw nothing special about them, but Marko ran for his camera to film the tower and made me dictate a record of the whole incident before he would answer my questions.

"That's a model of the terminal I saw—or thought I saw—where the grit brought us down on the moon," he told me then. "The seven clustered columns. The rising spiral of landing stages around the taller central column. That colored beacon at the top."

He frowned at me and shook his head.

"I'd like to know where they got that game."

We found the book about ships and stars, but there was no picture of a tachyon terminal. Carolina assured us that she had never told the children that much about the grit and the riddles of their origin. After a long and fruitless discussion, our reports went into the file of unsolved problems.

While that file grew thicker, year by year, COSMOS slowly crumbled. Politicians began to call it a nest of spies and traitors. Our budgets were sliced. Able people quit. Though we tried not to alarm the children with any news of outside dangers, I remember something Carolina said.

We were in the exobiology lab, where she still worked after hours. Blue sterilizing lamps washed the walls with a pale, painful light. Whispering from the filters, the air was still thick with the queer scent of the beta-life bubbling in the glass-walled incubators—a stinging reek like molding hay. She had been showing me her slides and models of those microscopic aliens with a glow almost of love, but her animation died when I spoke of the future of COSMOS.

"It's lak a san' castle, Mistuh Hodian." Worry brought back for a moment the soft Negro intonations she usually avoided. "Like the sand castles we used to build on the beach when I was a kid. The sea waves keep eating at it. I'm afraid of what will happen to the children when it's gone."

"Perhaps it won't go." I felt impelled to defend the future of the organization, not from any real faith in it, but I suppose because hopeful promotion had been my profession. "I know they keep cutting our budgets. But we can make a strong case for the seeker project at least, now that it's finally paying off."

I was thinking of the new wealth and knowledge that space had begun to promise. The diggers of those iron-walled tunnels into Mercury had yet to show themselves, but the seekercraft were reporting unbelievable billions of tons of iridium and gold in the nuggets that formed those craterlike ridges around the tunnel clusters.

Critics objected that gold wasn't yet worth its freight from Mercury, but Jupiter was already seeming to offer more exciting knowledge and cheaper transportation. Flying objects had appeared near that giant planet, gathering and wheeling as if to observe the spacemen towing the prefab sections of Jupiter Station One, flying with such remarkable speed and freedom that captured specimens were expected to reveal some radical new principle of space travel—if specimens could be captured.

The bold passes and swift escapes of those Jovian beings seemed to prove some kind of intelligence. The indications of advanced life on Venus and Saturn were not quite so clear. A second station in orbit above the newly mottled clouds of Venus had recently reported an unexplained loss of power before it ceased transmission. No Saturn probe had ever returned, or sent back any report at all from the close vicinity of the ringed planet.

"Why should we fear our neighbors in space?" I asked Carolina. "They've been next door to us for several billion years, and they haven't hurt us yet."

"It's not the planets I fret about," she said. "It's people. Being black, I can't see human nature quite as you do, Mr. Hodian. I'm afraid we're not so noble as the founders of COSMOS wanted us to be. That's why we must give the children a chance. I hope they'll be better than we ever were."

For a moment we stood silent, brooding over their uncertain future.

"Of course I want to know what dug those tunnels into Mercury," she went on suddenly. "And why our Saturn probes don't get back. But I think human nature is a bigger danger. To COSMOS. To the children. Maybe even to our sister biocosms."

She paused to frown at the incubator where her reeking beta-cultures grew in frothing flasks of milky liquid.

"We've had trouble for years with some unknown agent that kept killing off the cultures," she said. "Now I think I've found the killer. If the more advanced Venusians dislike human beings, perhaps they have a reason."

That was all she told me then, because she wanted to repeat some of her experiments, but she called me back a few nights later, along with Marko and Thorsen, to hear about her discovery. When we were gathered around a table in the lab, she tried to hand Thorsen a flask of pale fluid clotted with little brownish lumps. He held his nose and backed away.

"It can't hurt you, sir," she assured him softly. "It was a beta-culture, but it's dead. I killed it with a drop of human juice. The actual lethal fraction is a common enzyme. A human molecule that seems to multiply like a virus in the beta creatures. If the higher forms have no more immunity, one drop of human blood could spread a terrible contagion among them."

"So we're poison to 'em?" Thorsen relaxed, grinning now at the flask. "I suppose they'll learn to respect us."

"That depends on their level of evolution." She gave him an odd look, both baffled and sad. "Anyhow, we have other problems, closer home."

Thorsen himself was one of those problems. To understand the children, as Carolina said, we needed to know precisely what the grit had done to the seeker's three-man crew. Though my brother had disappeared, Marko and Thorsen were still under study.

Except for his sterility, Marko displayed no permanent effects of his experience on the moon. Though Thorsen angrily denied any effect on himself, he had lost flesh and youth and nerve. The flame of his hair and beard had slowly dulled to a rusty gray, and his old boisterous charm had died into a bleak taciturnity. We had watched that change with sharp concern, yet the outcome surprised us. He tried to kill Nick.

It was a warm autumn afternoon, the year the children were five. Suzie had arranged a picnic, hoping to revive Thorsen's fading interest in the children, and perhaps also in herself. Nick didn't want to go, but Kyrie thought Guy would enjoy the outing.

Trouble began when Thorsen commanded the children to dress. Kyrie slipped obediently into a sunsuit and brought shorts for Guy, but Nick came out naked. Thorsen lost his temper and shouted a new command. Nick said quietly that he didn't need clothes and wouldn't wear them.

Thorsen called him indecent and pulled him out of the car. He walked quietly back to the nursery. By that time, Suzie was crying and Guy had begun to moan. Kyrie ran after Nick and brought him out in a pair of red swim trunks.

I watched them drive away in Suzie's new electric car— a gift from Thorsen in the wake of some earlier domestic incident they wouldn't talk about. He looked grim and gloomy at the wheel, but Kyrie was soon happily excited, showing everything to Guy.

An hour before they were to return, the hospital called us. We found all three children laid out in the emergency ward, splashed with blood and grime, limp as death.

Carolina rushed to them and soon assured us that they were only sleeping. Marko and I left her to tend them, while we tried to learn what had happened. Suzie had driven them back in the car, but she was battered and exhausted, already under sedation. A police airtrac picked Thorsen up at the picnic spot. Deep facial scratches were still oozing blood. He glared at us sullenly and told the officers to take him on to jail.

We got the story next day, when Suzie and Kyrie were

awake. The explosion had come when the new car stalled on the last rocky climb toward the seep we called the Indian Spring, where they had planned to eat. Thorsen lifted the hood and read the fuel-cell handbook and finally said they would have to wait for help.

But Nick spoke up. He said the cell just needed adjustment, and reached past Thorsen to twist a relief valve. The motor hummed at once, but Thorsen came apart. Gasping with a wordless fury, he seized Nick's throat and swung him off the ground.

Suzie screamed, while Nick kicked and strangled, but Thorsen ignored her. She attacked him, clawing wildly at his face. He released Nick with one hand long enough to slap her off the road. Guy hugged his leg, mewing like a hurt kitten, as Thorsen shook Nick with both hands again.

Kyrie was more effective. She found the jeweled rescue gun in Suzie's purse—a gift from Thorsen himself, when he brought his bride back from the moon to the turbulent Earth. One quick jet knocked him out.

Nick was limp by then, but Kyrie knew he was still alive. She helped Suzie load him and Guy into the car, and waited until they were safe on the mesa pavement before she herself went to sleep.

Released by the police, when Suzie wouldn't file charges, Thorsen took a room at the Skygate Hudson. Marko and I tried to question him there. His patched face looked pale and drawn, and his breath had a faint whiskey reek. At first he wouldn't talk at all.

"No, I'm not drunk!" he burst out at last. "Yesterday I wasn't even drinking. The whole thing was just too much for me, when that smart-faced kid fixed the car. I can't stand 'em any longer."

"But they're our children." Marko blinked in owlish astonishment. "Little Kyrie's your own daughter."

"A damned cuckoo!" His face was red and twitching now. "They're all cuckoos. Something planted 'em in us—to be hatched in human bodies. But they're actually no kin. No more human than a crocodile!"

"You can't believe—"

"We've been damned fools!" He raised his voice to drown Marko's. "Trying to bring them up—to take the world away from us. They've got to be exterminated!"

We stood staring. I couldn't understand him. After a moment he staggered away, as if exhausted by his own trembling violence, and sank down on the side of the bed.

"I guess I was a fool today, letting that little devil tempt me to touch him, but they're all too much for me. Too clever and too quick. I saw that months ago." He paused to peer at us, bewildered and afraid. "Can you see what demons they are?" he whispered desperately. "Can't you see what they're scheming to do?"

Thorsen's assault on Nick revealed new fissures in the sand castle of COSMOS. The directors quarreled with the doctors at the space hospital about his sanity, and he was finally relieved of his post and transferred for treatment at a psychiatric clinic. The directors failed at first to agree on a man to replace him. They finally called Marko into a closed meeting, and sent him back as acting head, with a new program for the Center.

"Half the directors think Erik was right." He shook his head gloomily. "They'd like to get rid of the children. Since they don't know how to do that, they want us to watch them. We're to record every change we see. Report every word and every act."

The crumbling castle thus became a sort of prison, but we were able to keep the children safe inside it a little longer. Though the new joint research committee gave us no funds for formal research, Nick and Kyrie were turning sharper minds than ours to the riddle of their own existence.

Trying to shield the children, Carolina had often warned us not to talk to them about the alien biocosms and the riddle of their own origin. When they began asking questions about themselves, her first answers were evasive.

"Of course you three are different," she used to say. "You're the moon babies. Your fathers were the moon men. That's why you're all so special and so precious. You aren't like us poor dull earth people at all."

They outgrew such simple answers. The spring they were seven, Nick found Carolina's name in a child's book about "our neighbors in space." He brought it to me to ask if Dr. C. Marko was actually his mother. When I said she was, he and Kyrie demanded a tour of the exobiology lab.

Carolina reluctantly agreed, though she masked them cautiously against infection by some alien organism. Kyrie clung close to me, frightened into silence by the queer smells and queer machines. Nick was eagerly excited, shouting breathless questions through the gauze.

Huge-eyed, he peered at flasks of cultured beta-life. He squinted and prodded at a coiled iridium nugget from Mercury. He blinked at projected films of the snake-shaped creatures that had come out to circle Jupiter Station.

As we were about to leave, sudden bells jangled. Automatic doors thudded shut, sealing the hall ahead of us. A blinding violet glare flooded the glass-walled corridors around the incubators behind.

"Uncle Kim!" Kyrie gripped my hand. "What's this?"

I was unnerved, but Carolina seemed delighted.

"Don't fret." She gathered both children in her arms. "It's just the beta-life. Sometimes it changes shape, you see. Like tadpoles changing into frogs, or grubs into butterflies. Only in its own strange way."

She turned more gravely to me.

"We've been observing this for several months, though we don't yet have data for a formal report. The cultures bubble along for generation after generation, in single-cell form. But now and then something happens. The simple-seeming cells combine into an amazing metamorph."

"Let's have a look."

She made us wait while she got into a plastic gown and went back through double doors into the incubator block to bring a stopped flask to the glass barrier where we could see it. The children gasped and stared.

The milky fluid in the bottle had become a big scarlet bubble, oddly spotted with gold and black, fringed with silky silver tendrils. With an uneven rhythm, it expanded against the walls of the flask and contracted again, as if trying to breathe.

"Poor creature!" Kyrie whispered. "It wants out."

Carolina set the flask on a stand. We stood there outside the glass half the afternoon, watching that imprisoned thing while she made notes and photographs. Vigorous at first, its breathing movements became irregular and slow.

"That bottle's choking it." Kyrie looked almost accusingly at Carolina, when she came back at last to us. "Can't you set it free?"

"Our breath would kill it." Carolina patted Kyrie's golden shoulder, soothingly. "We'd all like to help, but it can't live in our biocosm."

We saw it die. Its last fluttering movements ceased. Its vivid colors faded into leadlike grays. Turning brittle, the bubble burst and shrank, its fragile membranes dissolving into a few drops of brown liquid mud.

Its odor reached us when Carolina opened the doors, a thin, revolting sweetness a little like rotten eggs. I wanted to leave, but Nick and Kyrie had questions to ask.

"We're getting two or three such changes a week," Carolina told us. "Each metamorph has a different color and shape. They're all trying to escape—that's why we've installed the sensors and the automatic doors. None has got away, or lived more than two hours. Really, we don't know much about them yet. You'll have to wait till we get data enough for a full report."

We followed to her office and waited while she put away her notebooks and cameras. Kyrie nestled uneasily against my knees, as if frightened by what we had seen. Equally troubled, Nick kept asking questions.

"Mother, what are we? Why do you keep us here, in our own special lab? Why do you watch us all the time?

Are we specimens too? Like the meta—" He tried again, careful with the word. "Like the metamorphs?"

"Don't you worry, dear." She tried to hug him. "You're our children. We love you very much."

"But we are different." He slipped out of her arms and backed uncertainly away. "You do observe us. You film us and tape us and test us. You keep records and file reports, just like you do for those funny bugs in your bottles."

I felt Kyrie shiver.

"Why?" Nick shrilled. "What kind of thing are we?"

"You're people," Carolina said. "But unique people. That's why you're so priceless to science. As well as to us."

"What makes us—unique?"

"Something happened to your three fathers, out in space." Carolina's eyes were as big and black as his, imploring him to understand. "They were the crew of a seeker survey craft, exploring the moon. They found a bed of queer black grit, splashed around an impact crater. Some force from that grit caught them and changed them— changed the genes of their sperm cells—so that you are their children."

"But they aren't exactly our fathers? We are not exactly human?"

"Not entirely human." Nodding reluctantly, Carolina caught her breath and tried to smile. "More wonderful than human."

"Who made the grit?" Nick demanded. "Who put it on the moon?"

"Nobody knows," Carolina said. "Though Yuri has a theory."

Nick dragged her off at once to look for Marko. Kyrie tugged me after them, her tiny hand trembling in mine. Nick pushed into Marko's office in the nursery, without waiting to knock. Coffee was brewing on his desk, bubbling fragrantly through a queer device of his own invention, a complex hookup of glass tubes and stoppered flasks. With a genial nod, he offered to share it.

"Father—" Something briefly checked Nick's high voice. "Yuri, we've seen a metamorph. My mother has been telling us about the moon grit and how it made us what we are. I want to see the grit and I want to hear your theory."

Marko turned off his coffee apparatus.

"The joint research committee keeps the grit in a vault." He blinked gravely at Nick. "What's left of it. Half what we had was used up in experimental study over the years, and spies were stealing the rest."

"How do you open the vault?"

"I petition the joint committee." Marko smiled a little at Nick's determination. "But here's a model of one grit crystal, magnified a hundred times."

The model was a shining black pyramid, two feet tall. It stood on a metal pedestal. Marko swung a slice of it out on hinges, to show its inner blackness intricately patterned with shining lines of gold and glass.

"The black mass is a granular allotrope of carbon, elsewhere unknown," he explained. "Seeded with microscopic thorium beads. Latticed in a very intricate way with those wafers of silicon and gold. Mixed with trace amounts of other elements."

Kyrie shrank back beside me, but Nick listened eagerly. "Your theory, Yuri?"

"The crystals were made somewhere," Marko said. "But not, I think, on any planet we've found. The splash pattern around the crater shows an impact from the south —the direction of our nearest star. I think the crystals were manufactured and shot to the moon by an unknown technology far ahead of us."

I felt Kyrie quiver.

"By the star folk?" she whispered. "Our own far people!"

"That was just a baby game." Nick glanced at her reprovingly. "We made up the star folk," he told Marko. "But we didn't know about the grit. What could it be for?"

"Maybe there is an interstellar culture." Marko smiled

soberly at Kyrie. "Maybe it is spreading across the galaxy, from star to star. Maybe the grit was contained in a messenger missile, shot from Alpha Centauri to make contact with us."

"Why the grit?" Nick peered at the black pyramid. "Why not a ship?"

"I've wondered for years," Marko said. "At last I think I see why. I think intelligent worlds are too rare and too far for ships to find them all. I think the messenger missiles must have been scattered like seed, across dead worlds and live ones, to be awakened by any evolving intelligence. Our seeker woke it."

"And we were born." Nick nodded slowly. "Now what are we?"

"The messengers, I imagine."

"So what is the message?" Nick looked tiny and puzzled and afraid. "What are we to do? If the grit made us, what are we *for?*"

"You'll discover that." Marko paused, with an odd look of owlish foreboding, before he added, "I think you'll find a very splendid destiny."

Nick smiled hopefully, but Kyrie was still afraid.

"Uncle Yuri—" Her small voice quivered and broke. "If Nick and I are messengers from the stars, what is poor dear Guy?"

Uncomfortably Marko shook his head.

"Tell us, Uncle Yuri. Tell us what your theory is."

"The messenger missile struck the moon millions of years ago." His eyes shifted uneasily from her to the tall black pyramid. "The grit had to wait for us to find it. Too long, I think. Most of the crystals were damaged by micrometeorites. If they are fission-powered solid-state devices —as I think they are—most of them are now defective." He looked unhappily back at her. "I'm afraid their defects appear in Guy."

"No!" Her voice turned sharp with pain. "You've got to be wrong, Uncle Yuri. Poor Guy is not defective. We love him exactly as he is."

Nick clamored to see the actual moon grit, until Marko filed a requisition. The joint research committee took three days to approve it, but then a security squad brought six crystals to the nursery, along with a receipt for Marko to sign.

All three children came to watch him pour the black grit from the test tube to a table top. Guy cried out when he saw the shining bits. More alive than I had ever seen him, he snatched at them and darted away with one clutched in each gray fist.

"They're for Nick." Marko looked at me. "Get 'em back."

Guy dropped to the floor, as I followed. He was moaning and quivering as if in ecstacy or pain. His eyes rolled blindly upward, and his barnyard scent rose rank around me. His hoarse breathing slowed and ceased. He was suddenly asleep, all his body limp except the knotted fists.

"Let him keep them," Kyrie begged. "He needs them so."

Marko agreed, and distributed the others to her and Nick. Their rapt delight almost equaled Guy's. Kyrie cradled the tiny tetrahedrons in her cupped hands, crooning plaintive little sounds I had never heard her make. Her palms and her bent face browned abruptly, as if tanned by some unseen radiation.

Nick was examining his own crystals with an air of alert intelligence, weighing them in his hand, listening to their ring when he tapped them with a fingernail, searching their bright triangles with a pocket lens. His skin was turning dark as Kyrie's.

"They are nexodes." She glanced delightedly at him. "Real nexodes!"

"What's that?" Marko started. "What's a nexode?"

"Something we made up." Nick shrugged. "In a game we used to play."

"What game?" Marko swung urgently to Kyrie. "Please tell me."

"You saw it." Her voice was faint and absent, her eyes

still fixed on the glittering crystals. "We were space folk, remember? Marooned and waiting for our people to come."

Marko nodded. "But I hadn't heard of any—nexodes."

"It looked like this." She showed the tiny tetrahedron on her small brown palm. "Only bigger—and bright with lovely light. A precious, precious thing. We used it to locate our people among the stars. And then to help their ship find us."

"How did you come to think of such a thing?"

She turned uncertainly to Nick.

"Just made it up." Scorn tinged his voice. "Baby stuff. Please, let's don't bother about it now."

He bent again, methodically testing each face of one pyramid against each face of the other, as if he expected them to stick together. When they did not, he produced a pocket magnet to try them with that.

That night in Carolina's lab we had a long discussion of those games and the grit. Marko argued for some unknown sort of cognition or memory expressed in the games. For evidence, he brought up those unexplained hallucinations that captured the seeker crew on the moon.

"The space terminal I thought I saw was too much like Nick's toy terminal," he insisted. "It can't be just coincidental. Through some medium too subtle for us, the grit communicates ideas."

"But your terminal on the moon wasn't really there," Carolina objected. "No more than Thorsen's space fort or Hood's gold meteor. The grit has been tested very elaborately for psionic effects, with negative results."

"Then how do you explain the game?"

"Nick says he made it up. Perhaps he did. Other gifted children have invented remarkable imaginary worlds. The Brontës, for instance. Nobody claims theirs was real."

We talked on, reviewing all our data and a hundred published theories, until my head throbbed from the blue glow of the sterile walls and the musty scent of the bubbling beta-cultures, but we came to no conclusions.

"Let's not fret about it," Carolina said, as we were leaving. "The grit shaped the children. Its meaning is for them, not for us. If it can help them find themselves, our real obligation is only to keep ourselves out of the way."

Next day, Marko tried again to question Nick and Kyrie. Still awake and still elated with the black grit, they seemed to understand it no better than we did. When he came to the games, Kyrie confessed a wistful half-belief that she and Nick and Guy were actual space folk, but Nick glibly quoted sources in books and films to prove that he had borrowed everything.

Carolina had seated them on the edge of Marko's desk, to bring them closer to our level. Kyrie kept eyeing her precious sample of the grit, reluctant to think of anything else. Nick sat impatiently drumming the front of the desk with his bare heels.

"We aren't bugs!" His bored annoyance flashed into abrupt resentment. "You can't cut us up to see what makes us tick—like the seeker crews want to butcher the space snakes they're hunting out around Jupiter. Why can't you leave us alone?"

"Nicky!" Kyrie caught his brown arm. "Don't!"

"To a lot of people, you are specimens." Carolina nodded soberly. "Fascinating exobiological specimens. We hope to protect you from such cruel people, until you learn why you were born. Trust us, please!"

"Of course we trust you," Kyrie whispered. "Don't we, Nick?"

His grin was almost sardonic. "We have to trust you!"

"One more thing," Marko said. "In those games, what was Guy?"

The teasing malice died from Nick's black eyes. He frowned as if he meant to speak, shook his head, finally turned unhappily to Kyrie. Her brown face faded as she raised it from the bits of grit, until she looked pale and almost piteous.

"That's the bad part." We had to lean to catch her stricken whisper. "Because Guy never liked the games. He didn't want to play. He said he was no kin to the space-folk, and he didn't want their ship to come and carry us

61

away. He wouldn't help us build the tachyon terminal. Once he kicked it and scattered all the blocks."

"Is that so bad?"

Her big eyes were a tragic black, and tears glittered on her whitened cheeks. She glanced anxiously at Nick. He made a face and shoved her shoulder as if to remind her that it was all a game, but the gestures failed to break her gloom.

"The bad part was more what I thought," she quavered miserably. "I thought Guy wouldn't play because he loved me and hated Nick. I thought he was afraid the space folk would take us both away and leave him all alone. I was terribly afraid—afraid he might hurt Nick."

"Don't cry about it." Nick pushed her again. "It was all just baby play."

Kyrie turned slowly to look at him.

"But Guy really does love me," she whispered. "And he really doesn't like it when I do anything with you, Nicky. That's why I'm so afraid. Afraid!"

Bad news came from space that year. COSMOS had reached no friendly worlds, and the cheerful assumption that the planets were oysters waiting to be opened was fading into fear that Earth herself might somehow become the oyster of some other biocosm.

The Pizarros of space had found no new Perus to loot. Though the flight mechanism of the Jovian delta-life had promised to be richer treasure than all the Incan gold, or even the nugget fields of Mercury, those elusive creatures still kept their secret.

Agile as shadows, they evaded every effort to capture or even to destroy them. No ship was swift enough to overtake them. No human weapon could reach or damage them. Near hits with nuclear missiles left them neither hurt nor offended.

As if reciprocating human curiosity, they kept darting close to the orbital station. Companionably, they escorted the seekers in flight around the planet's moons. They began flying out to meet arriving rockets. Finally they followed a returning ship, all the way to the Earth platform.

Even though the delta-form beings had never tried to take any human specimens, the news of that visit spread consternation. To head off panic, we released a theory of Carolina's that the Jovians had been to Earth before.

"They're at home in space," she said. "The evidence suggests that they can tolerate dry air at high elevations, at least for brief periods. They seem to look somewhat like the flying serpents of native Mexican art, and to move like certain UFOs."

To support the theory, she showed us the data that had come to her lab for analysis. Taken from the orbital station, one photograph had caught a snake-shaped thing in silhouette against the bright-streaked face of Jupiter.

The thick serpentine form was darkly transparent, a twisted shadow across the great Red Spot. It had an opaque nucleus—a dark jagged mass like an irregular crystal. From that mass there spread two wide luminous rays or plumes which to some primitive Aztec might have looked like wings.

"Everything suggests they've been making casual calls for centuries," Carolina said. "Without hurting anybody. I doubt that they can metabolize the products of our biocosm. Except for short visits to the highest, dryest mountains, Earth is not for them."

"Then why," I asked, "would they be interested in us?"

Her faint smile looked wry. "Perhaps because we're interested in them."

The news from Mercury was more disturbing. Computer analysis of the tapes from the seeker survey had revealed no life or motion on the surface of that hot planet. Now the COSMOS command on the orbital platform sent a landing group to test a notion that the tunnel diggers were either dead or departed. The notion turned out to be unfortunate.

The group reported a safe landing at their selected site on the rugged highlands, near the rim wall around the tunnel cluster they were to investigate. As the orbital platform moved out of contact, they had just begun blasting, to level the site and excavate a shelter tunnel of their own.

Two hours later, with contact restored, they reported evidence that Mercury was still alive. During a pause in the blasting, their seismographs had picked up a series of rhythmic tremors from the direction of the tunnel cluster.

By the time the platform came overhead, some kind of smoke or vapor was pouring out of the tunnels. It rapidly obscured the sixty-miles plain and began to spill over its circular wall.

Because of the small planet's close horizons, this cloud was not yet visible to the surface group, but the platform commander ordered them to stop drilling and prepare to take off at once if they did observe the cloud. What happened next was never discovered.

A narrow tongue of that bright fog was pushing toward the landing site, as the platform went out of range again. The commander tried to order an immediate takeoff, but laser contact was already broken. The landing group was gone when the platform came back over the site, and the last wisps of fog were disappearing from the crater basin, draining like a liquid back into the tunnels.

The commander decided not to risk another surface expedition, but photographs of the site showed a few small scattered scraps of wreckage, indicating that the landing craft had crashed or exploded soon after takeoff. The bodies of the men, along with most of the wreckage, had been somehow removed.

Relayed to the COSMOS directorate at Skygate, the reports of that incident set off a new debate. One faction wanted to withdraw all missions from Mercury. Another wanted to bombard the tunnels with nuclear missiles. As a compromise, orders were relayed for the platform commander to climb into a higher orbit and prepare to defend himself. What proved to be the last transmission from the platform had already been received. It was a routine signal that communication would be blacked out again while the platform passed behind the planet. Nothing else came through.

After another hot debate, the directorate canceled plans to send a rescue expedition. The exploration of Mercury ceased, the nature of the tunnel diggers still unknown.

In the wake of this disquieting disaster, COSMOS budgets were slashed again. The uncompleted orbital stations around Saturn and Neptune had to be abandoned, and plans were canceled for a series of transplutonian probes.

At Skygate, our difficulties multiplied. In spite of all our publicity efforts, people tended to identify the children with the enigmatic beings of those other biocosms. We ourselves were suspect. The security force received secret orders, as we later discovered, to watch us as well as our charges.

Nick was begging for permission to study a larger sample of the moon grit, but the joint research committee disapproved Marko's requisition for it. Some members doubted that a mere child could accomplish anything significant. Others feared that Nick might do too much.

Waiting fretfully, he spent most of his time in his mother's laboratory. He learned to culture the beta-life. He skimmed through all her reference books and her filed data on the other biocosms. He studied new closeups of the Jovian delta-forms, made from the Earth platform.

One of those photographs had caught the snake shape of a delta creature in outline against the cloud-swirled Earth. With sharper eyes or perhaps a sharper mind than anybody else, Nick discovered a puzzling structure of fine black lines that branched from the jagged nuclear crystal out into the serpentine shadow.

He spent two days mapping those barely visible lines, recording each with a microscopic exactness. For another sleepless night he sat cross-legged on the nursery floor, scarcely moving, "just thinking." Finally he approached his mother with a question.

"Do the COSMOS people still want to know how the delta-things propel themselves?"

Carolina said they did.

"I'll show them," he promised. "In return for freedom to study the moon grit."

She took that innocent offer to Marko. He carried it to the joint research committee. They referred it to the directorate. Nick slept while he waited, but woke instantly when Marko came back to accept his proposition.

We arranged the demonstration that same afternoon. Two engineers came from the research committee to observe it. They were not impressed with his preparations.

Clever enough with tools, Nick cut a round hole the size of a beer can in the center of a short pine board. He hammered a worn silver dime into a slot near one end of the board, and a copper cent into a slot near the other.

Marko and Carolina came along for the demonstration. Two security cars carried us out on the open mesa, a mile beyond the spaceport. I still recall the sardonic impatience of the engineers, as they watched Nick completing his device.

A thin, grave-eyed child, he looked too small for his seven years. His naked skin had been pale in the car, till the hot sun washed him with instant bronze. Squatting in the dust, he carefully fitted a can of warm beer into the hole in the board. With a soft graphite pencil, he began drawing an intricate system of lines that branched from the two coins toward the can.

His task took time. Less impervious than he was to heat, we watched and sweated. I had brought no hat, and my head began to throb. The engineers scowled impatiently through dark glasses. A security man snickered when Nick broke his pencil point.

Ignoring everything, Nick chewed his tongue and drew more lines till something happened. Though the gray horizon still shimmered all around us, I felt a sudden piercing chill. My mouth had a sharp metallic taste. Nick dropped his pencil and held his device up triumphantly.

"Watch!" he shrilled. "Watch it fly!"

White frost filmed and feathered the beer can. It burst, with a muffled thump, and brown ice jutted out. A queer edgeless dimness spread around the ice, veined with fine black lines that seemed to branch from Nick's pencil marks. Through that spreading darkness, I saw the board tugging upward. Nick clung to it, pale again with alarm. Flakes of frost swirled and crackled around him in that condensing shadow. Clinging to the ends of the board, Nick was lifted off the ground.

Carolina screamed. Nick let go. The board whistled out of sight. The sun blazed back, its heat strangely welcome. The sky rumbled for endless seconds. Silence came like a thunder clap. A dazed security man stood pointing at a puff of yellow dust on the hot horizon. I tasted that puzzling bitterness still in my mouth.

Nick gathered himself out of the dust, and the shivering engineers herded us into the cars. We jolted two miles across the mesa, to a shallow crater where the device had come down in a juniper clump. The engineers picked up a few pine splinters and a shred of twisted aluminum. Finally, they began asking what the gadget was.

"A sort of circuit," Nick said. "It picks up certain forms of energy. From light or heat or even gravitation. It changes them to kinetic energy." While the engineers muttered and stared, he added innocently, "The effect was stronger than I wanted. The broken pencil made the primary conductor marks too thick."

The whole affair left the engineers frustrated and, I think, apprehensive. They failed to translate Nick's description of the propulsion circuit or his drawings of the structured shadow-shapes of the delta-creatures into any terms they could understand. Their own copies of his device failed to fly.

Their reports, however, must have impressed the directors. The research committee approved a requisition, and an armored security truck brought Nick half a kilogram of the precious grit, in a thick cannister of yellow-painted lead.

* * *

67

Eagerly, Nick attacked the tetrahedrons. With access now to the big computer, he searched its data banks for every recorded fact about the grit. He repeated old experiments and invented new ones. Most of them failed. As weeks and months went by, his confidence ebbed into grim desperation.

Searching for help, he had us bring a series of scholars to Skygate. The first was Dr. Platon Papanek, an old colleague of Carolina's, recently back from Uranus. Nick bombarded him with anxious questions about the possibilities of intelligence in other biocosms.

"What's intelligence?" Still used to low gravity, Papanek shuffled laboriously to a chair and wheezed a garbled mixture of French and Czech that Nick translated for the rest of us. "A tool for survival. A sharper fang, a quicker claw. Each biocosm plays the survival game according to rules of its own. The successful adaptations of the beta and delta and gamma spheres can't be compared on our alpha scale. You don't measure poetry by the pound or wisdom by the yard."

"Is survival all?" Nick's thin face turned bleak. "I mean, sir, couldn't intelligence become a bridge? Couldn't it build a way for one biocosm to reach and understand and maybe help another?"

"I was once an idealist." Papanek shook his flaccid bulk and gasped for his breath. "I've been to five biocosms to look for cosmic altruism. I detected none. I conclude that benevolence is a negative factor for survival."

"Somewhere else?" Urgency quivered in Nick's voice. "Somewhere in the galaxy—couldn't universal friendship become a positive factor?"

"Who knows?" The heavy gravity of Earth damped Papanek's Slavic shrug. "The farther out we go, the queerer things we find."

He stayed three days. Listening to the questions Nick and Kyrie asked, I felt a sharper sense of the urgency of their desperate search for the makers of the moon grit, but I'm afraid they got no help from Papanek.

Nick sent next for an exiled Sino-Soviet geneticist, who

turned out to be as ignorant as we were about what the grit could have done to the sperm cells of the seeker's crew. He called in a professor of astronautics who cheerfully promised that intelligible signals could be sent to other stars within only two or three centuries, if space technology continued to advance. He invited a team of solid-state physicists, who disagreed scornfully with all his theories about the structure and the function of the grit.

His last guest was a mathematician, a big jovial Finn. They spent two days and nights in the nursery classroom, trading symbols in a haze of chalk dust. The Finn came out coffee-logged and reeling with fatigue.

"Was I expected to instruct that infant?" He blinked at me in red-eyed wonder. "In thirty minutes, he destroyed the work of my life—my model of the universe. I never met such power of mind. Yet I pity him." The Finn rubbed in a dazed way at his chalky jaw. "He doesn't know how to laugh."

Nick refused to send for anybody else. His feverish bouts of study and experiment almost ceased. He used to sit for hours in despondent thought or slip away from security to roam the moonlit mesa alone. Though he and Kyrie had always been immune to germs and viruses, Carolina thought he was falling ill of sheer frustration.

"Goodness, child, don't fret so hard," I heard her urge him one morning in the nursery kitchen. "You'll only kill yourself. No doubt you and Kyrie have tremendous things to do, but they had better wait till you are older."

"We can't wait." He pushed his untouched breakfast tray aside and stared at her with blue-rimmed eyes. "All the planets are on fire with danger for us. Earth worst of all. Our only hope is the message I think is in the grit, but time is running out for us to break the code. Mother, I'm afraid—" His faint voice cracked. "I'm afraid we'll die before we ever learn why we were born."

Such black moods distressed us all, but Nick was hard to help. Even when his problems proved impossible to solve, he would not forget them. He saw through the good news we tried to manufacture, and indignantly rejected most attempts to encourage or distract him. That year was difficult, though Guy and Kyrie brought us occasional relief from his gloomy moodiness.

Guy was heavier than I by now, and nearly as tall. Awake, he had the unpredictable vigor of a yearling grizzly and an appalling appearance. Though he enjoyed clothing no more than Nick and Kyrie did, he had reluctantly begun to hide his shaggy strangeness under a shapeless old raincoat when he was outside the nursery.

Carolina still worked when she could to train and study his sluggish intelligence. Sometimes she got him to fumble clumsily with a teaching device or an educational toy. More often he simply sprawled or squatted wherever he was, waiting dumbly for Kyrie. Nick's desperate plight did not exist for him.

Kyrie was desperately concerned, but Nick seemed not to want her with him in the lab or on his solitary walks. Trying to learn enough to understand his problems with the grit, she got Carolina to bring in a series of tutors for her.

Carolina helped her choose an international team of genetic specialists, and she begged them to tell her why Nick and Guy were so different. Those experts took new case histories of all three children, scowled at the grit, and muttered vaguely about anomalous genetic mutations.

Searching as urgently as Nick for any sort of understanding, she called in a group of noted composers, who turned out to like or understand her music no better than I did. She sent for philosophers and anthropologists, a female psychologist, finally a Chilean poet.

She liked the poet best. A sun-dried gnome with lank black hair and black child-eyes, he beat a many-stringed guitar to a whining chant about his own Homeric life. A onetime spaceman, he had ridden seekers around a dozen moons and asteroids, yet never discovered the meaning of life. Kyrie must have seen Nick and herself in his sad songs. When he was gone, she wouldn't send for anybody else.

"The wisest men aren't wise enough," she told Carolina.

"They can't help Nick. They can't tell us what we were born for. They can't explain why Guy is like he is." She sighed. "Really, you know—in spite of you and Uncle Yuri and Uncle Kim—the three of us are all alone."

Unable to do anything for Nick, she turned to Guy. His slow being quickened eagerly when she came near, and she seemed not to mind his backward strangeness. For months they were always together. They talked little— words, she said, were still too hard for Guy. But she used to sit crooning by him while he slept, and, awake, he used to whimper for her music.

Music—an odd word for the throbs and moans and howls that she beat and scraped and blew out of unlikely bits of junk, or even for the wailing songs she sang. Those tormented sounds were never melodious to the rest of us, but rather disturbing in a way I could never understand. But they set Guy to writhing and whining with an animal delight.

Uncontrolled, his gorilla strength had become a problem for security. When he learned to like working out in the gym, he broke equipment and threw balls too hard and fractured the jaw of a guard who was trying to teach him to box. The security chief was afraid he might hurt Kyrie.

She laughed at the notion of danger from her baby Guy, but Carolina, observing their sex development, began to take it seriously. Kyrie, too, had outgrown Nick. Still child-slight, her figure had matured distractingly. Carolina warned and cajoled and ordered her to wear bikinis anyhow. She obeyed now and then.

Though Nick had never given up his quest for the secret of the grit, it was Guy who made the breakthrough. It happened on a blazing summer afternoon. I was sitting in the publicity office, staring through the window at blue mirages on the mesa and not dictating my daily security report, when Kyrie burst in, screaming.

"It's the messenger stuff!" She was so breathless I failed to get the words at first. "Uncle Kim, the messenger stuff! Guy wants to show you. He's learned what to do with the messenger stuff."

I followed her back to a playroom in the nursery. We found Nick and Guy huddled over a child-sized desk. Nick sat on a chair, naked and alert and coffee-brown. Too big for the furniture, Guy was crouching over the desk, doing something with a handful of the tiny tetrahedrons.

"Guy knows how—"

"Shhh!" Guy hushed her, and we stooped to watch.

The grit was spread out on a sheet of white paper. Moving with a deftness that surprised me, Guy's stubby, short-furred fingers were pushing three tiny pyramids into a triangular pattern. Squinting with care, a new yellow gleam in his eyes, he lowered the base of a fourth pyramid upon the upright points, to complete a taller tetrahedron.

When that last crystal clicked into place, a soft blue glow lit the larger pyramid, brightest in its hollow center. Guy raised his browless head, with a thick grunt of satisfaction, and Nick snatched the thing he had made.

"We've got it, Ky!" His voice turned shrill as hers. "He can stick them together. In fours, like this. And the fours into fours of fours, the way they were meant to go. He's making our nexode—"

A savage growl unnerved me. In a blur of action, the little desk was splintered, black grit scattered, Nick flung to the floor. Kyrie bent over him, gasping and voiceless with terror. Guy lurched away, clutching that glowing thing against his belly fur.

Two security men burst in, shouting at him. He lumbered on toward their drawn pistols, until I called his name. He stopped then, mute and trembling. With Kyrie's aid, I managed to make peace. The guards put up their guns and helped gather the spilled grit. Nick said he hadn't meant to be rude, and begged Guy to finish the nexode.

Guy shook his head at first and clung moaning to the blue pyramid, but Nick brought the rest of the grit from the lab and Kyrie coaxed him back to work. He was at it all that night, painstakingly clicking the crystals into fours, and these into taller and taller steps, sixteens and sixty-fours. Each larger pyramid glowed with another color, strong at first but slowly fading, the sixteens greenish and the sixty-fours a tawny topaz.

Nick and Kyrie tried eagerly to help, but the art was Guy's alone. Though the undamaged tetrahedrons had always looked identical to each other, he selected each for its own place, turning and trying it as if to make some kind of invisible fit. He didn't explain what he was doing, and the black bits refused to stick together for the rest of us.

Guy changed as he worked, in ways that are hard to explain. Visibly, he shed his fumbling clumsiness. He looked more alive and happier. His fur seemed to shine with a sleeker luster. His ungainly frame grew straighter—after midnight, he moved everything to the top of a filing cabinet, so that he could stand at his task.

His brain was awakening, too, in ways less visible to me. I saw Kyrie watching the growing pyramids and Guy himself with a breathless fixity. Turning abruptly away, she wanted Nick and me to come with her to the kitchen for a snack.

"It's doing things to Guy!" she whispered, with an awed backward glance. "I don't know how to say it, but I keep feeling what he feels. When he touches the grit, I feel with his fingers!"

Nick looked blank.

"The slick cool blocks." Kyrie's golden fingers stroked and lifted an invisible pyramid. "The edges like black blades. The pattern of the faces—all three of threes. I caught other feelings, too."

Her amused eyes flashed at me.

"He likes you, Uncle Kim. He thinks you're more like him than anybody else. Not too smart."

"Ky!" Nick was startled. "How does he feel about me?"

Her brief smile went out. She sat down in a kitchen chair too big for her, suddenly forlorn. I brought her a glass of yeastract plus, but she didn't want it.

"He loves me," she breathed at last. "I never knew how much. But not you. Not you, Nick."

"It's nothing we can help." Nick stood behind the chair,

73

his brown monkey-hand just touching her golden shoulder, his voice quietly matter-of-fact. "There's one of you for two of us."

"How can you hate—" Pain stifled her. "How can you hurt each other, when I love you both?"

"I'll never harm Guy." His promise had a quiet finality that made him seem more mature than she. "I couldn't injure him, Ky. Not even for you."

Cheered by that assurance, she decided she was hungry after all. I left them at the table and carried a sandwich back to Guy. Busy with a new blue pyramid, he greeted me with a friendly grin but took no time to eat.

Before dawn, he finished the fourth topaz tetrahedron. Exhaustion had drained his new vitality by then. His gray paws were awkward and uncertain again, but he turned and tried his new pyramid above the other three until at last it snapped gently into place.

"Guy, Guy!" Kyrie gasped. "It's so very lovely!"

This final tetrahedron was four inches tall. A cool, rose-colored glow shimmered along its knifelike edges and filled its interior hollow, but lingering gleams of yellow and green and blue clung to the smaller triangles that made up its faces, filming all its intricately patterned blackness with a splendid flowing glow.

Nick was squinting at it critically.

"I don't think it's done," he said. "You could make it twice as tall. There's grit left over, and we can requisition more."

"I used all the good ones." Guy shrugged disdainfully at the handful of crystals scattered on the filing cabinet. "These went bad. See?" Though the crystals had been nearly diamond-hard, his pinching fingers crumbled two or three of those left over into soft black dust. "Burned out."

"May I, Guy?" Kyrie reached eagerly toward the bright pyramid. "May I just touch—"

"Please keep it for me." With a grace that astonished me, Guy set it in her quivering hands. "I'm dead—for—sleep."

His voice slowed and his body stooped and his yellow eyes grew dull, as he gave up the pyramid. He stood gaping vacantly at Kyrie. Like some trained animal, I thought, waiting dully for its next command.

"Thank you, Guy." Captured by the pyramid, she scarcely looked at him. "Go on to bed."

He shambled heavily away, already half-asleep. Turning to Kyrie, I was enchanted by the transformation flowing over her like some magic fluid from the rosy tetrahedron. She looked taller, rounder of buttock and bust. Her startled smile of sheer delight was quickly veiled with Mona Lisa's mystery. Somehow, the thin and wistful child had been clad in instant womanhood.

What I felt was a stab of desire, so sharp I turned away. When I dared look back, her golden gaze was on me, wise as Aphrodite's, aware of all I felt, her mocking amusement at my disquiet mixed with a silent pride in her new-gained power to kindle it. For one astonished moment I met her candid eyes, inhaling a wave of her lilaclike scent. Then she forgot me, peering again into that blazing pyramid.

"Nicky, this is better than the game!" she whispered eagerly. "It's our nexode—real! The record our people in the stars made for us. It will tell us who we are, and what our lives are for, and maybe how to find our way to them."

3

Iniquity

Nick and Kyrie worked all week with that great tetrahedron, while Guy slept. Nick failed to do much with it. Still convinced that it was incomplete, he got Marko to requisition the moon grit left in the vault, hoping that we could build the nexode yet another stage larger.

The joint committee released the grit with no delay, and security brought it to the lab in six lead drums. Nick opened the drums one by one, dipping an anxious hand into each, and sank on the floor beside the last, sobbing like any child who has lost a special toy.

Something had changed the grit in the vault. All the crystals had lost their glassy hardness; some were already crumbling into sootlike powder. Nick wanted no more of them, but Marko and Caroline tried to learn what had happened. Their tests showed all the thorium gone, most of the gold fused into microscopic beads.

"It's burnt out," Marko summed up their results. "By some kind of nuclear or partly nuclear reaction. The carbon residue is mostly graphite now, mixed with stable elements that must be fission products. I'd like to know what became of the energy released."

He crushed a dead crystal in his palm, frowning at the dull black dust.

"That energy could have exploded the cannisters like bombs. All it did was overload the gold conductors. Even the fission products don't show any residual radiation. Where did it go?"

Nobody knew. Yet, somehow, the assembly of the nexode had exhausted all the crystals in the vault. Security was uptight about it, suspecting fraud or robbery, and the joint committee demanded a full report. Next day we questioned Nick.

At first he wouldn't talk, though he seemed to be only waiting outside the lab darkroom where Kyrie was working alone with the nexode.

"You don't want me." He shrugged ruefully. "Ask Ky. Or Guy, maybe, when he wakes up. They can work the nexode. Somehow I can't get the knack of it. I don't know why."

"We've got to file a report," Marko persisted. "Tell us what you can."

Nick stared moodily at the darkroom door.

"The nexode's half machine," he said. "We knew that all along. It runs on nuclear power. The units are like computers—though each crystal has more circuits than any computer on earth. That's the part I nearly understand."

"The other part?"

"That's Kyrie's." His small bare feet shuffled uncomfortably, as if the floor had gotten hot. "Something locks the units together. Something reaches out, sensing and spending energy. Something almost alive."

"Alive?" Marko whispered. "How?"

"If the nexode's like a computer," Nick said, "it's also like a brain. The circuits in both are pretty much the same. I think the nexode is a sort of interface between the energy we call physical and something else. Another spectrum."

"You think the missing energy disappeared through that interface?" Marko squinted doubtfully. "I mean, the missing power from that fissioned thorium?"

"Where else?" Nick's worried scowl gave him the look of a small old man. "The laws of nature stand, though our notions of them change. The nexode channels energy in unfamiliar ways—as the space snakes do. But it's nothing more than a device—"

He stopped abruptly and ran to meet Kyrie as she came out of the darkroom. She looked like a tired and troubled child again, with no sign of that vital power which had flowed into her from the new nexode. She took Nick's hand, and they slipped away to stand for a while watching Guy's deep sleep. When they came back, Marko stopped Kyrie to ask what she was doing with the nexode.

"It's—hard." Trouble shadowed her face. "The room has to be very dark and very still, with nothing to distract me. I can't even think of anything except the nexode shining. I just wait, and wait, and wait. Sometimes something comes."

"A message?"

"Bits of one." She glanced unhappily at Nick. "Maybe most of it is lost, because the grit lay on the moon too long before anybody found it. Everything is dim and broken. But something—something tries to come while I sit there in the dark."

Marko had more questions, but Nick asked us not to delay her any longer. Neither slept, all that week. Kyrie sat hour after hour in the darkroom, while Nick waited at the door. Image by shadowy image, they put together a fragmentary picture. One breathless desert midnight, after Kyrie had taken her break and gone back to the darkroom, Nick decided to share it with us.

The day had been long and hot for me, with a suspicious security agent dogging me all afternoon with questions I couldn't answer about the affairs of my absent brother. I was longing for a quiet beer and bed, till Nick spoke.

"Ky's getting the hang of the nexode now." Beneath his offhand tone, I heard a throb of veiled elation. "We're learning who made the grit—and finding a bit of truth in our old baby games about our people in space and their tachyon ships." He grinned soberly. "I guess the grit did help me make them up."

We gathered close around him.

"Your old theory was pretty good." He glanced at Marko with a new respect. "There *is* a great galactic culture. A sort of superbiocosm. All kinds of races with different biologies, united in one universal civilization. They're bound together with the cosmic altruism that Pla-

78

ton Papanek couldn't find on any of our planets—maybe it doesn't evolve very often.

"Anyhow, the messenger missiles that carry the grit were scattered like seed through space to spread that great culture—to find any new races evolved far enough to welcome it. The ships do travel faster than light. Ky can't say yet whether they're really tachyon craft, but she says they can't come here without a proper beacon to guide them and a proper terminal where they can land.

"That's our mission—to build that terminal!" His lean face shone. "The grit was waiting for our fathers on the moon. If it was seed, they were the soil and we are the young plants. The grit made us like we are. We are part of a great plan that begins somewhere among the stars. It can't end till the starships arrive on Earth."

We were still up at three o'clock, debating the vast implications of that, when Kyrie took another break. Sudden clouds had veiled the moon, and we walked back to the nursery against a dry wind that smelled of brush and dust. Kyrie stood for a time over Guy, gently stroking his gray-furred face. Tears filled her eyes, when he moved and whined in his sleep. Her face looked pinched and bleak, with none of Nick's elation. He fixed her a tray when she came on to the kitchen, but she pushed it back untasted.

"What frets you, child?" Carolina asked. "Nick was so delighted with the message you were getting."

"But I'm afraid." She glanced anxiously at Nick. "Even if we get the terminal ready, I'm afraid our people will never come."

"But Nick says they promised—"

"A long time ago," Kyrie said. "When I'm reading the nexode, I forget how old the grit was. What it shows seems like *now*. But Nick says it lay on the moon sixty million years. He says it was old before men evolved on Earth."

"Is that so bad?"

She looked uncomfortably at Nick.

"Ky's a worry-worm." He made a face and gave her a playful push, but she refused to smile. "I thought she knew more about the grit. Now she's afraid our people won't know us, after sixty million years."

She nodded unhappily.

"Maybe they won't." Nick's own face turned sober. "It is a long time. Perhaps they're dead by now. Perhaps they've evolved so far they won't care about us. Perhaps they've forgotten all about scattering the messenger missiles. Anyhow, no matter what, we've got to build the beacon and the terminal. That's why we're alive."

"We must try," she whispered. "But I'm so afraid."

She reached for Nick to take her hand, and they were trudging back through the dark toward the lab as we went off to bed.

Guy woke at noon next day. As slow and bearlike as if he had never touched the grit, he opened my office door and peered vacantly inside, whining Kyrie's name. I called Carolina and we tried to distract him, but he wouldn't eat and he wouldn't come with me to the gym.

He shambled back to Kyrie's empty room and prowled the nursery hall until he came to the kitchen. There he found the chair where she had sat. He snatched it up to sniff at it and blundered out of the room, moaning and twitching, stooping to scan the floor as if his yellow eyes could trace her footprints.

Outside, he paused as if to sniff the wind and ran lumbering toward the lab. We saw Nick dart out to stop him, as shrill and ineffectual as a small dog trying to intercept a charging bear.

"Wait! Please! Ky's at work—"

Guy crumpled Nick with one careless slap and drove on through the doorway. Nick was flat on the concrete walk when we came up, a green fly buzzing around his head. Naked to the blazing sun, his pale body failed to tan.

Caroline gathered him into her arms. I ran past them into the lab. Guy had stopped in the hall, shaking his head and peering about as if the decayed-hay reek of Carolina's beta-cultures had washed out Kyrie's scent. His gray ears lifted searchingly. He turned and crouched and suddenly froze.

80

"Hold it, Guy—"

He ignored me. Somehow he had located Kyrie. His spread ears quivered. He plunged abruptly past me, toward the darkroom. I was close behind when he reached the door. Without pausing to try the knob, he went through it like a tank.

I followed him in, stumbling over the broken door. The rose-colored glow of the nexode was all I could see for a moment. Pushing into the dark, I found Kyrie's golden form. She sat on a high stool, staring into the great tetrahedron as if unaware of Guy.

Whining like a starving beast, he snatched it out of her cupped hands. The stool tipped over with a crash, but she came down on bare cat-feet. For a moment she stared up at him, the gold fading fast from her stricken face.

"Baby Guy!" she whispered. "What have you done?" She caught at his furry arm, her voice tremulous with terror. "What have you done to Nick?"

Guy swayed back and forth, clutching the rose pyramid in both gray paws. Peering into it, his eyes grew huge and dull, sooty-black and yellow-rimmed. His breath became a heavy rasping.

"Guy, Guy!" she sobbed. "You've hurt little Nicky!"

She darted out, but I stayed to watch Guy with the nexode. His slow paws turned it. His blank eyes blinked at it. He bent to lick its shimmering faces with a pink, dripping tongue. At last he cocked a furry ear to listen while he shook it, like some bewildered savage with a clock.

Waiting for the glowing pyramid to transform him again, I saw no change. When he put it together, he must have served only as a temporary tool, energized for that special purpose. The task accomplished, he was not energized again.

Instead, he ran down now. His noisy breath grew quiet. His frantic movements slowed. He stood swaying, staring dimly at the pyramid. Slow tears traced black streaks in his fur. At last he shook his head and shambled away. I followed him over the splintered door and out of the building.

Outside, the blaze of sun hurt my eyes. Carolina stood swinging back and forth, crooning softly, rocking Nick in her arms. His thin body hung limp, and the green fly still droned around his head. Kyrie was hovering over him, brushing at the fly, but she turned to face Guy with a look of sick accusation.

"You're bad!" she gasped. "You—beast!"

With a roar of sudden fury, Guy threw the nexode at them. It might have struck Nick, but Carolina swung him out of the way. It grazed her arm with one keen point and spun across the lawn. With a cry almost of pain, Kyrie darted to pick it up.

Trembling and sobbing, Guy shuffled after her. Turning her stricken face from him, she slipped around him and brought the nexode back to Nick. With a kind of howl, like a tortured animal, Guy swung abruptly away. Staggering blindly, he tripped over the curb and picked himself up and reeled out of sight behind the gym. His agonized bellows thinned and faded away.

By that time a security car had arrived. Nick's thin limbs hung sloppily as Carolina laid him on the rear seat, but I saw a faint tan beginning to spread where the sun had washed his body. She examined him back at the nursery, while we waited breathlessly.

"He's coming around." She gave Kyrie a comforting smile, and turned to me more gravely, "Better see after Guy."

The security men had reported Guy running toward the open mesa, and we followed in the car. He was far ahead when we saw him, a wild gray animal loping into a shimmering blue mirage. Bounding over boulders and juniper clumps, he almost outran us.

"Wait, Guy! Listen!"

I leaned from the jolting car to call when we were near enough, but he didn't stop. Instead, he swerved abruptly to attack an isolated clump of tall cactus. He dived into it, butting and slugging and kicking the spiny masses, finally embracing them, howling with self-inflicted pain.

His wild cries choked and died. He was asleep or unconscious when we reached him, lying flat beneath the thorny plant he had pulled down upon him. His arms and legs were locked around it, bristling with broken spines. His gray jaws were fixed upon a flaming purple bloom. All movement had ceased, but his barnyard scent hung in the heated air, stronger than any odor from the flowers.

We waited for an ambulance to take him back to the station hospital. Needing no anaesthetic, he lay three hours on the operating table, while the spines were removed. No sign of life appeared until Nick and Kyrie came to see him later, in his room.

They stood beside his bed until he moved and made some stifled sound. Kyrie reached to stroke his arm. His eyes came open then, yellow and empty, the pupils contracted to expressionless points.

"Guy!" Kyrie sobbed. "Dear Guy!"

His flat head turned. His gray ears rose and fell. His vacant eyes passed over her and Nick, without interest or even recognition. A dull growl came out of his throat. In a moment he sank laxly back, asleep again.

Kyrie crumpled down into a quivering little heap, and we had to carry her out of the room. Nick came with her to the nursery. He sat beside her all night. If he ever urged her to return to her work with the nexode, I didn't hear him, but she was back in the darkroom next day, behind a new door.

Guy slept most of the time for many months. His body shrank to knobby bones and shabby fur. His illness and regression puzzled me. Building the nexode, Marko suggested, had somehow used him up. The loss of the precious pyramid, Carolina thought, had left him with a psychic trauma. I wondered if losing Kyrie had not hurt him more.

When he began to recover, later during the winter, he wanted me with him. He used to lie watching me, hour after hour, with a dumb devotion. He liked to rub his fur against me, and he whined with delight when I scratched behind his ears.

Though Nick and Kyrie came several times to see him, he seemed not to know them. Kyrie brought the nexode once, and held it toward him hopefully. His yellow eyes glanced blankly at it and drifted indifferently away. Kyrie was stricken, and Nick begged her not to come back.

With Carolina's help, I taught Guy to speak again. We played with his educational toys and went to the gym and swam together. With food and exercise, he slowly regained his lost vigor and suddenly began to grow again. By summer, he was twice my weight.

An odd sense of humor came along with his returning awareness. He used his physical power to tease me, letting me nearly win a tennis game or even a wrestling match before he pinned me down. He played alarming practical jokes on the security men.

He found other interests, besides. One was a dark sturdy girl who had been hired to wash glassware in the exobiology lab. The name on her security badge was Veronica Geronimo. She claimed the famous Apache raider for an ancestor, though security later informed me that she came from the Bronx.

We saw no probable harm in this affair. Apache or not, Veronica looked competent to protect herself, even from Guy's rather alarming sex equipment. Marko thought Guy needed an emotional outlet, and Carolina seemed reluctant to inhibit the basic behavioral responses of a unique biological specimen.

I wasn't much surprised when Veronica disappeared, because Guy must have been a problem lover, but he was bewildered and dismayed. He wanted me to help him find her. When I went to security, I learned that she had been thrown off the mesa for peddling marijuana without a federal license.

Guy's distress produced a new crop of clinical symptoms for Carolina to record. For the first time in his life, he couldn't sleep. His fur lost color. His ammoniac odor grew sharper. He began breaking up furniture, absently twisting and snapping a lamp or a chair into fragments before he saw what he was doing.

He hadn't learned to read, and one day he brought me a note smuggled in by a cafeteria worker. The tinted paper reeked of cheap perfume. Veronica still loved her Papa Bear. She had lost her badge and she couldn't come to see him, but she was working at the Thunderbird Bar, out on the Albuquerque road. She had a room at the Starways Flytel, if her Papa Bear remembered his teeny weeny Goldilocks.

I tried to decline when Guy wanted me to come with him to the security office, but he carried me there on his shoulder. The security men snorted with indignant scorn when he asked permission to visit Miss Geronimo. Though they were not explicit, they seemed to feel that any union between Guy and a human girl would be wickedly unnatural.

The acting chief did say he'd be damned if he'd compromise security just to coddle a hairy half-man. He refused Guy's request and assigned special guards to keep him on the mesa.

Escorting us back to the nursery, those new guards wanted to know where Guy's girl was shacking up, but he was more astute than I expected. Assuming a blank idiocy, he managed not to mention the Thunderbird Bar or the Starways Flytel.

In spite of security, he left the mesa that night. How he went was never entirely clear. The guards put him to bed in a windowless room and stood their watch outside. Next morning they found a hole in the wall and an empty bed.

We were frightened for Guy. With his nonhuman look, he would be in danger everywhere. Though the government was suppressing news of the space invasion, facts enough were leaking out to kindle an antialien hysteria.

Carolina had kept us informed of what she knew about the invasion, which was enough to upset us all. As a distinguished exobiologist, she was on a special list to receive the classified reports. Low-ranking officials were streaming to Skygate to consult her about the dangers from space, and she was often called away to advise those higher up. Even she was perplexed and disturbed.

The Earth platform had begun reporting anomalous fogs at sea. Shallow but oddly dense, they occurred unpredictably, at points which made nonsense of the official theory that they were due to unexpected shifts in the cold ocean currents. Several fishing vessels were reported lost in them, before the censors closed the lid on such unsettling facts.

The news about the flying snakes was equally disturbing. Following our rockets home, those remarkable space creatures had explored the moon and investigated the Earth platform and had now begun diving into our own atmosphere.

When their appearances became too frequent for the censors to deny them entirely, COSMOS released an official opinion that they meant no harm. Perhaps that was true. Certainly they seemed more playful than hostile, although their intentions were never quite clear. They were evidently interested in human activities, and obviously attracted to heat—like Nick's flying plank—they somehow converted thermal energy into motion. They began diving out of space to escort our aircraft, as dolphins used to escort ships. Whatever their motives, the results were unfortunate. Drained of heat and power, the escorted aircraft often crashed.

The word "otheron" had begun to spread that year on the waves of secrecy and rumor and unconvincing denial. It denoted anything from another biocosm, moon child or space snake, cultured beta-form or imagined invader. Guy was an otheron, and we were concerned for his life.

He was gone two months. His disappearance was never widely advertised, for fear of touching off a panic, but Skygate security did organize an intensive secret search. Marko and I made several fruitless trips, following clues of our own and notions of Kyrie's, but Guy wasn't easy to find.

Our knowledge of his first seven weeks of freedom is

mostly inference, drawn from a trivee series screened the following year. Veronica Geronimo was the narrator of "I Loved a Monster," and her lurid drama must have been at least half true. Later, I saw Guy himself watching the program, chuckling silently. He confirmed a few details for me, though he would never talk to security.

It seems that he and Veronica covered most of North America, living and traveling in a series of rented or perhaps stolen helicabins. To the confusion of security, it developed that Guy himself had been on trivee half a dozen times during the manhunt.

Disguised with tigerskin shorts and stripes painted on his own fur, billed as Monk Tigerhide, he competed as a professional wrestler, dutifully winning or losing as Veronica and her friends desired, until he inadvertently damaged too many opponents.

In ways never revealed to Internal Revenue, the two collected a considerable fortune. Tax officials intercepted Veronica as she attempted to leave the country the following year with nearly six and a half million in unexplained World Bank globals.

Abruptly, on the helistage of the Manhattan Hudson, that grotesque comedy turned into disaster. Veronica must have been wearing too many jewels. A team of burglars broke into the helicabin. Guy collared one of them, but the other got away. He had seen Guy nude, and he spread the news of a moon kid in town.

With her own sure instinct for survival, Veronica escaped. The captured burglar seems to have gone along, replacing Guy as her consort. Guy himself was left to face the mob, naked and alone. Fighting bare-handed, he threw four men off the helistage and hurt a dozen others, but he was finally overcome.

Left for dead, if too tough to be dismembered, he was picked up by the riot police and finally shipped back to Skygate nailed up in a guarded box. Though his odor was overwhelming when we opened it, Carolina decided that he was still alive. The space doctors disagreed, but she made them let her keep him in a hospital room. After long weeks of something between death and sleep, he sat up to beg for a steak.

Carolina was gone three months from Skygate the next fall, on an unexplained assignment. Busy with security officials the day she returned, Marko asked me to meet her plane. She looked so tired and troubled that I asked what was wrong. She said nothing till we were alone in the car.

"It's the fog," she told me then.

Anxious to know more, but diffident about prying into confidential matters, I drove on without comment. She frowned hesitantly.

"Don't talk about it," she said at last. "But the government is getting the jitters. I was called in to lead a secret research group. Our instructions were to learn what the fog is and what to do about it." She drew a weary breath. "I'm afraid our report won't cure any jitters."

Again I waited, while she stared at the desert as moodily as if each twisted juniper had been some kind of space alien in disguise. When I had to brake and swerve to avoid a speeding security airtrac, she looked absently back at me.

"We tried." The flatness of her tone added that they had also failed. "The military called for an all-out effort. They gave us all the people and equipment we asked for, and all the data anybody has. We tried everything.

"Mapped the reported spots of fog. Photographed those we could find. Tested them for every sort of radiation. Dropped telemeted instruments into them, with rockets and parachutes. Towed scoops from aircraft to collect samples. Questioned every surviving observer, and every crackpot with a theory."

"And—?" I couldn't stop that query, when she paused again. "What is the fog?"

"We still don't know. The photographs show mostly splotches of featureless white. The radiometers found nothing unusual. The telemetry never worked. The surface samples weren't much more than a bad odor by the time we got them back to the lab. We got no deep samples at all—something caught the scoops and broke the lines.

"Don't ask me what." Her somber eyes swept me blankly and drifted back to the desert. "The military aren't very happy about it, but those negative results make up the main content of our report. We were asked to draw conclusions, but nobody liked our ideas. If you want to hear them—"

I said I did.

"I think the fog is a manifestation of life. Life from another biocosm—which one, I can't say. The surface samples died and decayed too fast to tell us much, but the evidence indicates to me that the surface layer is made of tiny bubble-shaped organisms, probably inflated with hydrogen. They're hygroscopic and very fragile. Dryness kills them."

I asked about the deeper layers.

"Nobody knows what's underneath." Her uneasy voice sank till I could barely hear. "But it must be something more than microscopic. Something strong enough to snap our scoops off the lines. Something hostile enough to seize every ship the fog overtakes. Something cunning enough to outwit all of us."

"You mean intelligent?"

"Call it whatever you want." Glancing from the road, I saw her shiver. "It unnerved us. The fog spreads in the dark. It has been reported creeping up on ships and isolated beaches, in a way that looks deliberate. It does retreat from the light—I think sunlight dries and kills those microscopic balloon cells. When the fog goes, nothing alive is left behind. Just a red, stinking slime."

She sat for a moment in foreboding silence.

"Another item," she added suddenly. "The fog doesn't like investigation. During daylight, it retreated from our parachuted instruments and even from a surface laboratory ship—which it later overtook in the dark. Every patch of fog that we tried to study melted very rapidly back into the sea."

As we came in view of the nursery building, she brightened eagerly.

"That's about it," she said. "If you want to know what the fog really is, all I have is the theory we cooked up from our report. The phenomenon is clearly an intrusion from some other biocosm. Wherever they evolved, the intruders have been changed—by mutation or more likely by metamorphosis—to adapt them for survival in the oceans of earth."

"Why are they invading—?"

"Let's get on to a more cheerful topic." She cut me firmly off. "How are Nick and Kyrie?"

As always now, we found them hard at work on their plans for the transgalactic terminal. In spite of all our warnings, they were determined that COSMOS could be persuaded to build it.

Kyrie spent most of her days and nights shut up alone in the darkroom with the great tetrahedron, groping for the bits and pieces of its half-erased message. Nick's drafting table was the floor of a room across the hall. He worked lying flat, often calling Kyrie in so that he could show her the emerging difficulties and tell her what to search for.

The following summer, as those problems began taking clearer shapes, Marko helped select a team of specialists to write the specifications and prepare the final drawings for COSMOS. Most of these experts had been with the famous "triple E"—Ex-Earth Engineers—the prime contractor for the seeker vehicles and several planet platforms. Accustomed as they were to vast space projects, they were dazed by the dimensions Nick demanded for the tachyon terminal.

After ten days of nonstop talks with Nick, they invited Marko and me to join a conference at the Skygate Hudson. Kyrie stayed behind in the darkroom, trying to fill some gap in the record. Nick sat between Marko and me at the long table, facing the engineers. In blue trunks, but pale and naked to the waist, he looked perilously young and small and vulnerable.

The seven engineers were sober and mature veterans of space, armed with rolled blueprints and entrenched behind portable computers and thick stacks of data. They shuffled their documents and scowled at Nick, waiting for their spokesman to begin. He was Ken McAble, a wiry brown dynamic Yankee who had tested his own hardware in orbit around several planets.

"I'll tell you why we're here." His ice-green eyes shifted uneasily from Nick to Marko and then to me. "We've got plenty of space know-how." He nodded approvingly at his fellow engineers, three on either side. "We've done some difficult things. I think we're competent to say what is feasible and what is not. I believe we all agree that this so-called tachyon terminal is just not possible."

The men around him nodded solemnly.

"But it can be!" Nick objected sharply. "It has to be."

"Just look at it." McAble fumbled through a stack of papers and held up a sketch of the terminal——the six outer towers with their landing stages rising like a spiral stair around the taller central beacon.

"Ten miles tall!" He pursed his lips and shook his head. "Equipped to dock and refit tachyon ships with diameters up to half a mile. The machinery works on principles we never heard of, and the specifications call for materials unknown on earth."

"Please, sir?" White and trembling, Nick stood up in his chair. "We'll explain the principles. We'll tell you how to make the new materials."

"Look at these dimensions!" McAble waved his sketch. "They reduce the Great Pyramid to a wart. Our preliminary estimates are still pretty rough, but they run to something like three point seven billion tons—of structural materials we don't have names for."

"We know it won't be easy, sir." Nick spoke too fast, as he often did when he was too gravely worried to remember the slow comprehension of ordinary men. "That's why we're asking COSMOS to take it over. All the nations must unite—"

"COSMOS!" McAble snorted. "COSMOS is already stinking dead. Its builders mistook the other planets for a free lunch. It looks like we're going to be the free lunch now, for all the other biocosms."

"But, sir! This trouble with the other biocosms is exactly why the terminal has to be built. The messenger missile was sent to prepare us for this very moment—when space flight is just beginning. Don't you see? Don't any of you see?"

Nick caught his breath and looked desperately along the line of doubtful faces.

"New biocosms need help to understand each other. The teminal beacon can bring that help—but we must have it soon. Without it, our own biocosms will probably kill one another. Can't you see that, sir? Building the terminal, we're running a race to save the lives of Earth and Venus and all our other neighbors. Don't you—don't you see—"

His forlorn voice slowed and stopped. I could hear a muffled clatter from the dining room. The sluggish air felt too cold and smelled faintly of fish. Nick gulped hard. I thought he was going to cry.

A pencil dropped and rolled. Two fattish engineers whispered together, and one of them passed a paper to McAble. He squinted at it and cleared his throat and scowled at Nick again.

"We do have one suggestion that might be productive," he said. "If you care to consider it."

"Yes, sir!" Nick gasped. "Of course."

"It has occurred to several of us that these plans are far too elaborate." He tapped his sketch and nodded at the fattish engineers. "This terminal we're talking about would dock a whole fleet of starships. It seems to us that we might begin with simpler facilities for just one ship. Can't you modify the plans?"

"I wish I could." Nick shrugged unhappily. "The terminal is large on our scale, but not on the cosmic scale. The stars are far apart. A tachyon beacon has to have a certain power, to reach ships or other terminals at all. A weaker beacon would be no good. Anyhow, we can't change the plans."

"And why not?"

"You see, sir, we're not designing anything ourselves. We don't know enough. We're only reading out the specifications recorded in the messenger missile sixty million years ago—and now partly lost."

"I think they should have been simpler in the first place."

"I'm afraid you don't understand, sir. There are too many billions of planets. Too many life forms always evolving—but too few that ever need or want to join the great galactic culture. The starships can't visit them all. Only those that build a terminal are considered worth an interstellar trip. It's how we qualify for transgalactic membership."

McAble frowned at that, and finally turned the meeting over to his fellow engineers. They began asking technical questions about structural materials for the towers, about the operation of the beacon, about tachyon propulsion and the minimum-energy shift to the tachyon state. Nick's answers were confusing to me and also, I think, to them.

Marko sent out for coffee, and later for sandwiches. With an afternoon break to let Nick assemble and demonstrate a second flying plank, the meeting lasted all day. Four of the engineers left Skygate that night, but McAble and two others decided to stay—"just for the hell of it," as McAble said. They worked nearly a year with Nick and Kyrie, producing detailed specifications and operation handbooks for machines they never really understood.

When their proposal was finally ready for COSMOS, the presentation had to be delayed because a jet carrying most of the European directors had been lost over the Atlantic. Official censorship veiled the details, but one survivor who had missed the flight turned up later to tell us that friendly space snakes and flown too near the plane, killing the motors and forcing it down into a patch of that anomalous fog.

Other members canceled out, until only the American and Sino-Soviet delegations came for the final presentation. The American group was headed by Erik Thorsen. Marko and I called on him the day he arrived at his official residence.

I barely recognized him. He was an old man now, stooped and slow, his face sternly tragic. His bloodless hands had a ceaseless tremor. I suppose the psychiatry had been successful, but I felt sorry for him. He greeted us stiffly and waited to see what we wanted, without asking about the children or Suzie or anybody else.

We tried to brief him for Nick's presentation. He listened silently, gray lips compressed, now and then shaking his cadaverous head. When we had finished he promised curtly to see us at the meeting, but I could see that he didn't mean to be convinced.

We met next day in the tarnished splendor of the Hall of Worlds, built when the great dreams of COSMOS were still alive. Clustered around the podium, our little group left the long chamber nearly empty, and its rolling echoes seemed to mock our fading hopes.

Maxim Petrov came in at the head of the Sino-Soviets. A vigorous thickset man, he shook hands cordially with all his old friends and smiled with a startled admiration for Kyrie when she and Nick came in.

One of his advisers surprised us more. A short stout brown man with thick untidy hair and dark sunglasses, he had arrived on Petrov's plane and spent the night in the Sino-Soviet residence. When he took the glasses off, I recognized my brother Tom.

Less cordial than Petrov, he waved a pudgy hand at Marko and me, lighted a long yellow narcorette, and put on another pair of glasses to study our terminal plans.

After all our preparation, that meeting was a brief anticlimax. The delegates frowned over the bulky handouts. Kyrie displayed the tetrahedron. Nick explained the purpose of the messenger missile, then called on Ken

McAbe to brief the delegates on our proposal for the tachyon terminal.

"I came in as a skeptic," McAble began. "But I've been convinced. I'll grant that the task of erecting this terminal will tax the resources of the planet. But I think it can be done, and I say we've got to do it."

He raised his voice above a murmur of startled protest.

"The alternative is death. Alone, we can't cope with the other biocosms we have encountered on Venus and Mercury and elsewhere. We don't know how to deal with the space snakes now in our own atmosphere, or with whatever is moving into our seas."

Thorsen stood up, but McAble wouldn't stop.

"I believe the creatures of our neighbor biocosms have found it hard to understand or cope with us. The exobiologists are suggesting that we have gravely disturbed the ecology of Venus, and I'm afraid we have given the other biocosms no reason to love us."

McAble still ignored Thorsen's quivering hand.

"Gentlemen, this is a turning point in the lives of our planets. The terminal can bring us the means to understand and bridge our differences. It can open a door to all the benefits of our transgalactic civilization—wonders I don't dare imagine. Without the terminal, I think we're dead."

Recognized at last, speaking in an old man's slow falsetto, Thorsen said there were too many space aliens already on earth. He didn't intend to import any more. The American delegation was voting to reject the proposal.

Maxim Petrov spoke longer and less vehemently. His technicians had discovered many items of exciting interest in the terminal plans, which would be carried back to Peking for additional study. He understood the grave hazards of contact between unaided biocosms, and he recognized a growing danger to the life of Earth. If Nick's proposal had been made just a few years earlier, the Sino-Soviet might have been able to support the terminal project. Unfortunately, however, in his opinion the crucial turning point had now passed. Already under increasing pressure from space intruders and divided by growing suspicions that the moon children and perhaps other space aliens were secretly meddling in human affairs, the nations of Earth could never unite to erect it. Regretfully, therefore, the Sino-Soviet was forced to join the Americans in voting to kill the proposal. Moreover, since the seeker surveys had failed to open up new living space for the human proletariat, or even to develop any important new industrial resources for the workers of the Earth, the Sino-Soviet and its allies were giving notice of withdrawal from COSMOS. Formal claims would be filed for the assets and privileges properly due them under the charter.

Nick and Kyrie should have been prepared, of course, for such an outcome, but they had never learned to make reasonable allowances for the ignorance and stupidity of ordinary human beings. Shattered, they clung together, sobbing piteously. Marko and Caroline tried to console them, but they wouldn't talk to anybody.

When Petrov gathered his delegates to leave the Hall of Worlds, my brother burst out of the group and scuttled across to Thorsen, begging for political asylum. Thorsen called him a traitor and turned his back on him. Sweating and gasping, he dashed to Marko and me.

"Kim! My baby brother!" He enveloped me in his fleshy embrace and the rich aroma of his armpits. "And my old comrade! Yuri! It's grand to see you both."

Marko took his offered hand, somewhat hesitantly.

"I need your help," he wheezed. "But you need mine— just as much. I can help you—help you build that terminal."

"Help us?" Marko squinted at him skeptically. "How?"

"I've got contacts." His calculating eyes rolled toward the Sino-Soviets. "I've got influence. I've got know-how. I've got everything you need to get the project moving. And that's a fact. Trust me, Kim. You've just got to trust me, Yuri."

Of course we couldn't trust him, but I saw no harm in listening. With our plans rejected, we had very little to lose. Though I had learned to fear his slippery resourcefulness, I couldn't help yielding to his old shrewd charm.

"What know-how?" Marko was demanding. "Contacts with whom?"

Tom shrugged evasively. This was no place to discuss such delicate matters, and the deal he wanted to offer us would take too long to explain. His hurried whisper turned frantic. He couldn't go back to the Sino-Soviet. If we refused to take him in, he was prepared to destroy himself.

"I'm your last chance!" he rasped. "Believe me, Kimmie. Without my contacts, you'll never get your terminal built."

Marko finally agreed to talk to Thorsen. Tom hung close to me, mopping at his wet face and watching the Sino-Soviet delegation as if he expected to be dragged away.

Petrov, however, accepted the situation with a fine diplomatic suavity. Returning to the podium, he announced that the defector was a running dog of capitalism and a proven enemy of the people. His ruthless criminal activities had betrayed the trust of the world proletariat, and he was no longer a welcome guest of the Sino-Soviet. Concluding, Petrov offered us an ironic farewell and departed with his delegation, leaving Tom behind.

Angered by the whole affair, Thorsen put Tom under guard and took him back to the American residence. We didn't see him again for several weeks, until the final dismemberment of COSMOS had been completed.

Title to the mesa and all the Skygate facilities reverted to America, as the charter provided. Suddenly recommissioned a Space Force general, Thorsen assumed command. He disbanded the old international security force and organized his own new security arm.

In the long squabble over the assets of COSMOS, Petrov demanded the tetrahedron for the Sino-Soviet. Refused that, he wanted Kyrie. When Marko pointed out that the tetrahedron was useless to us without her to read it, he offered to settle for Nick. Thorsen seemed willing to surrender him, but Caroline protested bitterly that Kyrie would die without him. There was no demand for Guy.

Petrov agreed at last to let America keep the children and the tetrahedron. In return, the Sino-Soviet took over the remaining space facilities of COSMOS, which had dwindled by now to the Earth and moon platforms and the half-abandoned installations on the surface of the moon.

When Petrov and his people were finally gone, Thorsen had us bring the children to a briefing room in the old COSMOS headquarters, which now flew his own flag. Nick and Kyrie sat perched on tall stools, squirming itchily in stiff white coveralls and a frilly pink little-girl dress. Carolina hovered behind them. The nexode lay on the table before them, one point of opulent splendor in that ugly, barren, military room.

Guy sat with me at the side of the room, too big for his chair, his odorous and hairy masculinity cloaked in a plaid raincoat. Flat and bright and empty, his yellow eyes weren't looking at Nick and Kyrie, or the armed guards around us, or anything at all.

A heavy cast-bronze ashtray lay on the table before us —a doughnut-shaped replica of the moon platform. He picked it up in his massive paws, turning it absently. Presently I heard a crack like a gunshot, and saw that he had snapped it in two. The guards around us were startled, but Guy sat fingering one of the fragments, unaware of anything. Before we left, he had broken the bronze into a dozen lumps.

The guards stood up when Thorsen came in with his new security chief, as if we were in court. Major Gort was a tall, lank, sallow man with sparse red hair and sleepy greenish eyes. He moved with an unmilitary slouch and spoke in a hoarse undertaker-whisper.

Thorsen had put on a kind of armored arrogance, along with his two new stars. Scowling at the children as if they stood accused of something unspeakable, he introduced Gort and laid down new rules for us.

"Skygate's a fortress now." Staring at the many-colored

pyramid as if hypnotized, he recovered himself with a spasmodic twitch. "We're setting up a strictly military effort to control all our space contacts, and we're on the front line here."

"Father, please!" Kyrie raised her hand like a child in school. "Won't we be allowed to work on the terminal—"

"Absolutely not!" He scowled bleakly. "We're losing a war with the space aliens already around us. Our mission here is to perfect new defenses." His sunken eyes flashed to Nick. "The engineers think your flying beer can might be used to propel a missile fast enough to knock out the space snakes."

"But, sir!" Nick's small voice shook. "We were born to build the terminal. We can't waste ourselves killing other creatures."

Thorsen's gaunt face lost color. He gulped and croaked and reached for a glass of water that Gort was hastily pouring. It shook and spilled over his hand.

"Now get this," he rasped at last. "COSMOS is dead. Skygate's a military post, and you'll all obey my orders. You'll forget that terminal. You'll waste no time on what you call pure research—on what you call knowledge for its own sake."

Carolina tried to say something about academic freedom.

"Get this!" His cracked voice rose to cut her off. "We're fighting for survival. Space war is a new game. We can lose it to a bug from Saturn or maybe win it with Nick's beer can. Every act will have to fit our total military effort. Get me?"

"I get you, General." Carolina stung him with her tone.

"All of you had better get—" His face turned dark and his old voice broke. He gulped water and cleared his throat and tried to smile. "Don't take me wrong. We used to be friends. I don't want to injure anybody. Remember I didn't trade the kids to Petrov. I'll try to keep you here as you are, if you'll only play the game. But get this!"

His dull eyes swept across us, one by one.

"Marko." He was a grim stranger speaking, no longer

99

Marko's old comrade on the moon. "Hodian. Carolina. If you fail to see things my way, you'll be replaced. You may not see the kids again. Am I clear?"

"You're clear, General Thorsen," Carolina whispered bitterly. "Very clear."

I hated Thorsen from that day, yet I felt a growing pity for him too. Bewildered and despairing, he was fighting desperately for the survival of the only world he knew. As much as I loved Nick and Kyrie and Guy, I too had come from his old world. I could feel his tragedy.

Guy growled once, softly, just before Thorsen rose to close the meeting. Even then he didn't look at Nick and Kyrie, but I could see them bending eagerly over the great tetrahedron, their intent faces turning brown again in its growing light. Absorbed in it, they started when Carolina spoke to them.

"Please! Let's go back to the lab." Kyrie whispered eagerly. "I think we've found something new."

"A weapon?" Carolina was sardonic.

Kyrie looked hurt and shook her head.

"We don't know." Nick was still staring into the tetrahedron, his eyes oddly dilated. "We don't know yet."

Major Gort sent a security car to take them to the lab, and they entered the darkroom together. They stayed all day. Late that night, worried about them, Caroline knocked and went in.

She found them lying like two children on the floor, the tetrahedron glowing splendidly between them. Their wide eyes were fixed on it, and they didn't move until she touched them.

She persuaded them to take a break. They came to the kitchen, walking dreamily together with intimate collisions of hips and shoulders as if what they were finding had been some delightful new awareness of each other. Silent about the nexode, they gulped a little orange juice and hurried back to the darkroom.

Next morning Thorsen called my office. My brother was to be questioned, and he wanted me present. The interrogation took place in the same briefing room. Major Gort presided. Tom came in between two guards, who led him to a chair and stood alert behind him.

He looked puffy with soft fat, rumpled and seedy. Squirming uneasily under Gort's sleepy stare, he caught my eye and grinned appealingly, turned nervously to beg his guards for a narcorette, stared defiantly back at Gort.

"Mr. Hood, we're considering your request for sanctuary," Gort began at last. "Before we can do you any favors, you have a good deal to explain."

"I'm no crook!" Tom's voice shook with indignation. "I'm an astronaut. I was trained by COSMOS. After retirement, I took a civilian job in a member nation—a right guaranteed by the charter and my COSMOS contract. Now I've come home to see my brother and my son. Is that criminal?"

"We've heard about your civilian jobs." Gort's cat-eyes were blankly alert, as if Tom had been a tricky mouse. "I believe one of them was smuggling pirated moon grit."

"But that was a kosher deal." Tom looked offended. "I was a legitimate agent, acting for Mr. Howard Hudson. He mined the grit on the moon. His operations there were legally licensed, with all fees paid."

"That grit was stolen from under the nose of Moon Control."

"Perhaps it was mined in the dark." Tom shrugged. "Hudson didn't make his billions sitting on his tail."

"You sold the grit," Gort resumed. "As part of your payment, you were employed, I believe, by the Sino-Soviet."

"I was hired as a space engineer." Tom's voice stayed level, but his fat dark face shone with sweat. "I soon found, however, that all they wanted was my genes—the altered genes I had brought back from the moon. I was sent to a lab buried under the Gobi, to breed more moon children."

"So we'd heard." Gort nodded sleepily. "What were the results?"

"Not good," Tom said. "The experiment lasted five years. A dozen creatures were born alive. None was even

101

semihuman. Three lived a year or longer, but they're all dead now." He hunched and shuddered. "Hideous little things. I couldn't bear to see them."

"You did other research with the grit?"

"Matter of fact, I did." Tom's bulgy eyes widened warily. "I had a fine staff. We repeated most of your early work here. We were able to assemble a couple of second-stage tetrahedrons, though none so large as yours. I think we learned a few things you don't know."

"Such as what?"

"New uses for the tetrahedrons."

"We'll get to that." Gort crouched a little, like a cat about to spring. "Now why did you defect?"

"The project had gone kaput." Tom's puffy shoulders drooped expressively. "My sperm had gone bad. All our moon grit had turned to dust—drained, I suppose, by your big tetrahedron. The Gobi lab was abandoned to the space snakes. My bosses got what I call space paranoia."

"Huh?" Gort drew slightly back. "What's that?"

"They couldn't cope. Their image of mankind didn't fit them to meet the creatures of our sister biocosms. When they encountered another intelligence, they expected to understand it. When they couldn't, their impulse was to attack. When nothing fought back—when the snakes just played hide-and-seek with their best missiles—they went paranoid."

Gort froze, as if the mouse had suddenly become an ugly rat.

"I believe I can be useful in your work here," Tom added smoothly. "Besides, as I told you, I was anxious to see my brother and my son. How about it, sir?"

Gort ruled at last that Tom would remain in custody while his case was under review, but Thorsen gave him leave next morning to see the children. I rode with him in a security car down to the lab. Nick and Kyrie ran out of the darkroom to greet him with a warmth that surprised me.

"Guy's father!" Kyrie hugged him eagerly. "I'm so glad you're here. Poor dear Guy will surely be happier now."

Nick shook his hand politely.

"Please, Mr. Hood. Tell us about your work with the moon grit." His voice quivered with interest. "Carolina says you've learned new uses for it."

"We put together two second-stage tetrahedrons." Tom paused to study Nick the way he used to study me when we played chess. "They were too weak to project a readable record, but we found a linkage between them nobody had expected. They turned out to be remarkable signal devices."

"That's no good to us." Disappointment erased Kyrie's eager smile. "We've only one nexode—"

Her breath caught. She and Nick stared at one another, eyes black and wide. Bright hope flowed back into her face. Nick turned abruptly back to Tom.

"Do you think other messenger missiles have reached the solar system?" His breathless voice was almost too fast for me to follow. "Do you think the other biocosms may have assembled nexodes of their own? Or do you think—" Emotion froze him for an instant. "Do you think our nexode might have power enough to reach the people of other stars?"

Tom gestured with the fluent assurance of some bazaar merchant proclaiming the unutterable worth of a smuggled emerald.

"I bring you these questions," he said. "And others equally exciting. I hope to help you answer them—with General Thorsen's permission."

They took him into the darkroom, where the nexode was. He spent three hours there. The waiting security men grew restive and finally sent Caroline in to learn what they were doing.

She found the lights on. Nick and Kyrie were seated on the floor, face to face, Nick holding the pyramid in his two hands and Kyrie leaning over it, her brown fingers touching and stroking the bright triangles of its patterned faces as if playing some curious musical instrument.

Tom sat near them on a stool, smoking his scented narcorette and calling out rhythmic syllables that Carolina thought were numerals and direction words in Mandarin.

He scowled with annoyance at her intrusion, but Nick and Kyrie gave her no attention. She watched for a few minutes and came out to report. The guards phoned Major Gort, who bustled over to discover what was going on. Nodding for us to follow, he burst into the darkroom.

Tom objected angrily, but Nick and Kyrie didn't look up until Carolina touched them. They seemed frightened then. Nick clutched the tetrahedron against his bare chest. Kyrie turned pale and tried to wave us back.

"What's all this?" Gort's hand was on his gun. "What are you up to?"

"I'm only showing them what we learned at the Gobi lab." Tom was sullenly plaintive. "A technique for operating the crystal. An orientation to the operator's brain. A sequence of contact points. A rhythm of relaxation and attention."

Cat-eyes narrowed, Gort drew back from the tetrahedron as if it had become a dangerous dog. "What does it do?" he rasped. "When you operate it?"

"That's what we were trying to discover when you stopped us."

Gort snorted. "You'll have to tell me more than that, if you want permission to go on."

"Sir." Nick stood up with the prismatic tetrahedron. "The nexode is a kind of machine. It communicates ideas, but not with anything quite like language. It uses its own sort of symbolic system for grasping reality." He hesitated. "I'd like to tell you more about it, sir, but the symbols are not translatable in any way I think you could understand, and the reality they represent doesn't fit any symbolic system you know. Mr. Hood is trying to show us a better way to operate the machine."

"To communicate with what?"

"So far, just with itself." Nick's intense black stare dropped back to the tetrahedron. "Now I think we can read parts of the record that we couldn't before. Mr. Hood thinks it might be linked with other nexodes, perhaps on other worlds. But we have not yet established any such contact."

Gort's greenish eyes blinked sleepily.

"Come along, Hood," his raspy whisper came at last. "I want to check with the general before you go any farther." He swung lazily to Nick and Kyrie. "Any attempt to use that object for communication with anything at all will have to be cleared with General Thorsen in advance. D'you understand?"

"Yes, sir." Nick glanced quickly at Kyrie. "We understand."

Grumbling under his breath, Tom left with Gort. Nick and Kyrie hurried back into the darkroom. Guy had been asleep for sixty hours, but he woke that afternoon. When he wandered into my office, I called Gort and got permission for him to visit Tom.

A security car took us to the old Sino-Soviet residence, and Tom's guards brought him down to meet us in a big room which the departing delegates had stripped of everything movable.

"So you're Guy! My son—"

Tom was waddling eagerly to meet him, fat hands reaching out, but he stopped with a gasp when Guy bounded toward him like a bear masquerading as a man. Before he could run, he was crushed in Guy's embrace. His breath came out in a frightened grunt.

"Father! Father!" Guy's slow voice was thick and strange with surging emotion. "I thought you would never come."

Tom squirmed with terror until Guy's arms opened. He tried to escape then, but Guy still held him with one great paw, stroking him eagerly with the other, whimpering like some tormented beast. Tom wheezed for his breath and offered Guy a trembling hand. Soon they were famous friends.

For the next three days, they were never apart. They walked on the mesa and worked out together in the gym and lounged in the nursery. The guards tried to protest when Guy followed Tom back to his room at night, but his rumbling growls persuaded them to let him stay.

Each day Guy came by the office and picked me up, with an air of apology for putting his father first. I watched them together, astonished by his emotion and searching for Tom's intention. Later security let me listen to the tapes of their talk in Tom's bugged room.

Guy's role was a doglike adoration. After lonely years, he had found his father. He sat for hour after hour, great yellow eyes fastened on Tom, begging for every detail of his life and Robin's.

Tom's tales amused me. Though the truth should have been sufficient, he made Gamal Hodian a martyred saint, our mother a comic peasant, Robin a wild nymphomaniac. In his stories of the moon and the stud farm under the Gobi, he made such an unlikely hero of himself that one day I warned Guy of his gift for fiction.

"Don't lose your cool, Uncle Kim." He winked one tawny eye. "I know what isn't true. I'm only helping my dad play his little joke on security."

I failed to guess the nature of that little joke—even next day, when Guy had a distressing encounter with Nick and Kyrie. He and Tom had stopped for me. As we were strolling by the lab on our way toward the gym, Tom began asking Guy how he had been able to build the great tetrahedron out of the grit. The questions worried Guy.

"I don't—don't remember." His slow voice thickened, and he stopped on the sidewalk outside the lab. His gray ears flared. A low growl rattled in his throat.

"But come," he rumbled suddenly. "I'll show you."

He darted into the lab. Tom gave me a searching look and ran after him. The security men shouted and fired a warning shot, but Guy was already gone. I followed them into the building.

In the darkroom, the tetrahedron lay blazing on the floor. Guy crouched over it, whining as if hurt. Nick was backing away, fingering a long red mark where a point of the crystal must have raked his naked chest. Kyrie fluttered between Nick and Guy, white with terror and dismay. Tom stood in the doorway, gesticulating with his reeking narcorette and trying glibly to talk the tension down, imitating our father's Turko-Yiddish accent to retell a peasant fable about three thieves and a stolen goat.

"Come along, Hood!" One of the security men jabbed a gun at him. "You're in real trouble now—"

Guy's gorilla roar paralyzed me. In a blur of motion, he reached past Tom, snatched the guard's arm, hauled him into the darkroom. When the roar died, the guard lay flat on the floor and Guy was snapping the stock off his gun as if it had been a candy toy. The other man had gone for help.

"Easy, now—" Tom had to wheeze for his own breath. "Let's get the goat back in the bag." He waved the narcorette and grinned at me. "How about it, Kimmie? Are you old Thorsen's stoolie? Or will you take a chance?"

I didn't know what he meant.

"Once a schlemiel—" He shrugged and turned to Nick and Kyrie. "How about you kids? You want to die for good old Gort? Or try your luck with us?"

"Our mission is to build the tachyon terminal," Nick caught Kyrie's pale hand, and they faced Tom steadily. "We won't let anything stop us. But I'm afraid you can't help us, Mr. Hood."

Sirens were screaming outside by then. Gort came catfooting down the hall, the alert squad behind him. He handcuffed Tom and scooped up the tetrahedron and herded us all outside to wait for Thorsen, who was just pulling up in his staff car.

"Erik!" Tom grinned and started toward the car, holding up his cuffed wrists. "I'm glad you got here. Your people are about to muck us up. Let me explain this incident—"

"Stand back, Hood," Savagely angry and visibly ill, Thorsen beckoned Gort to the car. "Hold this man under double guard," he rapped. "Check out your notion that he's spying for our space enemies. Charge him with treason."

"My friend!" Tom whined bitterly. "My old moon companion—"

"Lock that up in the headquarters safe." Thorsen's bony, bloodless hand trembled toward the tetrahedron. "Nobody is to touch it without permission from me."

"Yes, sir."

"You kids." Thorsen's dull stare swept Nick and Kyrie. "You've played too many games. I want your beer can drive developed into a missile propulsion system. Beginning tomorrow."

"Father!" Kyrie pointed at the long red scar across Nick's ribs. "Don't you see he's hurt?"

"Tape him up," Thorsen snapped. "Shop space will be provided. You can requisition what you need. But you'll be working under guard, without that lump of moon grit."

Standing hand in hand, tanning slowly in the sunlight, they said nothing. Thorsen barked at his driver and the staff car departed. Gort licked his lips and prodded Tom into his own car. Guy growled and started after him.

"No, Guy!" Kyrie whispered. "They'd only kill you."

Guy whimpered and blundered away alone. I walked with Nick and Kyrie back to the nursery. Silent and despondent, they refused a meal Carolina heated for them in the kitchen and soon slipped away to sleep.

A space snake buzzed the mesa that night. I didn't see it. I was reading a novel in bed when it came, trying not to think about the children and the terminal. I heard its screaming passage, felt the bone-deep chill of heat drained away, gulped at the bitter aftertaste in my mouth. The windows rattled. My reading lamp flickered and went out.

Barefoot, I ran to the door. Outside was black confusion. Automobiles had died. Men were cursing and running in the dark. Here and there a flashlight flickered. Random gunshots rattled.

Power line transformers had gone out, and the mesa was dark for an hour. When the lights came on, I went down to the nursery. Nick and Kyrie were sleeping undisturbed. I talked to a security man who had seen the diving snake.

"It wasn't like the pictures," he said. "You couldn't see the snake shape in the dark. Just that jagged crystal in the heart of it. And the plumes reaching out, like blue wings." He shivered. "Just one glimpse as it roared overhead—and nearly froze me to death."

I returned to bed, without looking into Guy's room. Marko woke me early next morning, breathless with the news. Guy was gone, along with Tom and the tetrahedron.

"Tom's guards were knocked out and expertly tied up," he said. "The headquarters safe was left standing open. Nobody knows how they got off the mesa. Gort thinks it all happened during the blackout." He gave me a troubled stare. "I don't know what your brother is up to, Kim. I suppose you don't. But Gort thinks he's working with the snakes."

4

Perplexity

Before Marko left, a security car came for me. I was held three days in a bare room in the old Sino-Soviet residence, while relays of men with tape recorders probed for facts I didn't know about Tom and Guy. The last day, Gort joined them.

"Mr. Hodian, your brother was heard inviting you and Nick and Kyrie to try your luck with him. He called you a schlemiel when you said no, remember?" His sleepy cat-stare searched me. "You'll have to explain what he wanted."

But I couldn't explain Tom's proposition. I didn't know why the snake had come to buzz Skygate on that particular night. I couldn't tell him how the headquarters safe had been opened. Or how Tom and Guy had left the mesa with the tetrahedron.

"Better talk," his hoarse whisper warned me. "Before we have to try the biochemical confessors."

I was sick with dread of a new ordeal next morning, when his men took me up to the headquarters building, but there were no biochemicals. Thorsen, instead, came shuffling to meet me at his office door, looking white and feeble and vaguely apologetic.

"Hodian, we're desperate." He gave me his unsteady hand. "I don't suppose you know that patches of that queer sea-fog have begun drifting over the west coast of Mexico. It rolls in at night and drifts back to sea when the sun comes up. It has covered two or three fishing resorts. When it goes out, the towns are empty. People and animals and even fish bait gone. Nobody knows what sort of things are in the fog—or where they mean to stop."

110

He tottered back to his desk and nodded for me to sit.

"We believe they're invaders—intruders from another biocosm. From Venus or more likely Mercury. We have evidence they're allied with the snakes. We suspect that your brother has been in contact with them—using assemblies of the moon grit for communication. That's why we've questioned you."

Slumped behind the desk, he paused as if to collect his wasted vitality.

"You're our best lead, Hodian. You're Hood's brother and Guy's special friend."

His shaking arm made a helpless gesture. "I hope—I hope you'll give us any help you can."

When I said again that I couldn't help, he merely shrugged and stared, with no more threats. I sat wondering whether this new mildness reflected Suzie's kindness. She had stayed on at Skygate through the years he was away, keeping busy in the nursery or the lab, sometimes joining our small social affairs but firmly declining dates, returning my open admiration with nothing more than friendship. She was back with Thorsen now, cheerfully patient with his new infirmities, tending him as faithfully as if he had been another moon child.

I returned to the nursery when he let me go. Kyrie was just awakening from the longest sleep of her life. I sat with her in the kitchen while she picked dully at a breakfast tray. She looked so bad, so pale and pinched, that I had to ask what the trouble was.

"Uncle Kim, I had a dream." She pushed the food away. "I don't dream much, but this—it was awful. About Nick and Guy. About the nexode and the terminal." She shivered. "It's too bad to tell you."

That was all she would say. I went with her to look for Nick. We had to wait for Gort's permission, but at last a security car took us out to an isolated building near the end of the strip, beyond the spaceplane hangars. Once a quarantine station for returning spacemen, it was now Nick's shop.

Guards at the door called Gort before they would let us

in. We found Nick with Ken McAble and two or three of his space engineers around a drafting table in a big windowless room. He kissed Kyrie tenderly and gravely shook my hand.

"We're supposed to be designing what the general calls my beer can drive," he said. "But we've got problems."

One long wall was lined with computer-driven metal-shaping machines that McAble had requisitioned from the spaceplane hangars, and benches were scattered with parts and half-completed models, all finished with far more care than Nick's first flying plank.

The big problems, he said, were assembly and control. When Nick had assembled and adjusted a unit, it somehow transformed any sort of radiation into kinetic energy, drinking up heat and screaming away until it hit something or went out of sight. When anybody else put one together, nothing happened at all.

"The gadget makes no sense to me." McAble had worked twice around the clock with Nick; he was bearded and hollow-eyed. "It violates Newton, acting without a reaction. It breaks the Second Law of Thermodynamics, decreasing entropy. Running energy uphill!" His tired eyes glared at Nick. "Can you account for that?"

"Newton didn't know all about the universe." Nick sat cross-legged on the table, child-small and naked to the waist but patient and grave as another Einstein. "Neither did Kelvin or Planck. Their laws are true for the cases they were able to observe. But somewhere in space-time, energy did run uphill, increasing entropy to make the matter we know. Otherwise our universe would not exist."

McAble bent groggily over the drawings again, asking about symbols that Nick seemed unable to explain. I watched for a few minutes without understanding anything and went to look for Kyrie. I found her in Nick's new office, huddled down on the floor in a corner, silently crying.

"It's aw-aw-awful, Uncle Kim."

She didn't want a tissue or a cup of water from the cooler or anything at all. She wouldn't even smile.

"We ought to be building the terminal before our time runs out. I thought the nexode would show us a way. I just couldn't believe poor dear Guy would do what he did. But now—" Her quavering voice was almost a wail. "I just don't know—"

When Thorsen came later to inspect the project, Nick begged him to give it up.

"Please, General! Maybe something in the fog doesn't like people, but we don't need weapons against the snakes. I don't think they mean to harm us—"

"They cause planes to crash."

"Not on purpose, I think," Nick objected. "I doubt they even know they're hurting anybody. I imagine the sharing of energy is their way of greeting—their plumes always glow with a brighter light while they're soaking up heat. Perhaps they're trying to tell us something."

"Bull!" Thorsen croaked. "Anything they want to say, I don't care to know. You just give us the drive. We'll decide what snakes to kill." He glared feverishly at me. "Come along, Hodian. I want you to draft a news story for us. Something to blanket the panic. Play down the fog and the snakes. Play up what we're doing here."

I waited to learn what that was.

"We're coordinating all contacts with our neighbor biocosms. We're analyzing all the data from space and planning a well-balanced program of energetic action. We intend to keep on top of the situation. There's no cause at all for public alarm."

He kept me busy for the next few weeks, rewriting bad news to make it look less alarming. The space snakes had diverted or disabled a salvo of nuclear missiles fired at a patch of fog drifting toward the Golden Gate. A pair of scouting submarines were overdue and presumed lost beneath an area of Atlantic fog. Space snakes were reported roosting on the summits of Aconcagua and Kilimanjaro.

I went back to see Nick and Kyrie when I could. To my surprise, they were eagerly busy as if they believed our press releases. Kyrie had learned to operate the computer console. The machines it controlled were grinding out intricate bits of metal and plastic for Nick and the engineers.

I watched Nick launch two or three more flying devices, one no longer than a pencil, which had a crystal of rock salt for a core. Each shrieked out of his fingers and vanished in the distance, leaving a chill in the air and a black taste in my mouth. But he was still unable to translate his description into any form the engineers could grasp or copy.

Absorbed in the project, Nick and Kyrie stopped coming back to the nursery for rest. Carolina made Marko move into the living quarters of the quarantine building to look after them. The last time I called, two security men stopped me at the door and sent Marko out to talk to me. He said they were asleep.

McAble overtook me on the parking lot as I was leaving. He wanted me to join him at the Skygate Hudson for a couple of drinks and a steak. He needed to talk. Keeping up with Nick and Kyrie wasn't easy. One by one, his fellow engineers had given up and gone. He felt ready to join them.

"Kim, I've got the jitters." He caught my arm and clung, as if seeking human warmth. "Not just from your double-talking press releases, either." His haunted face twitched, trying but failing to grin. "It's something here." He glanced uneasily back toward the angular building, stark and black against a blood-colored sunset. "Something I don't understand."

I waited for him to explain.

"Something makes sounds—a patter or a rustle or a sort of chirp behind you." Distractedly, he patted his pockets. "Something steals little objects—keys and coins and pens. Something watches you out of the shadows and scuttles away before you can turn on a light."

"Could be pack rats." I tried to cheer him up. "This desert's full of them. The building's been empty for years. They could have got into the basement. They're shy and they make sounds and they'll steal nearly anything."

"Rats?" He shook his head. "I don't think it's rats."

We drank too much that night in the hotel bar, talking

about the mocking promise of a high transgalactic culture, about the fog and the snakes, about what might have become of Tom and Guy and the tetrahedron, about Nick's impossible beer can drive, about pack rats or something in the quarantine building. Our troubles were hard to drown.

We never got to the dining room. While we were still in the bar, the lights went off. After one feeble flicker, when the standby plant tried to take up the load, they stayed off. I waited for the sonic boom of another snake flying by and sucking up our power, but no sound came. We had a few more drinks to the end of things, and I remember a bellboy with a candle putting me to bed.

McAble shook me awake next morning. My head throbbed and my mouth was foul. I didn't want to hear what he was saying.

"Your friend Gort's on the phone. He says get your tail back to the mesa. He wants to know why the power went off and what became of the quarantine building and where are Nick and Kyrie."

McAble drove me home to the mesa. We found traffic stacking up ahead of us outside the main gate. Nobody seemed to know why, but the guards were turning most of the civilian workers back. Tight-lipped and grim, they searched our car and called headquarters before they let us through.

Inside the reservation, we found tanks standing at the major intersections. At headquarters, troops were stringing barbed wire across the lawn and piling sandbags around the entrance. Behind the building, a quad of nervous men in combat gear were setting up a missile launcher on the parking lot.

They held us till Gort came down, trailed by a stocky Navajo security sergeant. Gort looked as bad as I felt, sallow-skinned and twitchy. His sleepy eyes were swollen, and his raspy voice was coldly hostile, as if he blamed us for everything.

I tried to ask what was wrong.

"Get in." He waved at his car. "We'll take a look."

The Navajo drove. Gort sat tense beside him, peering into each cross street as if he expected to see an alien invader. The headquarters area was crowded with military vehicles and men digging in, but the road to the spaceport was ominously empty.

"Something's out there." Gort gestured abruptly toward the old airstrip and the vacant mesa. "It cut the power lines last night. It demolished the quarantine building. It's still there."

"Nick and Kyrie! Where are they?"

Gort twisted to watch a beer can glinting in the weeds as if he expected it to take off for Jupiter. When we were safely beyond it, he muttered at the Navajo.

"Tell, 'em, Harry. Tell 'em what happened to you."

The name on the Navajo's badge was Harry Horse. In an awkward mixture of Bad English and worse Spanish he said he and Corporal Miraflores had come out in the night to relieve the two men on duty at the quarantine building.

He couldn't say what the time was, because all electric clocks and electric watches had been stopped, but the lights were still out everywhere and day had not come when they pulled into the parking lot.

Por Dios! It was an unlucky night. In the sweep of the headlamps, as the car turned, he saw that the quarantine building had fallen in. Flattened. Like a paper box under the cleats of a tank.

Leaving the headlamps on, he and Miraflores got out of the car to investigate. The building had been mostly steel. Scraps of metal and broken brick still cluttered the site. In the ruins—

Sergeant Horse was driving slower now, watching every weed along the road. Something had been swarming in the rubble of the fallen building. *Ratónes? Arañas grandes? Quién sabe?*

Rats, maybe. Great spiders. He couldn't say, because the creatures scuttled cunningly out of the light. Yet he and Miraflores could hear them working on the metal.

They made a sort of humming whine, like many small machines. He tried to imitate it.

Damn! He found the English expletive. While they watched, the lights of their car went out behind them. The creatures were eating it! He and Miraflores ran back to the airstrip, but nothing chased them. Daylight was coming now, and they ventured back near enough to watch the somethings consuming the car.

The light was not yet good, but he said *los demonios* looked like ants swarming over a dead lizard. They came along one path and took bits of the car away along another. Metal, tires, glass. Soon there was only the engine block and the naked frame, like the bones of the car. Before the sun came up, the last scrap was gone. *Toda la máquina.*

He wanted Miraflores to report the creatures while he stayed to observe what they did, but Miraflores was afraid Major Gort would not believe him. *Bichos*—bugs eating a car! They ran together, all the way back to the security center.

"Well, Hodian!" Gort turned to glare back at me. "What do you make of that?"

Without much to say, I looked at McAble.

"Major, we've had something—" He stopped with a gasp, when a dove flew up beside the car. "Something in the building. I was telling Mr. Hodian last night. Nothing I really ever saw. Something scuttling about behind me and stealing metal objects. Mr. Hodian said it was a pack rat."

"A pack— A pack—" Gort wheezed and twitched and finally broke into a stifled laugh, while Harry Horse drove stolidly on. "So Hodian said it was just a pack rat!" He gulped and wiped his eyes. "I wish to God it was just a rat!"

Abruptly, with a Navajo grunt, Harry Horse hit the brake. Tires squealed. The car lurched and stopped. Harry leaned out, pointing.

"God!" Gort breathed. "Look at the varmint. Flying!"

It dropped out of the sky ahead of us. A queer insect

flying with a piece of string. It looked larger when it struck the pavement, at least a foot long. The string was a ten-foot section of stolen power cable, which perhaps had been too heavy for it.

For a few seconds it lay still, not a dozen yards from us. Ant-shaped, it had three segments. The head segment was silver-colored metal, a bright eyeless hexagon. The thinner center segment sprouted dark stubby wings and a cluster of limbs like silver wire. The tail segment was a slick black ball.

"Una hormiga!" whispered Harry Horse. *"Una hormiga de maquinaria!"*

A mechanical ant! Moving now, it lifted and turned its blank metal head as if watching us. A single delicate bright antenna uncoiled above its middle section, curving alertly toward us. After a moment it darted back to the bit of cable, caught it with clustered limbs, dragged it off the road. Its tail segment turned white as it disappeared into the weeds.

"Did you see that?" McAble glanced at me and watched the weeds again. "The way it moved? And that white flash?"

"I saw it," Gort snapped. "So what?"

"It doesn't run," McAble said. "It flies—even on the ground. The limbs aren't legs. They're manipulators. The wings don't beat. They're probably just for balance and control."

"So what?" Gort repeated.

"Did you see the frost on its tail?" McAble asked. "I think it's kin to the space snakes. I think it flies with something like Nick's beer can drive."

"I don't give a nit how it flies." Gort's heavy-lidded eyes glared accusingly at me, as if he thought I had invited these invaders. "Hodian, what *are* the things? What are they up to here?"

"How—" My dry throat made only a croak. "How could I know, Major?"

All the reports of that ominous fog and the invading snakes had been disturbing enough, but they were still remote. This ant-shaped thing was here, as strange as they and probably still watching us blindly out of the weeds. A sense of creeping terror numbed me.

"Drive on," Gort told the Navajo.

"Nick and Kyrie were in the building." That recollection struck me like a club. "Yuri and Carolina, too. What's become of them?"

"Dead," Harry Horse muttered solemnly. "Killed when house fall in. Duckworth and Wiezell, *también*. Six people eaten *por las hormigas metálicas*."

"Maybe they got away," McAble said. "The things don't seem vicious."

Harry Horse doubted that. He and Miraflores had come back in another car to scout the perimeter, and military aircraft had been flown over and photographed the whole area. All they found were weeds and desert brush and *el hormiguero de acero*. The steel ant hill.

"I hope to God they're dead!" Gort grated suddenly. "If they're alive it means they've been dealing with these invaders."

"Huh?" McAble frowned at him. "How do you figure that?"

"In the first place, Nick and Kyrie aren't exactly human." Gort spoke with a whispery vehemence. "The general says they've never cared for anything except getting in touch with their own space kin. Hodian's brother was showing them how to use that tetrahedron for a signal device. Now who were they trying to signal?" His swollen eyes glared at me. "Maybe these mechanical ants—if that's what you call 'em!"

Harry Horse was stopping the car, near the end of the asterite strip. A weathered sign read "Quarantine Station" and a side road ran two hundred yards toward a mound of brown earth where the building had stood.

"Let's have a look." With a nod at me, McAble glanced at Gort. "You'll wait, Major?"

"Don't count on us," Gort growled. "If anything happens, you asked for it."

Not very eagerly, I climbed out after McAble. Harry

Horse turned the car around, ready for a fast getaway. McAble was walking toward that new mound, not looking back. I followed him, breathing hard.

The pavement was empty. Our feet seemed too loud on it. We passed a clump of tall dead weeds grown where rain had stood in the ditch beside the road. I jumped and stopped when something rattled them, but McAble said it was only the wind, or maybe just a rat.

I felt sweat trickling down my ribs, though the day was not yet hot. Ahead of me, McAble stopped to kick at the mounded earth. Still dark with dampness, it was packed smooth and firm.

"Three hundred cubic yards of excavation." He swept the mound with a calculating eye. "Maybe four. Plenty of room for Mr. Marko and the others, if they're alive."

I followed him up the smooth brown slope to a bright flat dome that crowned the hill. He made me hold a tape while he surveyed it. Twenty feet across, with a two-foot rise at the center. Six circular holes around the rim—the doorways—were sealed with metal plugs. He tried the metal with the point of a pocket knife, and knelt to put his ear against it.

"Listen!"

I caught a faint sharp odor when I bent, like hot sulphur. The metal felt slick and warm. With my ear against it, I heard a murmuring hum, fainter and pitched higher than the sound of bees. When McAble tapped one of the plugs with the handle of his knife, that busy whisper ceased for half-a-dozen seconds. It came back slowly, and didn't stop when he tapped again.

"Nick would know every sort of code," McAble said. "If he's alive, we ought to get an answer."

He kept rattling his knife against the metal and listening hopefully, but all we heard was that faint shrill drone, until Gort began honking impatiently for us and a military helicopter clattered overhead. McAble came reluctantly away.

"Move!" Gort barked as we came near the car. "The

general called. He's setting up a demolition raid on the ant hill. He wants us out of the area."

"Demolition?" McAble protested. "Is that necessary?"

"Get in," Gort rapped. "Quick!"

At his impatient nod, Harry Horse pulled away before we had time to close the doors.

"Shouldn't we wait?" I asked. "Suppose our friends are alive in that dome? Captives, maybe?"

"Their tough luck," Gort growled. "The general's afraid to wait."

We followed Gort through the barbed wire and sandbags, into the headquarters building. Thorsen's appearance shocked me. Wasted and shaking, he was a walking skeleton, animated now with terror. He clutched at McAble's sleeve and asked a few hoarse questions about the steel ant hill.

"I'll give you another look," he promised us. "After we've blown it out of the ground!" He shuffled toward the staff officers waiting. "The target area is now clear." His quavery voice turned violent. "Attack!" he gasped. "We don't know what the invaders are up to, but they've got to be exterminated."

"Erik!" I tried to protest. "General Thorsen! Your own daughter is probably in that dome. Along with Nick and the Markos and those security men. Captives, maybe. If they're alive, you'll kill them all—"

"Hold it, Hodian." He cut me sharply off. "The invaders have ignored our signals. They are a clear threat to the whole Skygate facility—perhaps to the human race. I refuse to be diverted by anybody. Our operation will proceed as planned."

We watched from the headquarters roof. Heavy mortars chuffed behind us. Shells rained on the mesa, raising geysers of yellow dust. A spottercraft wheeled over the target.

"Fire ineffectual." A laserman relayed the message to Thorsen. "Shells falling on target aren't exploding, sir.

121

We've had direct hits and near misses. But there is not a dent in that dome."

Thorsen scowled at McAble and me.

"You surveyed the target," his brittle crackled. "Can you account for this?"

"Maybe." McAble shrugged. "We saw frost on one ant's tail. Apparently they soak up energy the way the space snakes do. Probably they're deenergizing the fuses of shells that come within their range."

"Then I'll call in an air strike."

"I wouldn't advise it, sir." McAble squinted shrewdly at the wheeling spotter plane. "I see no advantage—"

Shrill with frustration and fear, Thorsen called in the air strike. The aircraft were invisible against the dazzle of the sun, their black bombs tumbling out of a serene and empty-seeming sky. Explosions winked and dust rose in yellow mushrooms and the mesa rumbled with dull thunder.

"Bombs not effectual, sir," the laserman reported. "Visible explosions come from wide misses. No apparent damage to target."

Thorsen called for napalm. Three flights of supersonic fighter-bombers crashed out of that smiling sky. Their bombs smeared the mesa with long streaks of yellow fire —which suddenly turned into drifting smoke.

"Spotter going down!" the laserman shouted. "Contact cut off—I don't know how, sir. But his last call indicates napalm not effective. Target still intact. Something snuffed the fire out, sir."

Shaking, Thorsen glared at McAble.

"I think it was that entropy-reversing field," McAble told him. "I believe its range has been increased. I think it put out the fire—and caught the spotter, too. I think you're beaten, sir."

"You keep thinking," Thorsen snapped. "I'm sending in the tanks."

The tanks went in, converging from three directions. The air quivered with their engines. Tracer fire streaked out of the golden dust that thickened over them. Under the rolling dust-cloud, their thunder-voices stuttered and died. When it lifted, the tanks stood frozen in a mile-wide circle around their goal.

"Have a look, Hodian."

The desert danced and blurred in McAble's binoculars, but at last I found the ant hill. Dead missiles had furrowed the mound of earth, but that metal dome showed no scar. I found a green-and-gray-splotched tank, tipped into a missile crater, dead. Something crawled along its level gun. A silver-headed insect—

"Watch out, Hodian!"

McAble caught my arm and hauled. The binoculars flew out of my hand. Men around me gasped and cursed and ran. A typewriter dropped out of the air, crashing into the roof where I had been standing. It rocked and clattered, as a bright-headed ant squirmed from beneath it.

I heard a fine mosquito-whine. The metal ant climbed over the smashed typewriter and darted at my knees, flying a foot off the roof. Numb with terror, I couldn't move. It stopped six feet away, hovering over the binoculars I had dropped. Its eyeless head raised and turned alertly. I smelled its hot brimstone reek.

"Back!" Dimly, I heard Gort's whispery shout. "Stand back, you fool!"

Stumbling back, I saw men drawing guns.

"All together!" Gort called. "Aim for the head. Fire!"

The sun dimmed and lost its heat. A deep unpleasant chill sank into my bones. Bitterness coated my tongue. Shuddering and ill, I waited for the shots, but all I heard was an empty clacking.

"Watch its tail!" McAble sounded far away. "Hot with sucked-up energy. That's why we feel so cold. And why gunpowder fails to burn."

Its orange-sized tail segment was no longer black, but glowing dimly red. It settled toward the binoculars. Its bright snaky limbs explored them, wrapped them, clung. Its fine high whine grew louder as it rose, and that sulfur scent took my breath.

"Grab it!" Gort shouted. "For a specimen."

123

Standing nearest, I took one unwilling half-step. McAble came plunging past me. He crouched and reached—and crumpled like an unstrung puppet. The ant shot upward with the binoculars to vanish over the mesa.

Behind it, the sun shone bright and hot. The rooftop crowd stood quiet for an instant. A sparrow was fluttering overhead, carrying a grass blade for its nest. I breathed again, gratefully—and saw Gort reloading and lifting his gun. Shattering that brief peace, his test shot exploded the sparrow.

Hysterical voices babbled. Thorsen hobbled into the elevator, half-carried by his shouting aides. McAble twitched and groaned where he had fallen. I helped him stand, and he stumbled clumsily away, rubbing his icy hands together.

"Hodian." Gort jogged my arm as we waited for the elevator. "We've got a rush job for you. The general wants a news release on the ants. Make 'em look harmless. Emphasize the fact that they aren't known to have injured anybody. Play down our failure to damage them. Don't connect them with the moon children, or the snakes, or the fog. We're taking adequate action to cope with them, and the general says they're under control."

I was sweating at my desk that afternoon, still struggling to give the story some hint of conviction, when Suzie Thorsen knocked and slipped timidly into the room.

"Please, Mr. Hodian. May I please speak to you?"

Though she had always kept me at a certain distance, I still admired her dainty charm and her clear-eyed joy in the comedy of life and even her patient fidelity to Thorsen. She wanted to talk about him now.

"Erik's sick, Kim—and I don't know what to do." She looked pinched with worry, her eyes dark-rimmed. "The doctors think he has some unidentified exoform virus in his blood. He can't sleep and he can't eat and he has such dreadful headaches. I sometimes think he's not quite sane. He ought to be hospitalized, but he won't give up his job."

There was nothing useful I could say. Though Thorsen's sickness had been evident to me, he wasn't likely to take my advice. All I actually did was take Suzie over to the nursery for a cup of coffee.

Military cargo craft were rumbling across the sky. Down the street, men in battle dress were loading trucks with files and boxes from the exobiology lab. Two sentries at the nursery door scrutinized our badges.

The kitchen inside was quiet, however—too quiet, with the children gone. Suzie made coffee. I poured a big slug of Mexican rum into mine, but she waved the bottle away. We sat a long time at the table, talking over her problems and my own.

The children had become the center of our lives. Involved in their long search for themselves, suffering with Kyrie in the conflict between Nick and Guy, excited by their splendid dream of the transgalactic terminal, we had been content to forget ourselves. Without them now, without Marko and Carolina, we both felt lost.

We needed each other. What we said was commonplace. I don't recall many of the words, but I do remember the comfort of her smile and the candor of her voice and the delightful conviction that she was really fond of me.

We didn't talk much about the ants. Their arrival was a final, unbelievable blow, so completely devastating that I had scarcely felt it yet. Trying not to think about them, I was pouring myself a second slug of rum when all three doors of the kitchen splintered inward.

"Hands up, Mr. Hodian!"

Men stormed in, guns pointing. Most of them were Space Force regulars, but the leader was one of Gort's lieutenants. He looked sweaty and jittery but somehow startled and apologetic.

"You're under arrest, sir. Verbal orders from General Thorsen. No charges specified. We're taking you to the security center. You aren't allowed to communicate with anybody."

Suzie begged them to wait while she called her husband, but they marched me out while she was on the phone. At the security center, they took me to Gort. He was rummaging his office in a harried way, dumping drawers on his desk.

"Okay, Hodian." His swollen eyes glanced once at me. "Here's the situation. Ants are reported in the spaceplane hangars. Thorsen is calling in a nuclear strike. We're evacuating Skygate ahead of the missiles. I'm escorting you to another post. Our plane should be ready now. The guards will see that you don't talk to anybody."

"What—what do you think I've done?"

"I don't know, Hodian." His savage eyes flashed back to me. "Whatever you've been up to, I intend to find it out. We've no time for any formal charges now. But you're Tom Hood's brother. You've been involved in space research, and you've been close to all the children. You're our best link to the ants."

"Believe me, Major. I don't know anything—"

He turned his back on me to dump another drawer. Our plane took off half an hour later. It was a big military transport, loaded with records from headquarters and the exobiology lab. The other passengers included McAble, as well as Gort and a dozen of his men.

McAble was beside me in a window seat, still shaken and subdued from his skirmish with the ants. As we climbed, I caught one glimpse of the mesa above a tipping wing—the zone of black craters and the circle of dead tanks around the untouched dome of the ant hill, which glinted in the sun like a lost coin.

"So Thorsen's going to throw in the nukes." McAble made a grim brown face. "He might as well throw in napalm to put out a fire. His missiles will be bread-and-butter for the ants."

Nobody had announced our destination, but the wheeling plane turned east. Trying to avoid the snakes, we flew cautiously low through the mountain passes and on across the square-patterned brown and green of the plains. Occasional turbulence began to rock us, and presently I saw the dark cloud-towers of a weather front standing all along the east horizon.

The turbulence increased. Rags of cloud whipped by. We bored into a blue wall of storm. The plane pitched and shivered. Rain streaked the window. We turned and climbed and burst out at last. Above the dazzling pillars of white, the sky was darkly blue.

"Uh-oh!" McAble frowned. "We're too high."

Not much later, everything grew darker. The cloud summits lost their dazzle. Fangs of cold sank into me. My tongue turned bitter. I heard the engines cough and die, and knew a snake was diving on us.

I was numb and shuddering from loss of body heat, nearly as dead as the plane. Wrapped in its eerie quiet, I was barely aware of the rushing wind, of Gort's whispery curse, of McAble's sudden nudge. Turning painfully, stiff as if my tingling skin were already ice, I saw the snake.

A long serpentine shadow, transparent as black-veined glass. Its heart was a jagged crystal mass, smoldering with dull inner fire like an uncut diamond. Two plumes of blue light spread out of the crystal, wings of cold fire. Powered with our own stolen heat, it swept in fast.

A bright pulse beat in the wide blue sprays. Perhaps the creature was sending some signal of friendship or warning. Perhaps it felt companionable. Perhaps it simply needed our heat. Its alien grace was as meaningless to me as the bitterness lingering in my mouth.

The plane nosed down and the snake was gone. The snowy clouds were dazzling again. I gulped and shuddered and got my breath. Gort lurched past us toward the cockpit, shouting orders at the crew, but the engines failed to start.

We spun down through a storm, through boiling clouds and battering winds, through darkness and lightning and jarring thunder, through rain and savage hail, to a rough belly landing.

I recall jumbled fragments of sensation. A vague dark line of wind-whipped trees. A ripple of blue lightning, illuminating a toy-sized train creeping toward a toy grain elevator. Ripe wheat beaten flat with hail. A jolt, a pitch, a dazing blow—

The time after that crash is still a shadowy nightmare in my memory. The plane didn't burn, perhaps because the snake had drained so much of our heat. I believe McAble and Gort both lived—the recollection is dim as a dream, but I think they came together to visit me in the hospital, Gort on crutches, McAble with his arm in a sling.

As I try to look back, my own survival seems surprising. I believe I had a brain concussion. For a long time I lay in traction, with both legs broken. On top of such injuries, I contracted a severe gamma-form infection. Perhaps it saved my life.

Dr. Ram Narasimachar was my physician. I knew him first as a brisk foreign voice, as a hand very deft with the needles that went into my veins, long before I saw his darkly arrogant face. Gort may have told him in the beginning that I was someone worth saving, but his passion was the space diseases. The mutant gamma-forms in my blood made me a laboratory specimen.

Living in my own delirium, for a long, long time I didn't care where I was, or what was happening to the planet. Though I must have heard talk about the space war, its appalling disasters were never quite so real as my lurid private dreams of the children and the ants.

A quiet old Dane named Andy Elving used to clean my room in the morning. He had been to the moon as a systems engineer on the seekercraft. Now his wife was dead of a space infection and his son was gone to the war. He lived alone in a small white house we could see from my window. He was growing roses in his back yard, and he used to keep a vase of them on my window ledge.

He talked about roses and the town. Pitman had been a prosperous argicultural center. There was a militia camp near it now, and a new munitions factory below it on the river. A long way from the mountains where the snakes had begun to nest and the seas where the fog kept spreading, it offered all the security he could find.

Even the ants had never come to Pitman, Andy Elving said. Their lust was for metal and power. As if fed by the nuclear strikes, they had scattered at first to Albuquerque and Los Alamos ànd White Sands. Later they swarmed unpredictably into larger cities, leveling everything to build their impregnable nests. Now, however, they were leaving the cities to mine the earth itself. With no ore bodies near, Pitman was probably safe.

A year and a half had passed when I began to care about the calendar. I started asking questions then, about the moon children. Andy Elving remembered reading about Guy's stealing the moon jewel. Nick and Kyrie had been killed, he thought, in the bombardment of the ants at Skygate. But that was all he knew.

Nobody had heard about any transgalactic terminal. I began to feel that the messenger missile had lain on the moon for sixty million years for no result at all, that the children had been born for nothing. I thought we had lost our race to stop the chaos of conflicting biocosms. For a long time, I didn't even want to recover.

Andy Elving didn't like to talk about the war. Dr. Narasimachar was too sick and self-absorbed by now to talk much about anything. He had an acute gamma-form infection, probably picked up from me, and he was trying desperately to immunize himself with transfusions of my blood.

My first real news of the war came from other patients, after I was well enough to be moved out of isolation. Clayton Carter was a sunburnt ghost when he came into the ward, but his weakness came from hardship and exposure, not from any space disease. He was out of his head at first —maybe most of the time—but his unbelievable story rekindled my interest in the world.

A veteran Space Force pilot, he told me how the mechanics of his militia unit had built what he believed was the last spaceplane in America—out of salvaged wreckage. When it was ready, his first test flight was a scouting mission across the Rockies. Flying low and fast, he hoped to evade the snakes and bring back a report on what the ants were doing in the Skygate area. A diving snake killed his jets and forced him down, however, somewhere beyond the Rio Grande.

As the spaceplane went down, Carter glimpsed something that strained his faith in his own sanity. Even now, he couldn't quite believe what he had seen, and I had to coax the story from him. He was sitting up in bed that day, a black-bearded skeleton smeared with chalky ointments. I remember the tortured hesitation in his hoarse cattle-country drawl—he was a native New Mexican.

"The army don't believe what I saw—or thought I saw." His inflamed eyes peered uneasily at me. "A building on the mesa where Skygate was. A kind of tower—taller than the Rockies! Call me a liar—"

"Was it white?" I whispered. "Was it seven columns in a cluster? Did the tops of the outer columns make a kind of spiral stair? Did the center column have a pointed, shining dome?"

"Have you—" He gulped and wet his ulcerated lips. "Mister, have you been there?"

"That's the transgalactic terminal!" My voice was rough and breathless as his own. "The station the moon children were born to build, so the tachyon ships could come from the stars." For the first time, I tried to sit up in bed. "Are you sure it's really there?"

"It's there, all right." Awe echoed in his voice. "Taller than I dare fly and shaped exactly like you say. Except —" He paused to frown. "Except for that high dome. It wasn't bright or shining at all. It was black as midnight."

"Just so it's there!" I was trying to climb out of bed. "Now the tachyon ships will come—"

"Not for us they won't." He sank back against the pillows. "Because that terminal don't belong to no friends of ours."

I had to wait while a nurse sprayed his sadly damaged feet, but then he went on with his tantalizing story.

"I was tom fool lucky in a way," he said. "The plane came down dead, but the ejection gear did kick me out before the crash. All I got was a twisted ankle and a few cracked ribs. Not bad, considering the rocky arroyo I came down in.

"I scrabbled around in the wreckage, but I never found my survival kit. The desert got hot and my ankle swelled and I began to wonder how lucky I really was. But when I climbed out of the gully, I could see that tower. Taller than the clouds!

"I waited till sundown, afraid it might be a mirage. But it stayed there. The sun blazed on it, long after the desert was dark. Mister, it was something! Golden up high where the sun still struck, with zones of red and purple slowly climbing out of the night around me. I never imagined the towers of heaven quite so beautiful.

"I made a sort of crutch out of parts from my ejection shell. When dawn came, I started toward the tower. The top of it was already blazing before day came, gold and rose-colored under that dead black dome.

"It looked about a mile off when I set out. I hobbled along till sundown, and it still looked a mile away. By that time my tongue was thick and my ankle was killing me and the tower didn't seem so pretty any longer.

"I hadn't seen a sign of a human being anywhere, or even any animal bigger than a pack rat. I guess the fallout from Skygate got most of the larger life. It may have been still active—I had no meter for it. That next day might have been my last, if I hadn't stumbled into the old Albuquerque road.

"There wasn't any traffic. Hadn't been, for a long time. Rocks washed into the highway dips. One funny thing—all the bridges had been taken out. I was still sane enough to wonder why. I limped on till I came to the old Dos Lobos trading post.

"I used to stop there on vacation trips, but I barely recognized it. Everything metal was gone. Signs and gas pumps and the tin roof off the buildings. Even the junk cars piled up behind the garage.

"Rain sometime had begun to crumble the 'dobe walls, but I dug in the dried mud with my crutch till I uncovered a bottle of apple cider. That saved my life. I sipped and

131

slept all night—and dreamed about people with golden wings letting me into that tower, like old Saint Pete admitting the children of God.

"In the morning I dug again. Most of the metal cans were gone or rusted through, and rain and rats had spoiled a lot of the rest, but I found three more cases of cider and enough other stuff still good in glass and plastic.

"I stayed there at the 'dobe walls, lying in the shade at noon and watching that tower the rest of the day, till I could leave the crutch and carry a pack. I walked on, then, following the old pavement and climbing through the dry canyons where the bridges were missing.

"A half-moon was out, the night I came to the mesa. Feeling too eager to stop, I climbed the old mesa road by moonlight. The moon was low when I got to the rim—but there it was!

"The foot of it was still a mile or two away, but that black dome was lost in the stars. I got a crick in my neck, looking up at it. Mister, I wish I could tell you how I felt. Crazy with wonder, but somehow afraid—"

At that point, the nurse came back. She told Carter he was getting too tired. Though he protested, she turned his pillow and lowered his bed and snapped her sleeper gun at his head. Next day, after his feet were sprayed, I begged him to go on.

"You ain't laughing at me, mister?" He squinted suspiciously through his wild black beard and his chalky facial dressings. "You don't think I'm nuts?"

"I knew the moon kids," I assured him. "I watched them working two years on the plans for that terminal, hoping COSMOS would build it. I hope—I hope it's real."

"It's plenty real." He punched the button to raise his bed, and sat glaring strangely at me. "But the builders ain't human," he muttered. "They ain't setting it up for us."

I waited uneasily till he went on.

"They were working overtime, the night I got there. I couldn't see much, because the moon was nearly down by then. But I could hear—" One bandaged hand made a

132

hesitant groping motion. "A sort of humming whine," he said. "Like a million dentists drilling. Or a billion hives of bees. Then there was a kind of booming beat, deep and slow, like the biggest drum that ever was.

"I dropped my pack at the mesa rim and started toward the tower. But I didn't get far. I began to wonder why those workers used no lights. And why I heard no human voices. Then the wind must have changed, because I caught an odor that choked me. A scent like burning sulfur.

"All that was too much. I picked up my pack and scuttled down the road to a sort of shallow cave I had passed. I crawled in there to hide. It was cold, but I couldn't risk a fire. Finally I shivered myself to sleep.

"Something woke me, about sunup. Something crawling on my chest. I batted it off, before my eyes were open. It had a cold metal feel. I heard a whine and smelled sulfur and saw it hovering over my head.

"A damn' mechanical ant! I'd seen news pictures, but still the thing shook me up. That blind six-sided head, watching me with no eyes to watch with. The legs of it like a bunch of thin wire snakes—coiled around the coins and keys it had stolen out of my pocket. Even the class ring off my finger!

"It watched me for maybe half a minute before it sailed away with the loot. I was sick, after it left. Lost my supper and what little strength I had. But finally, after an hour or two, I nerved myself to climb back to the rim for another look.

"The tower wasn't heaven to me now." Carter shivered under his sheet. "It looked more like the gate to hell— with all those metal ants for junior demons. They were swarming as far as I could see, swirling like dark clouds all around the bottom of the tower.

"Near me, so close I could see their flat bright heads and their black tail-balls, they came and went from a metal-rimmed pit. In one stream they brought materials— hundreds of them clinging to a rusty ingot or a mass of ore or a scap of junk that might have come from my own

133

spaceplane. In another stream they came out with fabricated parts they carried to the tower. Bright metal and big white blocks. Their noise shook the rocks under me, and their hot reek burned my eyes. They're building an ant hill —into the stratosphere.

"Standing there, I forgot to be frightened, till one of them came whining around my head. I was afraid it wanted my gold tooth. When it flew back to the pit, I turned and ran. Nothing followed me—but I nearly died getting out."

Carter sighed as if still exhausted.

"I wandered out of the desert and over the mountains and all the way back. The ants had scavenged all the metal everywhere and I never saw a human being. Water and food were hard to find. After my shoes wore out, I had to tear up my clothes for bandages—that's how I got cooked with the sun. I was nearly back to Oklahoma when the militia scouts picked me up.

"That's it, mister." He sat up, glaring fiercely through his chalky mask. "The militia don't believe me, and I ain't got no proof. The snakes have downed our last airplane. But that tower's standing there where Skygate was. Taller than the clouds! I ain't no liar, mister."

"I'm sure you aren't," I said.

But suddenly I wasn't sure. Something about his angry challenge made me think of Yuri Marko, who had once been just as positive that he had found a transgalactic terminal on the moon.

With new skin grown on his feet, Clayton Carter went back to his militia unit. He wanted to lead a mounted party west. Neither the snakes nor the ants, he thought, would interfere with horses. He hoped to photograph the terminal and perhaps to try communicating with the ants, but I never learned what became of him.

The next man by me lay three days in a heal-sleep tent. "His name's Ballou," old Andy Elving told me. "He's got friends. They brought him on a horsecart from back east and threatened to burn the hospital if Doc Narasimachar wouldn't take him in ahead of the war refugees that are dying in the streets."

"A space case?"

"Some woman carved him up. Slashed his face and stabbed him in the gut. He came in with peritonitis, and it took some fancy surgery to save him."

Awake, Ballou was an angular waspish man with thick dark hair and a complaining nasal whine. He fumed when the doctor hurt his face, peeling off the bandages, and demanded a mirror to inspect himself.

"Look what you've done to me!" He fingered the forked blue seam across his cheek. "I used to be a fine-lookin' man. Folks said I coulda been a trivee star. Now look what a fright you've made of me." He threw the mirror at the doctor. "You clumsy bastard vet!"

Narasimachar ducked the mirror, which shattered on the floor. My blood had failed to stop the gamma-life teeming in his flesh, and his worsening palsy had in fact begun to spoil his surgery. I saw the stifled fury on his own dark face, and the way he clutched his gaunt hands together to stop their shaking. He stalked out silently.

"Call him back," Ballou snarled at the nurse. "I won't be insulted. Not by any pill-pushing quack. I'll have you know I'm somebody. We're the Fairfax Ballous. I guess you've heard of us—"

"I've heard plenty."

The nurse whisked out, and he turned fretfully to me.

"I'm Spiro Ballou." An ingratiating smile twitched across the unscarred half of his face. "Call me Spike. Back in Fairfax, I was somebody. People didn't insult me there. Not twice!"

I was about to introduce myself, but his plaintive voice ran on, quivering with self-pity now.

"All this crap is hard for me to take, because of who I was. My old man was president of the Fairfax National Bank and chairman of the board of Fairball Industries. He owned the best half of the town. When I married, he

135

bought me the Poppy-Cola franchise for a wedding present. But look at me now."

He sniffled and fingered his scar.

"My wife was Billie Fran—the sexiest doll in town. I had four acres out in Faircrest. An eight-room home of hand-laid brick. I drove a Cadillac Hydrocat, and traded twice a year. I thought I had everything, till the Moon King came along—"

"The Moon King?" I had been thoroughly bored with Spike Ballou, but that jolted me awake. "Who's the Moon King?"

"You remember the moon kids? Two cute little scamps, and one like a hairy bear? There used to be moon kid dolls, and moon kid toys, and moon kid picture books—"

I said I remembered the moon children.

"People sort of turned against 'em as I grew up. I guess just because space didn't mean fun and games anymore, after we got into the other biocosms. Anyhow, a couple of years ago this animal type ran off with what he calls the moon jewel—"

"Have you seen it?" I interrupted him. "A glowing pyramid—"

"Billie Fran saw it." Rancor growled in his throat. "Most of the women in Fairfax did. But he never showed it to me. He don't take to men—"

"Is Guy—" I caught myself. "Is this jewel in Fairfax now?"

"It sure is." Ballou nodded bitterly. "I hear he stores it in the vault of my old man's bank. Billie Fran says it keeps the space things out of Fairfax. The killer fog and the flying snakes and them iron-eating ants. She thinks it cures the space diseases."

"This moon boy has it?"

"He ain't no boy. Big as a grizzly. But he come to Fairfax with the jewel a couple of years ago. About the time the world began to fall apart. Only I didn't know him then. One that did was Billie Fran. My own wife—"

Ballou gritted his teeth.

"That was when she turned cold to me. If you can

imagine——" He choked with indignation, as if he couldn't imagine. "They were slick enough. It was just lately anybody found out about 'em. My wife——and that hairy beast! They should have been buried alive."

He sat up in bed, breathing hard and glaring at a nurse who had stopped to listen at the door, until at last she sniffed and disappeared. He lay back to get his breath.

"Seems the moon thing come into the country with some circus. Like the animal freak he is. Billed as the Siberian talking bear. One night a college professor got to asking questions he didn't like. He smashed the guy's face against the bars, and broke out of his cage before the cops got there.

"That was off in another town. He slipped into Fairfax through the woods. Dressed in a floppy hat and an old rain cape to make like a human hobo, he was working the alleys, begging for food. I must have been playing gin at the country club that day. Anyhow, Billie Fran was home alone."

Rage seethed in him.

"I guess she let him into the kitchen first. She filled him up with a roast and potatoes she'd been cooking for me. She never told me all they did, but finally she put him in the little apartment behind the garage, where her old lady had stayed till she died. She kept him there——if you can picture that!

"How could she do it?" He blinked at me, his glaring fury clouded with a dim bewilderment. "A sweet girl like Billie Fran——singing in the Presbyterian choir, and teaching the toddlers' Sunday school class, and crying like a baby every time she found a spot of lipstick on my shirt. How could any woman love that circus freak? When she had me!"

I didn't try to answer.

"She kept him there the best part of a year, before I ever knew. But she wasn't the only one he had." A sullen amazement slowed his voice. "I guess it was the cleaning woman, first. Then her Thursday bridge luncheon. Then her Sunday school class——the young married women." He

137

grimaced with a certain bitter smugness. "So I wasn't the only sucker."

I couldn't help asking how he found the moon child.

"Billie was just too damned happy." He scowled savagely. "Too damned healthy. Too damned beautiful. As if she had discovered the fountain of life. Her sinusitis cleared up. She was singing to herself all the time. Doing little things to please me. She tried to cook what I liked, and she saved out of the house allowance to buy a new shockproof chronoscope I wanted for my birthday, and she quit nagging when I come in late. Things like that made me wonder, but then a stranger tipped me off.

"A fat black little guy with a hook nose and a bad odor. When he first come out to the Poppy-Cola plant, I thought he was a federal nark. But it turns out he don't care how we spike the stuff. He's a private eye, hired to find the moon jewel."

"Hunh?" I had begun to wonder how my missing brother would fit into the picture. "Was his name Tom Hood?"

"The name he give us was Todhunter Hoke." Ballou peered at me sharply. "He knew all about that educated Siberian bear and he'd talked to that bunged-up college professor. He snooped around till he located that moon beast and his harem.

"I saw red when he told me about Billie Fran. I tried to hit him, but he ducked away and tossed me a picture of her and the beast. He'd bugged the room, too, and he played me a tape that made me sick. That beast and Billie Fran making love and laughing at me!"

Ballou sat silent for a moment, his scarred face dark and twitching.

"Hoke called a bunch of us together. My golf and poker buddies—that hairy brute had all our wives." His stifled voice was hoarse with hate. "I wanted to catch him and burn him alive, but Hoke said he'd be too hard for us to handle.

"So finally we called in the law. My uncle was the chief of police, and the county sheriff had a note at the bank, so we got cooperation. We closed in on that garage apartment with twenty men in six cars. I had buckshot in a pump gun, and I meant to gut-shoot the beast.

"But he got away." Ballou writhed with frustration. "Somebody yelled that he was running into the woods behind the barbecue. We all dashed in like fools. Shooting started down in the brush by the creek, but when we got to the dead man he was just a deputy sheriff.

"That beast had outfoxed us—them damfool women musta tipped him off. Our cars had been rolled over and set on fire before we got outa the woods. And all that was just for openers—"

Perhaps I had smiled, because he stopped to glare at me.

"It ain't no joke," he whined angrily. "Not to none of us. Nor to them women, when our turn comes. We'll make them sluts hate the day they ever saw that stinkin' brute."

"It's more than a joke," I agreed. "Did you ever catch the moon man?"

"Not yet. Nor many of his crazy bitches, either. The sheriff tried to round all the women up and get 'em out of town. He swore us into a special posse and sent us up and down the streets, but all we caught was a handful of little girls and smooth-mouthed grannies. All the rest was hiding or shooting at us.

"That monster hunt went on all day. A dozen men was hurt or killed in a shoot-out at the city park. The sheriff got hit in an ambush down by the bottling plant. A big fire was set on Main Street, while we were outa town.

"We had 'em surrounded once, in the Red Raven Tavern, out on the airport road. The police tossed riot bombs into the place and went in shooting. But that brute was too much for 'em. He breathed the gas and took the bullets and used the chief like a club to smash his way out. A hairy devil! Big as a Brahma bull.

"And them women—you can't imagine what he's done to them! Most of 'em pregnant. Blown up with their own baby beasts. But that don't slow 'em down. I seen the

Presbyterian pastor thrown outa the tavern through a plate-glass window by his own young daughter.

"By night, they was hunting us. Gangs of them hot bitches took the courthouse and the city hall and the militia armory. They sniped at us from the water tower and the elevators and the roof of my old man's bank. They run us out of town."

Ballou lay back and closed his eyes, wheezing for his breath as if defeated all over again by the violence of his own narrative.

"Run us out—and kept us out. They burned the bridges. Piled up wrecked cars for road blocks. Posted snipers in trees and silos. Them crazy women and their hairy stud— that's why we call him the Moon King."

"So he's still there?"

"The gov'ment ain't about to help us catch him—not when they're busy losing the space war. The militia's been trying to fight a patch of the killer fog spreading over Lake Ballou. So Hoke helped us organize our own mounted patrol.

"I'm the captain, of course. We forded the river early one morning and slipped down through the woods where the snipers couldn't spot us. We surprised three women picking beans in a little garden patch. They yelled and ran, but we caught one of 'em.

"Billie Fran, about to bust with her own monster baby. Her second kid by him—she never wanted none of mine. We took her back to camp. She wouldn't talk at first, but she opened up when Hoke got hold of her. She told us all about that brute and the moon jewel—how they keep it in the bank vault while he sleeps once a week, two or three days at a time.

"I felt sorry for her when Hoke got through—what a fool I was!" Ballou's quivering fingertips explored his scar. "I was guarding her that night, in the barn where we was camped. Somehow she got untied and come at me with a rusty old gelding knife she musta found under the hay. She cut me up and got away on our best horse.

140

"That's how come I'm here—and I like to died on the road. But we ain't through. Hoke's setting up another raid right now, but he'll wait for me to lead it. He's overhauling a broke-down army tank the militia left when they run away from the lake. We're going in with that, on a day when the Moon King's asleep. I don't think them bitches know how to stop a tank—"

"Nap time, Mr. Ballou!"

He glowered at the bustling nurse as if she had been one of Guy's girls. Smiling sweetly, she smoothed his sheets and read his monitors and spread his tent for another heal-sleep treatment.

Three of his commandos come to pick him up when he was discharged. They were brown sullen men, bristling with knives and guns. The tank had been checked out, one of them said, and Hoke was figuring the days when the Moon King would be asleep. If the hairy bastard ever woke up, he'd learn he'd lost his marbles.

My next companion was Dr. Narasimachar. The gammaforms were eating his nerve tissue now. Most of the time he was twisting and moaning in an agony the nurses couldn't relieve, or howling in delirium, but sometimes he was sane and calm enough to talk.

"You know, Hodian, I hate to go now," he told me, during one long midnight interlude. "Just before the world ends. I'd rather be the last man. Anyhow, I'd like to live long enough to see where we went wrong."

Drowsily, I pondered that.

"I was a research man," he said. "I never cared much for individual people—you learned not to, in the Indian cities where I grew up. But I did have rather large ideals. That's why I tackled the space diseases. We had to conquer them, I thought, before we could hope to make friends with our neighbor biocosms. Now I guess we'll never win."

He sighed and fell silent. I lay contemplating Spike Ballou and his tale of Guy's kingdom of women, who were somehow protected by the moon jewel from both space creatures and space diseases. The whole story seemed too complex and improbable to bear retelling to a dying man, and I said nothing.

"I've always been an optimist," Narasimachar went on suddenly. "I believed in science. I hoped it would show us our world and our nature. I tried to make it a bridge that we could follow, from the animals we are to the gods we could be."

I heard him move and felt his tormented eyes on me in the dark.

"Hodian, do you think I was wrong?"

I had to say I didn't know.

By morning he was frothing and whimpering again. Two days later he died. Andy Elving came in to pull the sheets over his face and draw the screen around his bed, but nobody took him away. Sometimes I heard feet and thumps and whispers in the corridors, but nobody answered my buzzer.

The screen blocked my view of the window, but for a time I could hear sounds in the street. The drum of fast traffic. An angry blare of horns. Now and again, squealing tires and the crash of a collision. These noises ebbed and finally eased.

By afternoon, the silence was stifling. I strained for the clink of a dish, the echo of a footstep, a voice on the street, for any sound at all. All I could hear, with my head on the pillow, was the slow throb of my own blood.

Before nightfall, Narasimachar had begun to smell. Not, however, with any odor of human decay, but with the sour and overpowering scent of the gamma-life which had consumed him, a scent like a mashed beetle.

Goaded by that odor, by hot thirst and cold terror, I struggled out of bed that night. Giddy with weakness, clutching at chairs and the wall, I swayed around that blocking screen and reached the window.

Outside, a full moon shone on a sea of snowy fog. It lay flat across the river valley and covered most of the town. Here on the low hill where the hospital stood, the tops of trees and the roofs of a few drowned houses stood dark above it. Covering the first floor of the hospital, it came nearly to my window ledge.

Far away across it, faint lights twinkled on the black hills where I suppose the refugees were camped. Though no wind stirred the trees, that vast white lake was alive with lazy waves whose slow rise and fall became almost hypnotic. Cold as the moon, serenely soundless, it shone with an unearthly loveliness that almost invited me to jump.

5

Fatality

Andy Elving woke me next morning, out of a long nightmare in which a sweet high voice like the baby Kyrie's kept enticing me to dive into that snowy fog. I found myself where I must have fallen inside the window. Along with all the familiar discomforts of my gamma-form infection, I was bruised and chilled, too numb to move.

Elving wore a mask against the overwhelming beetle reek of Dr. Narasimachar's corpse. Pale and grim beneath it he didn't try to speak, but he moved with a methodic calm, hauling me into a wheelchair and pushing me down the empty corridors and ramps, out to the hospital parking lot. It was deserted, except for an abandoned funeral coach that must have come for the dead doctor.

My stiffened limbs jerked with shock when I met the fog. Its odor struck me first—a heavy rancid scent that made me think of overripe muskmelons rotting in a garbage can. Then I saw it through a screen of trees—a gray uneven sea that heaved and billowed as if agitated by more wind than I could feel.

Its surface layers, darkened to a leaden colors, were shredded into tattered, crawling wisps, as if somehow dissolved by sunlight. Its level had sunk perhaps a dozen yards, leaving the hospital on a low island rimmed with a red, slick-looking residue where its deeper layers had lain.

Beneath those writhing tongues, its depths were still milk-white, opaque as ever. Lapping over the roofs below the row of trees, its dull flood filled the valley and still covered most of the city. A forlorn little group of buildings in the business district rose out of it, the tallest topped with a sign somehow still flashing: PITMAN TRUST.

144

"A bad night, Mr. Kim." Elving had torn off his white mask when we came into the open. "Sorry I couldn't get you out yesterday, but I was trying to save a few of my roses." He was loading me out of the wheelchair into the long black hearse, and I saw a stack of his rose bushes already there, neatly bagged in burlap. "The militia had warned us, but the fog came in faster than anybody thought. I spent the night on the hospital roof."

I felt a pang of dismay when I learned that the motor keys were missing, but Andy Elving had been an astro-engineer. He lifted the hood and started the motor with a pair of pliers. I watched with a little more hope as he got under the wheel and drove us off the parking lot.

The fog surrounded us. He tried one street and then another, turning back when it dipped below that restless sea. On three sides of us, everything was covered. Southward, however, the ground was higher. At last we found one residential street where dripping trees and soiled roofs marked out a hazardous lane across it.

Elving stopped the hearse above that street to study the crawling tongues of dull-colored mist that still intermittently hid the red-slimed pavement. Stolidly calm, he pulled a plug of tobacco out of his hip pocket and bit the end off of it.

"A filthy habit," he muttered absently. "Picked it up on the moon. We couldn't smoke in the spacecraft."

He sat there half an hour, chewing steadily, spitting unobtrusively, watching those tossing rags of fog. At last he expelled his wad into the street, closed the window, gripped the wheel.

"Hang on, Mr. Kim," he called to me. "The stuff has gone down as far as it's going to. I guess it's now or never for us."

Too weak to hang on, I dropped flat. The trucklike hearse lurched down the street. Gray tongues licked at the windows. Suddenly everything was white. Elving sat hunched and rigid, driving blind.

We hit something. The hearse lurched and quivered with the impact. Above the whine of the racing motor, I

145

thought I heard another sound—a thin fading wail, like the cry of some small creature in pain.

Perhaps that was just my excited imagination, for the hearse was skidding, the tires screeching on the unseen pavement with a far louder sound. Elving grunted and struggled at the wheel. We jolted against the hidden curb, and that rancid muskmelon odor was suddenly nauseating. But the hearse roared on till I saw blue sky.

A mile up the street, Elving stopped. He rolled the window down and mopped his calm brown face and bit off another chew of tobacco.

"Well, Mr. Kim." He looked around at me, almost casually. "What now?"

"I think I know a place where the fog and the ants won't come. A place where nobody gets the space diseases." Briefly, I told him about Spoke Ballou and the Moon King.

"I've heard that yarn." He frowned in disbelief. "These times you can hear anything."

"But I know the moon children. Guy Hood is my nephew. I've seen the object they call the moon jewel. I believe the story's true. I'd like to see Guy again, if we can get to Fairfax."

"My son was married there." He squinted deliberately at the fuel gauge and turned to peer at the uneasy sea behind us. "Just a couple hundred miles. Travel ain't as easy as it used to be—but why not?" A slow shrug announced his decision. "I guess we've nowhere else to go."

For a good many miles, the land was empty. We stopped two or three times to investigate abandoned vehicles. Elving loaded spare cans of fuel from one of them, and lugged a case of dehydrated beef and a plastic bag of water from another.

At the crest of a long hill, a militia roadblock stopped us. Three hollow-eyed young boys manned it. They stabbed bayonets into the pile of rose bushes and asked nervous questions. When Elving told them about my gamma-form infection, they stepped quickly back and waved us on.

For miles we drove beside refugee camps. Rocky hills we covered with tents and parked vehicles. Stragglers were still on the road, and once a militia convoy held us up again, crossing ahead of us with water tanks and trucks of crated food.

On one hilltop, an enormous crowd swarmed around an open-air tabernacle, so near the road that I caught snatches of a hymn brayed from a speaker system, and phrases from a screaming preacher warning his congregation to prepare themselves for the end of the world. It had never seemed so near.

Dusty militiamen at a second roadblock told us that snakes had been reported nesting in the higher hills ahead, but Elving refused to believe it. This whole region, he thought, was too low and humid for the snakes. When he warned the men about my space disease, they let us drive on.

We met no snakes. Those bare hills were vacant, until we saw a half-dressed girl standing by the road, waving for us to stop. Elving slowed the hearse, but suddenly speeded again. Hidden men sprang out of the weeds as we went by, and glass fragments sprayed me from sudden holes in our rear windows.

Out of range, Elving stopped to look for damage. When he found nothing serious, he opened a tin of dried meat and offered to share it with me. All I wanted was water, but he ate with evident relish and washed his dentures carefully before we went on.

Beyond those hills, the road fell into another wide valley. To my relief, there was no fog. We drove through miles of weed-grown farmland and then across an oddly empty space ridged here and there with mounds of broken brick that looked as dead as Babylon.

"Transplanet City." Elving nodded at the red mounds. "Transplanet Chemical was located here. The main industrial center in these parts. Till the ants cleaned it out."

The ants had removed the old metal bridges. We had to leave the pavement and jolt down a rocky detour to a log trestle the militia must have built. The road beyond climbed into rocky hills that looked vacant until hammering bullets dusted me once more with broken glass.

A tire was punctured, too, but we kept going long enough to outrun three ragged gunmen who chased us on an old farm tractor. Elving fixed the tire where we stopped that night, in a clump of trees behind a burned and looted country store. He slept a little while I sat up to watch, and we went on at dawn.

That day we crossed grassy hills that must have been cattle ranches, though I saw nothing larger than a frightened rabbit. In late afternoon we reached a level prairie that sloped gently toward a dark shadow along the horizon.

"Yonder's Fairfax." Elving had stopped to check the tires and do what he could for me. "Just beyond that ridge —it's the old Greenway Park." Thoughtfully, he rolled the tobacco in his jaw. "Fairfax could offer us a problem. I don't say this Moon King ain't you nephew. But how do you aim to identify yourself?"

Set against all the other hazards we had faced, that seemed at first a trivial question, yet I found no easy answer. We were men. Guy's women, expecting no friends, would probably shoot without warning. Andy Elving shrugged and drove silently on before I could think of any reasonable solution.

We passed abandoned farms, fields unplowed and buildings burned, and crossed another strip of pastureland where no cattle grazed. Abruptly, near the ridge head, Elving stopped the hearse and climbed out to inspect the pavement.

"Cleat tracks," he muttered. "Your brother's tank."

Sitting up to look, I saw the double scar the tank had made, wallowing across a muddy field toward the woods. Elving grunted and pointed, and I discovered the tank itself parked beneath a tree, sloppily half-concealed with a few broken branches. A bullet slapped the top of the hearse and whined away.

"Your friend Spike Ballou." Elving slid under the wheel, with a nod toward a group of horsemen riding out of the trees beyond the tank. "I'd rather not meet 'em."

They rode hard to intercept us, but the hearse was faster. We lost sight of them as the road wound into the wooded ridges beyond the tank. In happier times, this had been a pleasant recreation spot. It was nowan empty buffer zone around Guy's kingdom. We plowed through the frost-seared weeds and vines that clotted the unused pavement and detoured the burned-out vehicles and felled trees that blocked it. Elving braked to a quick stop at last, where a bridge was gone.

The gap was only thirty feet, but we found no way across it. Upon all my fatigue and pain, that final frustration was almost too much for me, but Elving was quietly hopeful that Guy's girls would reach us ahead of Ballou's men.

Patiently, he went to work on a signal. My name, we decided, was our best password. Using charcoal from the burned bridge mixed with motor oil, he set about printing it on a sheet.

Amid the space war's madness, that spot was a paradoxical island of peace, sweet with the cool natural odors of terrestrial life and decay. Clear water gurgled over the pebbles. The frost had not touched the blue morning glories still shining in the deeper shadows. A jay was scolding Elving as he stretched our sign from a tree. Somewhere a woodpecker drummed.

We waited. Dull with pain, I must have been dozing. I sensed a sudden stillness, then a clatter of hooves on the pavement behind us. That stopped. There was only the murmur of the stream, until I heard my brother's voice.

"Now hold your cool!"

He stepped from behind a screen of morning glories, a rifle in his hand. As fat as ever, he moved with a surprising cautious agility. His shapeless coveralls were stiff with grease, perhaps from the tank, and his filthy brimless hat crowned his dark Levantine head like a fez.

"Well, Kimmie. I thought you were dead—and you don't look good." His slow drawl reflected neither pleasure nor surprise. With a wary glance at Elving, he stopped outside the bullet-shattered window. "What are you doing here?"

"We're refugees." I nodded at Elving. "From the fog over Pitman. We're looking for Guy."

"If you find him, you'll be sorry." His soiled face grinned as if to some gloating recollection. "I don't think you'll ever see him. His women don't like us human men. But I'm in position to persuade Ballou to let you try, if you'll carry a message for us."

I waited.

"A message from Captain Spike Ballou." Tom fumbled the crumpled butt of a narcorette out of his pocket. With no light for it, he sprinkled the last blue grains into his grimy palm, sniffed them into his nostrils, and sprayed me with a sneeze.

"A message to the women—we figure Guy is sleeping now." A slow grin of dull joy had spread over his bloated face. He closed his glassy eyes, and we waited while he snuffed his dripping nose two or three times, with a kind of concentrated greed to save the precious juice.

"Tell 'em Ballou wants the Moon King," he panted. "Tell 'em to let us at him before he wakes up. If they'll agree to that, we'll promise to be tender-hearted. Ballou says he'll let Billie Fran come back and take what's coming. But if they won't agree—"

He leaned through the broken window, and I caught pungent narcotic fumes already mixed with his own stale goatishness.

"If they won't play our game, we won't stop with just taking care of Guy." A smothered violence burst into his voice. "We'll slaughter all his bastard brats—and every slut that's pregnant by him. Tell 'em that!"

I shrank from a spray of acrid spittle.

"If they don't fall for that one—and I don't think they will—here's another offer you can pass along." He chuckled thickly, leaning too close to the broken glass. "This one personally from me."

With a cunning glance at the screen of vines behind him, he lowered his voice.

"Personally, you know I wouldn't hurt Guy. My own dear son." He winked at me slyly. "I sure don't want his

150

women—no man will ever please 'em now. All I want is the moon jewel—that lump of grit he put together. Tell Billie Fran to slip me that, and I'll guarantee that Spike Ballou will never trouble her again. Personally—my pleasure!"

I wiped my face and asked what good the nexode would be to him.

"Still a schlemiel!" His tone and his sardonic shrug might have been our father's. "Kimmie, that crazy crystal is the only thing worth wanting in this crazy world. It's knowledge—when you learn how to use it. It's power—look what Guy does with it. It's safety—from the fog and the snakes and the space diseases. What good is the moon jewel?"

He slapped his greasy leg and chortled.

"Anyhow, Kimmie, here's our proposition." Grave again, he waved his rifle for emphasis. "We'll put you across the creek. If you get a chance to talk, give the women a choice. Tell 'em to give up their king or the jewel. Give 'em till sundown. If they balk, tell 'em we're coming in tonight with something they can't stop. You'll do that?"

I looked at Andy Elving. He shrugged in noncommittal acceptance. Tom made us back the coach, and put us on a gravel side road which took us down to a shallow ford and back to the pavement beyond the stream.

"I don't care for your brother," Elving muttered. "In fact, I wouldn't claim him."

He drove slowly, tooting the horn. Once we stopped to wait at an old park-service camp site, but nobody came out of the trees. He gnawed off another chew, and our hearse lurched on. Before we got back to the pavement, a pile of rocks stopped us. A little beyond them, a heavy chain was strung between two trees to bar the narrow road.

Elving tried the horn again. When nobody answered, he climbed over the chain and vanished beyond the screen of vines. He was gone a long time. I lay in a feverish do listening to the wind above the trees and a dove cooing softly far away, till voices roused me. When I propped myself up, Elving was coming back, walking modestly in front of two girl guards, each uniformed in a single wide green garter and a singular aura of vibrant joy.

A short redhead with a rusty old double-barrel shotgun, the cracked stock bound with black tape. A slim long-haired dark girl with a bright-tined pitchfork. Aglow all over with the pure spirit of youth, they handled their weapons with a playful gaiety that almost alarmed me.

"Here they are, Mr. Kim." Elving had to look at them now, and their vital beauty crinkled his brown face into reluctant admiration. "But they can't quite believe who you are."

"Sir?" The redhead bent to inspect me doubtfully through the shattered glass. "Honest, are you really Mr. Hodian?"

"Guy's Tío Kim?" The dark dirl had a soft Spanish accent that made it *Keem*. "From Skygate?"

When I nodded, the redhead laughed with sheer delight.

"It's just too grand to be true," she gurgled. "One night Guy told me a lot about you. How you helped him learn to talk. How you were good to him when he was still too young to help himself and how you cared for him when other people hurt him. He said he was afraid you were dead. He'll be so glad you came!"

"Maybe *si*, maybe *no*." The dark girl shrugged to toss the sleek black mane off her face. "If you are Guy's Tío Keem, I think you better prove it. Tell us facts about him."

"You knew Guy when he was tiny?" The eager redhead widened immense blue eyes. "I bet he was as cute as a baby bear!"

"Not really," I said. "The beautiful moon children were Kyrie Thorsen and Nick Marko—"

She looked disappointed, and the dark girl scowled.

"Who? Who you say?"

As I discovered then, they knew very little about Guy's actual past. Though he had told them something about his father and me, apparently his total rejection of Nick and Kyrie had caused him to deny that he had ever been one

152

of the famous moon kids. The girl guards apparently believed him.

"Maybe you lie." The dark girl stabbed her pitchfork into the sod and bent so close that I caught the clean fragrance of her glossy hair. "Guy's own *bandido* father try to rob him. Maybe he send you to try again."

Weak and sweating with alarm, I looked at Andy Elving. He was chewing steadily, and his broad stoic face gave me nerve to go on.

"We're refugees," I said. "We're running from the space invaders and our own fellowmen. We need Guy's help. I think he'll let us stay here, if you'll just take us to him."

"I'm sure you'll be welcome—"

"Meester, you better make no fonny business." The dark girl cut the redhead off. "Maybe you don't tell us everything." Her jet eyes squinted with suspicion. "Who show you where to cross the river?"

"We did meet Guy's father." I nodded uncomfortably. "He gave us a message from Mr. Ballou, to take to Guy's women." I caught an uneasy breath. "Will you let us deliver the message?"

The dark girl was clearly in command. She frowned at the redhead thoughtfully, and sharply back at Elving and me.

"We give you a choice," she decided at last. "We let you turn around and go back now. Tell Ballou and Guy's *bandido* father the mothers want no message from them. Or else we take you to the mothers—"

"Take us," I said.

"The mothers have Guy's children." She shook her head, with a hard look at Elving and me. "They share the power of the jewel—enough to know fonny business. Maybe they say you both okay. But maybe they see you not okay. Maybe they keel you."

I turned to Elving. Delicately, he spat away from the girls, in the general direction of my brother and Spike Ballou.

"No choice," he muttered. "If it's the mothers or the fog, we'll take the mothers."

*   *   *

The redhead clapped her hands.

"I think you're both okay," she burbled happily. "I just know the mothers will let you wait for Guy. You'll have to wait, because he's sleeping now. He'll sleep for two or three days, and his sleeping place is secret. Only the mothers know—"

"Shhh!" The dark girl hissed at her. "Lib, I think you talk too much." She pointed the pitchfork at us. "Maybe they work for Guy's *bandido* father. Maybe they come to spy out his sleeping place. We wait for the mothers to say."

"We wouldn't hurt Guy," I kept insisting. "And he used to be fond of me. I believe he'll want to help us now. He always was a strange creature, but I believe he means to be good—"

"He's grand!" Lib swelled with pure happiness. "Just too grand." Her bubbling eagerness moved her closer to the hearse. "If you knew him always, tell us how he used to be."

Wondering how much to tell, I looked at the dark girl.

"Say what you like." She flung back her veil of hair, with a gesture of spectacular indifference. "The mothers will decide."

"Thank you, Eva." Lib beamed breathlessly at me. "I so want to know about Guy, when he was a baby."

"He wasn't a pretty baby," I began uncertainly. "Though I did learn to love him, it wasn't easy. He always seemed—well, more animal than human."

"He's more than human now." Devotion rounded her enormous eyes. "In every way there is!"

"Perhaps he has changed, since I knew him." Their absolute worship had begun to puzzle me. "I can't quite understand how much you seem to care for him."

"My father used to speak of heaven when he prayed," Eva said. "He lived on *frijoles* and died fighting weeds in another man's field. But Guy—" She caught her breath, and I saw the dark blaze of passion in her eyes. "Guy makes a little heaven here."

"Look at me." Lib preened herself, lifting her pink-nippled breasts and combing the fingers of both hands through her flame-colored hair. "Before Guy came, I was a miserable thing."

She made a fetching face at what she had been.

"Bad skin. Ugly freckles. Stooped shoulders and dry hair and crooked teeth. Allergies the doctors couldn't cure. And I was afraid of men. Just one date was all I ever had. A pimply grocery clerk wanted to walk me to a church supper. When he came to pick me up, I got sick at my stomach. I vomited, right there in front of him." Shaking off that depressing recollection, she glowed again. "Guy does more for me."

"Maybe you like to look at me." Eva arched her tawny torso, as if to challenge Lib. "Guy makes heaven for all of us. Maybe you like to know what he did for me. You know Spike Ballou?"

She waited for my nod.

"Back before Guy came, Ballou found me waiting tables in a helibar and picked me to be what he call a Poppy-Cola girl. I was supposed to be on trivee to sell Poppy-Cola, but he wanted to have sex all the time, at the conventions of Poppy-Cola salesmen, and up in his helicabin, and even on the sofa in his private office. Most of the time he was too drunk, but he did get me pregnant. When his wife found out, he let me go. With an EZ-Abort gun and a fifty-dollar bonus. I got another job waiting tables at the Red Raven—and he wouldn't even look at me when he came in." She spat on the ground. "Guy's better."

Her luminous eyes narrowed warily at me.

"Maybe now you see why we watch the border." She gestured at the chain across the road. "Guy makes a small heaven here, but it's for women only. Men—they all want to kill Guy and steal his jewel."

"Men don't like Guy." Lib nodded, as if with a passing regret. "Take our Presbyterian pastor. I used to adore him, before Guy came. Such a refined, handsome, godly man. His voice when he prayed used to give me goose pimples. But he joined Spike Ballou—I can't imagine why."

As if dismissing some idle puzzle, she tossed her fiery curls.

"He slipped across the river on an old gray mule and found his wife in the barn milking the cow. He prayed over her till he got her convinced that Guy was the devil incarnate. He made her hide him in the house and help him spy around till he found where Guy was sleeping with the jewel."

"If you plan such tricks as that—" With a feline ferocity, Eva waved her pitchfork. *"Adiós!"*

"The pastor's wife had come to her senses by then," Lib bubbled on. "But he tied her up and broke into Guy's hiding place. If you can imagine a minister—he stabbed Guy and grabbed the jewel and tried to get away."

Merriment began to ripple in her voice.

"Guy's as hard to wake as he is to hurt, but the pastor pulled a boner. Left the knife sticking in him. That bothered Guy so much he roused up long enough to call the mothers. They sent a squad of us maiden guards to catch the pastor.

"It was the middle of a dead-black night, but we could see the shine of the jewel. He had it in a sack, but somehow it lit him up, and even the mule. We caught up with him right about there." She nodded at the rocks in the road. "I sort of hated to hurt him, but we've got to defend Guy's country."

She slapped at a fly crawling down her firm pink flank.

"We hanged the pastor from a live-oak tree. Next day the mothers tied his body on the old gray mule and let it wander back across the river as a warning for men to keep out. I don't know why, but they just can't learn."

Very briefly troubled, she frowned toward the road behind us.

"Just last month, Ballou and his raiders carried off Billie Fran—she's the first mother. They hurt her terribly, trying to make her tell where Guy sleeps now and where we keep the jewel. But she finally found a knife and fought Ballou and got away."

"Maybe you see now why we don't like men." Eva leveled the long-tined pitchfork toward Elving, as if half-

156

inclined to use it. "Maybe now you change your mind. Maybe you go back to Spike Ballou."

Elving turned to spit carefully aside.

"We'll take our chances here." He glanced gravely at me. "I told you Mr. Hodian is sick. He's had a long fight with a gamma-form infection. You can see he's not able to hurt anybody."

Both girls peered at me. Eva's eyes narrowed doubtfully, but Lib's grew round with sympathy.

"You do look awfully pale and bad," she said. "But you'll feel better fast if the mothers let you stay. Fairfax is a healthy place since Guy came. A happy place too—for women, anyhow. Our lady doctors can't understand just how the jewel works, now that we keep it locked up—"

"Careful, Lib!"

"He's no spy!" Squealing at Eva in a flash of resentment, Lib turned pinker all over. "But we do have to defend Guy's country." She smiled soothingly at me. "We have to guard the jewel, because it's really wonderful. Look what it did for my Grandma Bloodworth."

Lib turned her graceful back on Eva, who was stirring restively.

"Ninety-two years old, the day she first saw Guy. Dying in a rest home. He didn't even touch her then, or let her see the jewel, but she got well. Her fractured hip knitted. Her cancer went away. Her weak heart got strong again. She moved out of the rest home, back to the farm. Now—"

Lib turned to giggle at Eva.

"Guy likes music—a queer sort of music we never heard before. He's been teaching some of us to play it. Eva used to be the best. But Grandma Bloodworth is his favorite fiddler now. And I think she's pregnant again."

"Who isn't?" Eva snapped, but in a moment she was reflecting Lib's happy adoration. "I told you Guy makes a little heaven here. The mothers say even the weather is changed since he learned to work the jewel. Maybe they're right. The rain seems to come when it should, and the hail and the frost don't come when they shouldn't."

I sat wondering vaguely what sort of unexplained interface might have been established between the forces of the atmosphere and the unknown energies of that ultimate artifact from the stars. Elving spat deliberately and spoke to Eva. "Will you take us to the mothers now?"

"Your choice." She shrugged, with the lazy grace of a bored tigress. "Maybe you be sorry."

With an effortless strength that amazed me, the girls rolled two big stones out of the ruts ahead. Eva removed a padlock to lower the chain. I settled gratefully back against my pillows, and the hearse lurched ahead.

When the rocks and the chain had been replaced, Eva searched the hearse for weapons and slid cautiously into the rear, her pitchfork ready at our backs. Lib perched on the front fender, bright hair blowing, beckoning casually with the old shotgun to guide us.

We were soon on the pavement. As Elving drove us on toward Fairfax, it seemed to me that we had entered a phenomenal circle of joyous and abounding life. Early frosts had already browned the arid uplands we had crossed beyond the river, but here we came out of the trees into a lush green landscape.

Lib beckoned us to stop beside a gnarled old tree, where sprays of young leaves and white bloom shaded ripe red apples. A mockingbird in the tree kept on trilling while she picked huge apples and tossed them into the hearse. I bit into one of them, when Eva handed it to me. Even though I had no appetite, its sweet juice made my saliva run.

Gravely weighing the apple in his hand, Elving leaned slowly to spit his cud into the dust and impulsively tossed his gnawed plug after it. Munching the apple, he drove impassively on.

By that time I was sitting up again, feeling unexpectedly refreshed and sharing Lib's bright delight in the exuberant life around us. Gaily waving the old shotgun, she pointed to a covey of quarter-grown quail running beside the road as if it would be spring forever. She smiled at a young calf suckling a black-spotted cow, laughed at a sorrel colt frisking across a green alfalfa field, clapped at a black stallion mounting a mare.

Though Ballou and his raiders had managed to burn most of the buildings near the river, we were soon rolling through an unscarred zone where dairy cattle grazed near white-painted barns and half-clad women sang as they tended the fertile soil. A young girl and a dog watched a flock of white sheep. Red-painted combines were crawling across fields of ripe wheat. We overtook two women on a wagon loaded with full bags of grain.

In contrast to all the waste and chaos we had left beyond the river, Fairfax itself was a welcome island of peace. The streets were clean. Naked children scampered about a school playground. When we passed a bakery, the smell of new bread set my mouth to watering again.

A little group of women on horseback met us near the courthouse square. They carried haphazard weapons—a police pistol, a hunting knife, a hatchet, a slung deer gun. Their leader was a tall attractive sun-browned girl with long yellow hair and a bright ironic face. She had a short bow slung behind her and a tiny child in her arms.

Lib beckoned for us to halt, and Eva ran ahead to speak to the women. After a few minutes, the yellow-haired girl dismounted and they came back to the hearse together. I saw long welts across the girl's back, not fully healed, and ugly blue marks at her wrists and ankles.

"The first mother." Eva was crisply respectful. "Mother Billie Fran Hood. She'll decide about you."

"So you are Guy's favorite uncle?" Her pleasant voice had a slight, childish lisp. She paused to catch some murmured word from Lib, and a quick concern changed her tone. "Eva says you've been ill." She peered into the hearse, and I watched her doubts dissolve. "You do look bad. I think you need the jewel's power. If Guy wants you —" At last she nodded, slowly smiling. "Eva will find a place for you to wait till he wakes up."

"We have a message," Elving reminded me uneasily.

"We talked to my brother back at the river," I said. "A man who calls himself Todhunter Hoke—"

Her blaze of fury checked me.

"Go on," she snapped. "What's the message?"

"Spoke wants Guy," I said. "My brother wants the

159

moon jewel. They're demanding that you give up one or the other before sundown. If you refuse, they're coming in with an army tank. They're threatening to kill all Guy's children—"

"Let 'em come." Her scarred arms tightened on the lively golden infant, which was peering at me as brightly as another baby Kyrie. Her smile turned defiant. "They've been here before. If they come back, they'll get another lesson."

Calm again, she paused to bounce her wide-eyed child. Elving had turned to listen, frowning. Though I had noticed no sound except the ring of fever in my ears, he said he could hear the rumble of the tank, crawling toward us over the ridge. I wasn't sure anything could stop it.

Lib and Eva escorted us to the Fairfax Manor. Twelve stories tall, it overlooked the courthouse square. The lights flickered now and then, as the women had some minor difficulty with the standby generators, but we had no other ground for complaint. With Lib and Eva standing guard, we were fed abundantly and put into the penthouse suite to wait for Guy's awakening.

In spite of the impending attack, I felt relaxed and oddly happy. Though I hadn't seen the tetrahedron, I believe some abscure effect from it had begun to help my body overcome that old space infection. Whatever the cause, my pain had gone. My head was clear. Once more I enjoyed eating. I even found a certain delight in contemplating Guy's girls and the radiance they wore. That night I slept well.

A thudding concussion woke me before dawn. The windows shook. Somewhere a woman screamed. The roar of Spike Ballou's tank was unmistakable now, and I knew it was firing into Fairfax. I shouted anxiously to find Elving.

"Out here, Mr. Kim." His calm voice came from the terrace. "I think the women are attack— Hunh?"

A startled gasp cut off his reply. Grateful for a sense of health I had not felt in two years, I left the bed to join him. At the street corner across the square, yellow flames exploded out of a shattered building. Women ran around the corner dragging a hose, but dropped suddenly flat.

White fire geysered out of a new crater in the pavement near them, where another incendiary shell had fallen. Glass shattered and the floor quivered and shell fragments whined. Stumbling toward the parapet, I stopped to stare at Elving. He wasn't watching the action in the street. His eyes were lifted to the moonlit sky.

"What—" For the first time in my experience, his voice was shaken with amazement. "What unholy thing is that?"

Dread blew cold on the back of my neck, when I saw what he was watching. A silver globe brighter than the moon, it dropped out of the sky, veered away from the dark courthouse, hovered over the blazing building at the corner. Elving watched it for what seemed a long time, before he turned slowly to me.

"I'm a plain man, Mr. Kim," he whispered hoarsely. "I always done my little bit, here or on the moon. I think I've earned a few quiet years. All I wanted now was time to grow my roses. I thought we had found the place to do it here."

Sobs broke his voice.

"I—I don't like them flying snakes, Mr. Kim. Or the metal ants, or the killer fog, or all the space diseases. Now here—here's this thing in the sky. At first I thought—thought I was outa my mind. But it ain't me. It's the whole world gone wrong, Mr. Kim."

He clung to me, shuddering.

Down in the street, the women had vanished. That bright sphere dropped again, as if to observe the abandoned firehose where it writhed like a broken snake on the pavement, jetting water at random. The globe hovered as if to inspect the towering flame, and drifted slowly upward.

At about our level, it slowed again and wheeled over the courthouse in a curiously hesitant way, as if somehow hunting. It came so near that I could see the pattern of its silver surface—a curious honeycomb of small hexagons.

Elving gasped and shook his fist, but it ignored us. I heard a faint shrilling as it went by, like the whine of the mechanical ants, and I caught a sharp sulfuric scent in the air. The ants, I thought, had somehow come to invade Guy's kingdom.

Not far from us, the object paused. It hung still while another shell came wailing down to tear a new crater in the courthouse lawn. Abruptly then, it shot away into the northward sky.

We saw no more of it, but I heard the tank again. Its engines roared briefly. Its cannon thudded rapidly a dozen times. Smaller arms crackled in the distance. But those sounds died. No more incendiaries fell into Fairfax.

Across the square, the women returned to the recoiling hose. We watched until they had the blaze under control. Uneasily searching the sky, we saw only the pale moon setting and a pink dawn glowing. My wonder and alarm slowly ebbed into a sense of mystic peace and fitness I didn't try to understand. Sleepily serene, I went back to bed.

Elving woke me at noon with news and food. A swarm of metal ants had attacked Ballou's tank and scattered his men. Guy was still asleep, his kingdom now secure. Elving himself had recovered his slow-spoken calm. Listening with a new tranquility, I cleaned every crumb from the tray and fell asleep again.

Next day I was up before Elving, feeling almost drunkenly well. We went down for breakfast with Billie Fran and our two green-gartered guards. When we had eaten, Elving drove us a few miles out of town in the hearse to see what the ants had done to the tank.

It had plowed through a hedge into a field of alfalfa. Its cleats had torn the dark earth, where it attempted to turn. Its fleeing crew had left footprints in a muddy ditch, but nothing else. We found no metal, no ants, not even a brimstone odor.

Elving drove us slowly back, looking for a spot where he could replant his roses. Ballou's men were scattered, Guy would soon be waking up to greet us, and we all felt secure in the shelter of the tetrahedron.

The space war seemed far away. Billie Fran sat beside me, aglow with the alluring new vitality that all Guy's women shared, happily dandling her little golden daughter. The child's likeness to the baby Kyrie still astonished me, and I wondered if the moon grit had created Guy to father a superhuman race, destined to inherit the solar system, if not to open a way to the stars.

Those idle speculations were cut rudely short. As we parked the hearse beside the hotel, the child screamed in sudden fright. Billie Fran gasped and snatched for her knife. Elving shouted in hoarse alarm. Something bright flashed overhead.

I heard a whine and caught a sulfur scent and saw a bright globe skimming past us. It paused across the street, above the massive cube of glass and granite that had housed the Fairfax National Bank, and came gently down outside the drive-in window.

A long panel of joined hexagons flexed and dropped to form a ramp. Two people stepped lightly down it, out of the shadowy ball. A man and a girl. Neither was clad, though the man carried a folded blanket over one arm. They looked very fair at first, but the sun washed them with glowing gold.

Nick and Kyrie!

Dazed, I could hardly breathe. I had not expected to see them again, and their arrival here was as unbelievable to me as their vehicle itself. I ran to meet them, stumbled over the curb, and reeled to a halt in the street—not yet so strong as I had felt.

"Uncle Kim!"

Illuminated with joy, Kyrie darted to hug me. Nick gave me a vigorous handshake. I stood gaping, because they had changed. Both stood taller. No longer the skinny, big-eyed, troubled child, Nick was poised and confident, a golden god.

Kyrie—I looked at her with an ache of delight. Long ago a woman, she had grown into a goddess. Yet what touched me was not her lean, high-breasted perfection. Kyrie loved me. The light in her eyes filled my own with tears.

163

"What's wrong, Uncle Kim?" Her lilac scent enveloped me, and her dear voice was a warm caress. "Have you been sick?"

"I'm all right now," I told her. "Now that you are here."

When I looked around for Elving and Billie Fran, the street lay empty behind me. They had fled into the hotel. I turned back—and saw a thing that jolted my senses.

Behind Nick and Kyrie, the edge of that flexible ramp had frayed into darting fragments. The fragments were ants. A stream of them came whining toward us through the air. Kyrie held out her hand, and one lighted on it.

The whole globe, I now discovered, was made of ants. Sealed into a honeycomb pattern, their bright hexagonal heads formed all its outer surface. Their sleek black tail balls made the inner one. Interlaced limbs knitted them together.

"Ants!" I swayed backward, choked with their hot scent. "Are you—prisoners?"

"If you could see yourself!" Kyrie gurgled with delight. "These are ours." She smiled fondly down at the thing in her hand. "I suppose they are a little like ants, but Nick calls them replicating machines."

She was trying to hand the whining thing to me.

"It won't bite you, Uncle Kim." She laughed at my alarm. "Actually, it won't harm anybody."

To my relief, Nick waved it away.

"Kyrie found the design recorded in the nexode." He spoke with a casual brisk assurance. "After COSMOS had come apart. We built the first units at the shop on the mesa. They do reproduce themselves in underground centers, somewhat like insects. But really they are only tools. We used them to build the tachyon terminal."

I couldn't quite grasp that, until the saga of Clayton Carter began to emerge from the fading nightmare of my long confinement in the Pitman hospital.

"It's already—already built?" Staring at that bright ball of ants, I shuddered in spite of myself. "I knew a man," I whispered. "A spaceplane pilot, forced down near Skygate. He nearly died, getting out of the desert. In the hospital he was out of his head. He talked about watching the ants at work on the terminal tower, until they frightened him away. But I was afraid to believe—"

"It's there," Kyrie told me. "Ten miles high."

Awe blew cold on the back of my neck.

"Too bad your friend lost his nerve," she added. "Nick's parents and my mother have been gathering a little colony of refugees. They hoped for a long time that you would turn up."

"The starships—" Wonder caught my throat. "Have the starships begun to come?"

Suddenly troubled, Kyrie shook her head.

"The terminal's complete, but not yet operational." Nick frowned too. "We haven't got the beacon going. It turns out that we must have the nexode, to modulate the tachyon signal. We've failed to find a substitute. I thought the whole project was dead, till Kyrie located the nexode here."

He nodded toward the bank building, as if he already knew where Guy and his women kept the tetrahedron.

"You can't have the moon jewel," I was gasping. "Guy won't let you!"

"It's bad, Uncle Kim." Kyrie's lips quivered. "I knew poor dear Guy would be hurt, and I made Nick look for another way. But he says there simply isn't any other way. We've come to take the nexode—"

Her shivery whisper died. Lips parted, eyes black, she stared up the street. The golden glow drained out of her skin, leaving her a figure of frozen terror in white alabaster. She had seen Guy.

I had been vaguely aware of a flurry of footsteps and hushed voices behind us, but Guy was alone when I turned. He came down the middle of the silent street, walking with a sort of rolling swagger. Naked, he was as male and nearly as huge as a bull.

Though little taller than Nick or Kyrie, he must have weighed a good quarter ton. The short glossy fur had turned black across his back and his massy shoulders, cream-colored over his great belly. His yellow eyes slitted warily as he drew near, and his black-tipped ears cocked toward the ball of ants.

Their high-pitched song grew sharper. That black gangway rolled itself swiftly up and sealed itself neatly back into the round bright honeycomb. The globe rose a little, floated lightly forward, settled again beside us, where it blocked Guy's path.

He roared. His belly-deep rattle wasn't loud, yet it chilled me, even in that hot sunlight. It had the menace, I thought, of a starved lion challenged for his kill. Guy rolled on, unstoppable as an avalanche.

Kyrie darted suddenly to meet him.

That savage rumble died. He stopped, trembling and breathing hard. As his red lips drew back, I saw that even his teeth had grown. He stood grinning down at Kyrie with long white fangs, saliva drooling.

"Ky!" Nick cried out beside me, sharply. "Come back!" But she ran on.

"Dear Guy!" She laughed with evident delight. "How strong you've grown—"

He wrapped her in his bulging arms. She reached up to stroke his shoulders, tiptoed to kiss his sleek-furred cheek. He shuddered and whimpered and crushed her fiercely against him.

"Guy, don't! You're hurting—"

He moaned and let her go. Growling, he glared at Nick. His yellow eyes blinked when he saw me. His ears cupped toward me. With a ferocious smile, he shambled to meet me, extending his gigantic furry paw—it had grown great black claws, which now were safely sheathed.

"They told me you were here." His slow thick voice was almost as alarming as his roar. "I'm glad, Uncle Kim. You were always good to me. You're welcome here."

Snarling ominously, he swung back toward Nick.

"Shake hands!" Kyrie gasped. "Please—"

166

Gravely, Nick offered his hand. Guy made no move to take it. He swayed slowly back and forth, his narrowed eyes flickering between Nick and the globe of droning ants.

"Why did you come?" His voice was a modulated growl, barely intelligible. "What do you want?"

"I hope you can forgive us, Guy—" Nick began.

"Please!" Kyrie stopped him. "Let me talk to Guy."

Guy bristled his stiff gray neck hair at Nick, flared his ears toward the strident globe, swung slowly back to Kyrie. His wide face twitched beneath the fur, and tears welled out of his tawny eyes. Poised on the balls of his feet like a boxer, he bent his ears toward her.

"Guy— Dear Guy!" Her low voice broke, but she gulped and went on. "Don't you know why we exist? The grit from the messenger missile had been lying millions of years on the moon, waiting for anything intelligent to come. It changed our fathers when they got there, so that we were born. We're here for a purpose. Can't you see that, Guy?"

His only reply was to bounce slightly aside, as if evading a blow.

"You know why we were born." Her voice turned desperate. "We're to set up the transgalactic terminal, so the starships can come. That's all we're for."

His ears flicked toward the clustered ants.

"The starships will bring peace between the biocosms," she promised him. "The transgalactic culture will help us understand our neighbors and ourselves. It will stop the space war, Guy. It will end all our troubles with the snakes and the fog and the alien bioforms—"

"But, Ky, they don't bother us." Guy grumbled and erupted like a volcano finding a voice. "We've got a good place here, so we don't need the starships. I want Uncle Kim to stay. And you, Ky—" He uttered a low, hoarse sound, half sob and half moan. "I want you—so much it kills me, Ky." He shuddered and blinked and swung toward Nick like a boxer feinting. "Nick had better take his things and go."

"Please, Guy!" Pale and shaking, Kyrie clutched his arm. "You aren't so safe as you think. Not for long. We had to send the replicators—the ants—to stop a tank attack while you were asleep." He was ducking back, but she clung to his arm. "Guy, Guy! You've just got to understand."

He trembled and stood still, quivering ears lifted toward her.

"The star people sent the grit." Her high voice quavered and raced too fast for Guy, who stood shaking himself in a dull, bewildered way. "They knew young cultures often kill each other on contact—before they learn to understand one another. The grit was sent to help us save all our planets. But we've already made too many mistakes. If we don't get the terminal open soon, Guy—very soon— we'll all be dead."

"Get—away!" his great throat rattled. "Just leave—me alone."

"We can't, Guy." Kyrie wet her pale lips. "We've got to have your help. You see, the replicators have the terminal almost done, but we can't light the beacon to guide the starships to earth without—without—"

She faltered and stopped, quivering with pain.

"We need the nexode, Guy." Nick's level voice was slow at first, clipped and intense. "Ky made me try everything else, but we can't energize the beacon without it." His words came faster and faster, as they always did when he was under stress. "I hope you'll try to be reasonable, Guy. Perhaps we won't need the nexode long. When the ships arrive with new equipment, we should be able to return—"

"You always had everything." Guy drowned him, thundering like a rising hurricane. "You had brains. You had charm. You had a father and a mother. You had each other. You could talk and you stayed awake and you did things—"

"Guy, Guy!" Kyrie cried. "You know I always loved you—"

His ruthless paw swept her aside.

168

"You always took everything." He danced like a fighter at Nick, moving with a surprising tigerlike grace. "You took the jewel, when I was slow to use it. You took Ky."

"No!" Kyrie sobbed. "Guy, you don't realize—"

"Now I do." His drumming boom cut her off. "I realize the jewel is mine. I made it. My father helped me take it. I need it. Now I mean to keep it. I won't give it up. Not for you, Uncle Kim." His yellow eyes blazed at me with a paralyzing power. "Not for Ky. Not for anybody."

The street was quiet for a moment, except for Guy's harsh breathing and the shrilling of the ants. The hot air stirred around us, and I caught a whiff of Guy's barnyard rankness.

"This will hurt you, Guy." Nick was brisk and cool. "It will hurt Ky, too. I don't like it, either, but you've left us no alternative. We've come for the nexode. We're going to take it."

Guy crouched toward him, like some great cat.

"Ky has it located, here in the bank vault. The replicators won't take long to dig it out. We don't intend to hurt you, Guy. I hope you won't attempt to interfere—"

Guy charged.

"Stop it!" Kyrie screamed. "If you love me—"

Nick jumped back. Though I observed no signal, that bright ball exploded into individual ants. Whining like hornets, they swarmed around Guy. Their sulfuric reek burned my eyes.

Bellowing, Guy plowed into the swarm. Ants dived at him. The bright sun dimmed, as they sucked at his energy. I staggered back, numb and shuddering from the sudden cold in my bones, sick with the bitterness in my mouth.

Guy bawled with rage and pain, but the ants failed to stop him. I never knew why. Perhaps some effect of the tetrahedron shielded him. Perhaps some effect of Kyrie's terror slowed the ants. More simply, I suppose, Nick couldn't kill Guy, while Guy had no inhibiting compunction.

His furious paws batted the ants away from his head. When Kyrie darted in, he flung her aside. Cruel claws open, he caught Nick by the throat, shook him till I heard his neck snap, flailed at the flying ants with his lax body, tossed him toward Kyrie's feet.

Nick jerked and lay still. Kyrie shrieked and dropped beside him. A stranger thing—the ants died. Their shrilling ceased. Their bodies clattered on the pavement, jangling like a shower of old clocks.

Suddenly the sun shone bright again. Beneath its heat, the courthouse square lay hushed and desolate. Kyrie knelt over Nick. His flat body looked small as a child's, its color slowly fading to a frightful whiteness. Guy towered over them, rocking back and forth like a groggy boxer. All I could hear was his rough breath and Kyrie's piteous sobs. Black bitterness lingered in my throat.

Sweat ran down Guy's heaving barrel body, painting black uneven streaks in his pale ventral fur. His gamy musk clogged my nostrils. His panting breath was now accompanied by a broken vocal sound, a slow and meaningless moaning. He shook himself at last and bent slowly over Kyrie. Long claws sheathed, he fumbled her quivering shoulder.

"Why, Kyrie? Why?" His moaning became a tormented voice. "You knew I couldn't give the moon jewel away. Why did you—?"

"Murderer!" she stiffened beneath his clumsy paw, and her slashing shriek cut him off. "You stupid monster! You've murdered Nick! Murdered the terminal! Murdered the world!"

Guy's ears drooped. He shook his great flat head in a dull, bewildered way, like a punch-drunk fighter. Reeling backward, he stumbled over one of the fallen ants, picked it up with an awkward paw, stood blinking at it blindly. With a sudden stifled howl, he hurled the dead machine against the granite wall of the bank and ran blundering up the street.

Andy Elving and Billie Fran had taken refuge in the

hotel. They came back when Guy was gone. We carried Nick inside and called a doctor. She confirmed that he was dead, his neck broken, his heart stopped, his skull caved in when Guy slammed him against the pavement.

Intrigued by Nick's different anatomy, the doctor wanted to do an autopsy. Kyrie objected wildly. She stayed beside Nick, I think with some desperate hope of his recovery. Recalling how often the children had baffled common human medicine, I shared that hope till it was gone.

When the body began to swell and decompose, even Kyrie gave up. Elving had nailed a plain wooden coffin together, and we carried Nick to the Fairfax cemetery in our own hearse. Guy and a dozen of his women walked silently behind it.

We held no formal ceremony. The forms we knew seemed not to fit. I did breathe a prayer, however, to whatever powers might be concerned with the moon children and the survival of mankind, and I saw several women kneeling. Guy and Kyrie stood bowed by the grave for a long time after it was filled, and they walked away hand in hand.

"—to show you're truly sorry," Kyrie was saying, as they came within my earshot. "You can bring the nexode and come with me back to the terminal. I don't know what we can do without Nick. But at least we can try to light the beacon."

Guy halted, and she swung anxiously to face him.

"Now you're the silly one, Ky," he rumbled gently. "I don't like hurting you, but I can't leave Fairfax. Did you know I was happy here, Ky? For the first time ever. Because people needed me. Because they loved me like I am. They still do, Ky, even if I did kill Nick."

"But, Guy—"

"Anyhow, we can't get to Skygate." His rising growl drowned her protest. "It's too far. The fog is coming up the rivers and the snakes are on the mountains and men like my father are hunting other men. Sorry, Ky."

Sullen now, he stalked away. His silent women followed. Kyrie stood there, marble white and marble quiet, staring bleakly back at the grave, until Elving and I urged her into the hearse.

We returned to the hotel. As we left the hearse, she picked up one of the lifeless ants. She examined it with an air of absent and indifferent wonder, as if it had been perhaps the fossil skeleton of some long-extinct trilobite.

"Could you start the ants again?" A spark of hope had stirred me. "They could carry some of us back to Skygate, maybe with the nexode, if Guy would ever let it go—"

"I can't, Uncle Kim." A cold finality dulled her voice, and she dropped the motionless machine. "Because they belonged to Nick. His brain controlled them through resonant interfaces with the nexode spectrum. In a way, they were members of his own body. They all died with him."

We took her into the hotel. She wouldn't eat and she didn't want to talk. When we found her a room, she locked herself in. For several days, I didn't see her again. In fact, I found it queerly hard to remember her grief.

In spite of all the staggering impact of her tragedy, the nexode must have still been at work. Though the nature of its effect was still a riddle to me, I felt as if it were somehow radiating life and love and joy, to bathe us all in an invisible ambiance of vital optimism.

Immersed in that atmosphere of blithe tranquility, Elving genially declared he never expected to need his tobacco again. He had found a bed for his roses in the city park. I spent two or three sunny afternoons with him there, watching him prepare the soil and sharing his pleased wonder at all the plants budding and blooming around us as if they were immune to winter.

Though Leb and Eva still escorted us, they were becoming more playmates than guards. Their petty tensions at the border had mellowed here into a purely sisterly affection, and they had begun to smile at us so warmly that I was almost afraid Guy would be offended when he woke.

As for myself, I was still convalescent, eating well and sleeping most of the time, half-intoxicated with a joy of life I had almost forgotten and no more concerned with

172

the space war and the dead beacon than if they had been forgotten incidents in the history of another planet.

Relaxing in Guy's world, I had begun to feel that it might become a small terrestrial heaven for Elving and me, as well as for his women—until one night the weather changed.

The day before had been bright and fine. I had gone to bed in our penthouse suite with the windows open. About midnight, a howling wind woke me. Icy gusts whipped me as I tried to close the windows, and my throat was choked with bitter dust. The storm had died when I woke again, but a hard glitter of frost had fallen over the city.

If Guy's kingdom had been a shielded oasis of eternal spring, some inexplicable thrust had shattered the shield. Reluctant to get out of bed, I thought I could feel that space infection aching in my bones again. Elving looked dull and depressed when he wandered in to go down to breakfast with me, and he confessed that he hankered for a comforting chew of tobacco.

We found Lib on guard alone. Eva was in the hospital, she told us, after a sudden miscarriage. As wan and bleak as if she herself had been the patient, she doled out more tales of disaster while we were slowly discovering we had no appetite for breakfast after all.

The unexpected storm and frost had blighted crops all around Fairfax. Scores of young animals were mysteriously dying. A crazed stallion had thrown a twelve-year-old girl and trampled her to death. The mothers reported that Guy had been tossing and moaning all night in his sleep.

"We don't know what has gone wrong." Lib gnawed her bloodless lips. "Mother Billie Fran first thought perhaps the jewel had been stolen, but the mothers on guard say it's still in the vault. We're afraid it's somehow ruined or broken. The mothers say its light flickered and dimmed, an hour before the storm hit." She shrugged dismally, hunched and shivering as if she needed more than a garter to keep her warm. "Guy's still asleep, and nobody knows anything."

Even Guy had been aroused, however. We were still sitting over our unfinished meal when I heard him booming in the lobby. His belligerent bounce was gone, when we went out to greet him, and his yellow eyes looked bleared and hollow.

He was waiting for Kyrie, and he didn't want to talk. We stood there a long time, shuffling about and watching the elevators in uneasy apprehension, until at last Billie Fran brought her down. Looking pinched and pale, she came out to face him with an expression of blank apathy, as if he had been some unpleasant stranger she didn't care to meet.

"Ky, I've been asleep." His voice was flat and too loud, as if to challenge some unuttered apprehension. "I dreamed—I dreamed I was Nick."

Kyrie gasped and stared.

"I dreamed about the tach—the tachyon terminal." Guy shook his head and paused to peer around him, as if uncertain where or who he was. "I dreamed we had to get that beacon working."

"Yes?" Kyrie breathed. "Yes?"

"That's what we've got to do, Ky." His forced, toneless voice almost denied his words. "We're going to Skygate. We're taking the jewel. We'll try to energize the beacon for Nick."

"Oh, Guy!" Kyrie swayed and caught at the back of a chair. The disbelief on her thin face changed to breathless wonder and at last to a dazzle of delight. "Nick would love you," she whispered. "He'd forgive you—if we can only light the beacon!"

Guy's women were less enthusiastic. Already stunned by that unexpected storm, they were soon furious or weeping. Guy was sick and out of his mind. His place was here with them and his babies. They all adored him, and they couldn't live without him.

Yet, here in his own kingdom, Guy was clearly the king. When he raised his voice, the uproar ceased. With a level of intelligence he had not displayed to me before, he began discussing plans for the trip, at first with Kyrie only, but soon including Elving and me.

We decided to drive the hearse, the sturdiest vehicle available. Elving set about collecting spare parts, tires, drums of fuel. Guy called on his women for weapons and supplies. We pooled our scanty knowledge of the fog areas and the militia posts and the roads possible still open.

For weapons, we had two hunting rifles, an ancient but accurate target pistol, and a lightweight missile launched that Guy had captured when he ambushed an earlier raid of Spike Ballou's. There were only two or three boxes of ammunition for the guns and nine rounds for the launcher. Against fog and snakes and bandits, that seemed a very meager arsenal.

Guy's new determination remained surprisingly firm, in spite of all the hazards ahead of us. Yet his behavior troubled me. His normally voracious appetite was gone. His movements seemed weak and uncertain. His great paws had developed a tremor he couldn't control. His eyes looked swollen and dull, and his voice had lost its old booming power. I began to wonder if he had contracted some unfamiliar space disease.

When everything else was ready, he waddled heavily across the street to the bank, where two or three of his women had been guarding the vault, and returned with the nexode. It was hidden under a rack of aerosol bombs, beneath the false bottom of a trick box my brother must have made for it, a salesman's display case for Narcaroma inhalation kits.

Kyrie cried out with delight when he put the splendid pyramid into her hands. Its radiation swiftly browned her bright face, and somehow restored most of the vital beauty that Nick's death had drained out of her. She stood clutching it, peering raptly into its glowing hollows, until Guy replaced it in the box.

Billie Fran ran after us, when we went out to the coach, holding up Guy's bright-eyed daughter. Hysterical, she wanted to go with us. She loved Guy. So did little Valkyrie. If he left them, they would die. Spike would come back and murder them.

Guy stopped and turned to listen. His shaking paws

175

took the naked baby for a moment. Suddenly he pushed it back at Billie Fran. With an inarticulate howl, he blundered blindly after us and squeezed his odorous bulk into the hearse.

Armed women crowded around the coach, as Andy Elving tried to pull us away from the curb. Lib and Eva were there, both white-lipped with stifled fury. Eva threw a rock that might have smashed the windshield, if Kyrie hadn't leaned deftly out to field it. They all fell back, however, from Guy's bellow—which I thought echoed more agony than anger. He was sobbing convulsively as we drove away. Most of the women stood silent behind us, but Billie Fran was shrieking, waving Guy's naked child over her head, as long as I could see her.

Andy Elving was driving us through Greenway Park, a dozen miles out of Fairfax, when we splashed into the river ford. Halfway across, he gasped and collapsed. The hearse stalled. Guy lifted him off the wheel, and I drove the hearse out of the river.

He was conscious again by the time we reached the bank, rasping brokenly that he would be okay, but I saw that his haggard face had turned cyanotic. Over his hoarse protests, we bundled him in blankets and drove ingloriously back to Fairfax through the storm-leveled, frost-blackened fields.

The nurses at the hospital squealed with delight to have another glimpse of Guy and dutifully rushed Andy into the cardiac room. I shook his lax blue hand and promised to have his roses tended while he got well. In another hour, badly shaken and deflated, we set out once more.

At the wheel when we crossed the ford again, I was thinking of all the hard miles and unknown hazards ahead, missing Andy very much. Kyrie sat with me, forebodingly silent as I was. Guy was lying in the back, breathing heavily and apparently asleep.

Kyrie caught her breath as we lurched up the rocky

bank, and I saw a man stumbling into the road ahead. A reeling monument of pure disaster, he was hatless and tattered, slick with dripping muck, splashed with blood. When his thumb jerked up, I recognized my brother Tom.

Reflexively, I speeded the hearse and twisted the wheel to veer around him. Wildly waving both muddy arms, he jumped into our path again. I hit the horn and tried to nerve myself to run him down, but Kyrie was tugging at my arm.

"Stop! It's Guy's father."

Unwillingly, I stopped. Tom came limping to us. He was short of breath, scratched and torn, coated with evil-smelling mud. Bright blood smeared his sleeves and his hands and the hilt of a knife in his belt. Clinging to the side of the hearse, he smiled grimly through his mask of red-spattered grime.

"Kimmie!" His wheezy voice tried to be ingratiating. Kyrie, doll!" He ogled her lean golden nudity and turned to peer into the back of the hearse, where Guy was stirring uneasily on a blanket. "My son! How is my dear son?"

"We were better," I said, "before we met you."

"Now don't play the nudnik, Kim." He frowned impatiently at me and turned more hopefully to Kyrie. "All I need is a ride. Seems I've worn out my welcome here. I saw you here before, and I was hoping you'd be back." He touched his knife and leaned again to grin slyly at Guy. "By the way, your women won't have any more trouble from our friend Spike Ballou."

"You killed him?" I recoiled from that casual implication. "Why?"

"Why not?" Tom turned to listen warily at the green wilderness behind him, new sweat gleaming on his face. "Let's go." His lowered voice grew urgent. "Before somebody gets around to cutting us off. Whatever you're up to, I'll lend a hand." He swung persuasively back to me. "How about it, Kimmie?"

His smooth appeal recalled all the times in the past when he had spoiled things for me, and I wanted to say we had no time to help him.

"Please, Uncle Kim," Kyrie stopped me softly. "Maybe he can take Mr. Elving's place." She looked gravely up at Tom. "Listen, Mr. Hood. We're on our way to Skygate. The tachyon terminal is standing there, complete but dead. We have to get there with the nexode, to light the beacon. Maybe you can help us."

"The nex—" Something took Tom's breath. His fat face flickered with a dozen conflicting expressions, the last a bland smile. "You have the moon jewel? Here in the car? Of course I'll go with you. A chance I never expected. My last chance, perhaps to pay my debts to the human race and maybe to see a better world than I was born in."

"I think we need you, Mr. Hood."

I wanted to object again, but Kyrie had already opened the door on her side of the coach. Serenely undisturbed by Tom's rank filth, she slid over to make room for him at her side. All I could do was drive on.

Tom asked about weapons, and Kyrie had Guy pass a deer rifle to him. He tested the action and loaded it expertly. A few miles farther on, where the trees began to thin, he made me stop while he took the rifle and slipped ahead. After half an hour we heard three rapid reports, muffled by the foliage.

Kyrie nodded for me to go on. We found Tom waiting where the road broke out of the trees half a mile ahead. He had acquired a well-worn hat, a police pistol with a cartridge belt, and a blood-smeared deck of narcorettes. Smugly silent, he lighted one of them and climbed in with Kyrie.

Delayed by missing bridges and turned back by roadblocks, we made camp that night in the burned ruin of a barn not fifty miles from Fairfax. Speaking for Guy, Kyrie announced that she and I and Tom would stand equal watches. When I woke at daylight, the camp was silent. I couldn't find Tom.

In disdain of such inventions as sleeping bags, Guy and Kyrie lay side by side on the scorched concrete that had been the barn floor, and I stood frozen half a minute,

178

shocked by the contrast between her long-limbed loveliness and his gigantic bestial naked maleness.

Shuddering to obscure emotions stronger than my anger over Tom's defection, I shook them awake. We searched the camp. I found Marcaroma bombs spilled on the ground beyond the parked hearse, and the display case tossed into a pile of charred rubble, its secret panel gaping.

"Tom's gone," I told them, my outrage tempered with a certain secret satisfaction, because I had wanted not to pick him up. "Gone with the nexode!"

Guy rumbled with speechless fury, ready to join me in pursuit, but Kyrie advised us to wash and make breakfast. While we were eating, Tom came back, waddling wearily, swinging the nexode in a burlap bag. With an air of sullen submission, he rolled it out of the bag at Kyrie's feet.

"Gevalt!" He shivered and wheezed, shrinking away from the blazing tetrahedron. "I've gone mechuleh. That damn thing's too much for me."

Kyrie picked it deftly up and paused to blow and brush the dust from its bright triangles. It washed her skin with a richer tan, as she smiled across it at Tom.

"I was depending on it to bring you back," she told him gently. "We've got a long way to go, and we still need you, Mr. Hood."

"I'll do what you say." Tom's instant agreement astonished me. "Anything you say."

She pointed at the water trough and found him a pair of clean coveralls that had been packed for Andy Elving. In half an hour, we were on our way again.

6

Futurity

The interface between Tom and the tetrahedron was too subtle for me to grasp—if "interface" is an adequate word for that invisible link between man and thing. He was strangely changed, almost a human metamorph. Unwontedly subdued, he rarely spoke, and then generally with the Yiddish intonations he had learned from our father and abandoned in his youth. He obeyed Kyrie's soft-spoken requests without objection, and sometimes he even listened to me.

Guy became our leader, displaying a resourceful cunning that surprised me. I suppose his long war with Spike Ballou had taught him how to deal with bandits, but I never understood where he had got his new insight into people, or his uncanny sense for traps and ambushes.

His huge eyes shone at night with a golden phosphorescence, and he could see to drive through blackness that seemed absolute to me. Again and again he stopped us to wait while he crept through the dark ahead to break up a roadblock and return with a captured weapon or a sack of supplies.

We moved very cautiously, keeping away from streams and valleys when we could. Often we had to turn back from an unexpected lake of fog. One frosty moonlit night we crossed a wild white river of it, on a long highway bridge the ants had somehow left.

Again, trapped by an uneasy white sea rising behind us, we waited through most of a day for the wind and sun to clear the fog from a shallow wash still damp from rain. Guy had gone to sleep in the back, as inert and odorific as something dead, and Tom took the wheel to drive us through the gray wisps and tatters still crawling out of the mud.

As we lurched and splashed through the pools of thin red slime the fog had left among the rocks at the bottom of the wash, I saw scattered bones beside the road, bones of a horse and a man. Beneath one lifting shred of mist, I caught sight of something else—a flat and endless ribbon of livid red flesh, trapped there in the clotting mud, writhing and squalling among the red bones as if tortured by the sun.

I was shivering and nearly ill for the rest of the day, from a shock I couldn't understand. I had seen space aliens before, and far too many remains of my unlucky fellowmen. What unnerved me was the agony in that thin squalling. It sounded like a human child.

At the beginning, Guy was awake and active for two or three days at a time, exhausting all the rest of us. As we went on, however, he slept more often and longer at a time, with no benefit that I could see.

He always woke petulant and feverish, parched with thirst. The tremor of his paws was always worse. He complained of weakness and giddiness and strange aching pains in every part of his body. Always, too, he had been dreaming.

He used to tell Kyrie about his dreams, hoping she could explain them. He was never himself, he said, but always Nick. He was always on his way to the terminal tower or already there, working to energize the tachyon beacon.

"It frightens me, Ky," I heard him mutter. "Everything is too plain—too real. I see every part of the terminal the way I know it really is. I understand all the parts of it the way Nick did."

He drew a harsh, uneven breath.

"In those dreams, Ky—I *am* Nick. I think the way he did. I remember all he knew. And the worst—the worst part is what I think of Guy." His paws came up in a searching way to rub his furry face, as if he had to identify himself. "I'm sorry for Guy. The poor, stupid beast, born all wrong. I know he's good for nothing. I try to tolerate him. Because Kyrie used to like him. But I'm afraid of him, too. I know he hates me, because he wants Kyrie. But I don't know what he can do to hurt us, because even he doesn't know his own power."

He struck at the air with great open paws, as if fighting off some unseen enemy, his long hooked claws unsheathed and shining like black glass.

"What's wrong, Ky?" he whispered hoarsely. "Am I crazy?"

"I'm sure you aren't insane." Consolingly, she stroked his trembling arm. "Though I'm afraid you've picked up some space infection. But I think perhaps the nexode is causing your dreams, Guy. I think it has begun to make an interface with you."

"What face?" Raw terror rasped in his throat. "What's an interface? What's happening to me?"

"I don't know, Guy." Her stroking hand drew quickly back, as if she shared his dread. "I'm afraid to guess."

Strangely, as it seemed to me, each long period of dream-ridden sleep left Guy more like Nick. Most obviously, he spoke faster and used longer words and displayed a better brain. Sometimes I thought I heard Nick's intonations in his voice. As he lost weight—for he had almost ceased to eat—I sometimes thought I caught subtle hints of Nick in the way he looked and moved.

Though I never quite understood Kyrie's philosophy, she had come to accept Nick's death with what looked like a quiet fatalism. She no longer hated Guy—I wasn't sure just how she felt. Remarkably serene, she often ignored the rest of us, and all the hazards of the road, while she sat for hours with the tetrahedron in her golden hands, great eyes lost in its luminous hollow.

"Why fret so?" she asked me once. "I don't understand what's happening to poor Guy. I'm not sure we'll be able to reach the terminal, or that we can light the terminal even if we do get there. Not at all sure. But we're trying. That's what I was born for, and it's enough to make me happy."

Sometimes she was happy enough for childish play. Once she tried to teach me a numerical game Nick had invented. Though I was never able to master the rules, it seemed to involve a race between the players to find large prime numbers that would complete certain intricate symmetrical sequences.

"Sorry, Uncle Kim." She smiled affectionately when I gave up in disgust. "I had forgotten how much you hate to think."

She began to pass the time as she did long ago with her incomprehensible music, blown and beaten out of an odd set of instruments she had picked up along the way. Now the helmet of a dead militiaman made a melancholy drum. Empty cartridge cases and beer cans became sad pipes. A thin scrap of bullet-punctured armor vibrated in her deft brown hands, moaning and howling and wailing.

I never learned to like her music, though it sent Guy into twitching and whimpering ecstacy. But I could never forget it, either. Its eerie sweetness and its painful dissonance and its ungraspable scales are still alive, throbbing in some dim corner of my mind, and they come back to burn my eyes with tears whenever I think of Kyrie.

Somewhere we had crossed an unmarked frontier, out of the region where the scattered militia forces still tried to guard the refugees from the rising fog and their lawless fellowmen. We had come into the higher, dryer western uplands, stripped of metal by the ants, abandoned by mankind, and as yet penetrated only here and there by probing tongues of fog.

This was the region where the pilot, Clayton Carter, had nearly died in his flight from the ants, but rains had come since his ordeal. We found water in the prairie lakes. With no human marauders now in the way, we made good time. I had nearly forgotten the snakes, until a bright autumn afternoon brought us into view of the mountains of central New Mexico. Though they were still blue and far, I knew the snakes were now nesting there, and suddenly I was cold and giddy again with recollection of that disaster when the passing snake brought our plane down into the hailstorm.

Guy was asleep in the back of the coach. I wanted to stop until he woke, but Kyrie had recognized the mountains and she was anxious to press on for at least a glimpse of the terminal tower before we camped. Tom agreed with Kyrie that our motor probably ran too cool to attract the snakes, and we went on.

Gaps in the pavement delayed us. At sunset, Tom gave the wheel to me and went to sleep in the back with Guy. Kyrie sat silent beside me, the glowing pyramid cradled in her hands, her anxious eyes on the dusky horizon. We crept on by the faint gray light of the low crescent moon.

Here the ants had leveled everything. With no road signs, we were half lost. But the moon guided us west, and I could tell from the pull of the motor that we were climbing steadily. At each new crest, I felt something of Kyrie's eagerness to see the tower.

Yet the strain of driving tired me. As each moonlit summit revealed nothing more exciting than a higher one ahead, I began to feel a desolate sense of hopeless isolation. Kyrie became an untouchable stranger. The nexode was a riddle I could never hope to solve. The transgalactic culture was a fantastic myth that didn't really matter. The loneliness of the arid and abandoned landscape crept into me, until I could almost feel myself becoming the last man alive.

"Uncle Kim!" When Kyrie caught my arm, I almost recoiled from her warm hand. "There it is!"

I saw the terminal then, through a break in the hills to our left, its vastness diminished with distance. Though we had been driving a long time in the dark, the sun still struck its upper stages, so that they were outlined in purple and splendid gold.

"Tomorrow—" Her voice rang with joy. "Tomorrow we'll be there!" But then I heard the startled catch of her breath and heard the sudden trouble in her tone. "What's that shadow? Did you see it, Uncle Kim?"

The dead beacon was the highest point of the tower, its dark onion dome hard to make out against the night sky. What I saw was a queer veil of darkness slipping down from the black beacon, dimming and blurring the upper stages of the terminal.

"It's probably just the twilight," I said.

"No." Her voice was sharp with fear. "The natural shadow of the earth comes up from the foot of the tower. That darkness is crawling down from the top. It must be something else."

She glanced at the pyramid in her hands, and I felt her shiver.

"I think it's the snakes!" she whispered sharply. "I think they're nesting on the tower. After all, it rises almost into empty space, where they feel at home. I'm afraid we'll have trouble with the snakes."

That trouble came sooner than I had expected. The terminal tower dropped for a time below the moonlit hills as we drove on. The zoned rose-and-purple of twilight had risen higher when we could see it again, and the stranger darkness of the snakes had crept lower from the beacon dome, filming the whole tower with a ghostly unreality. I was trying, with no success, to imagine an actual tachyon ship landing on its fading stages, when a snake buzzed us.

Acrid bitterness flashed across my tongue. A chilling numbness brushed me. The headlamps went out. I had the briefest glimpse of its serpentine shadow dipping and lifting against the moon-washed sky. It was gone before I heard its sonic crash.

It left us stalled on the road. Tom woke, grumbling Yiddish that I couldn't understand. We lifted the hood and struck matches. Though nothing else was visibly damaged, all the batteries were drained. Even our flashlights were dead. We failed to start the motor.

Dead-tired and still shivering with that bone-deep chill, I wanted to make camp. But we were near the summit, Kyrie said, so high the snakes might descend on us again.

She shook Guy awake, and we pushed the hearse a mile or more, over the highest crest.

That far-off phantom tower had dissolved into the dark by then, but we pressed on down the winding canyon road toward the valley of the Rio Grande and the ruins of Albuquerque. Guy was asleep again, groaning and twitching as if pushing the hearse had been too much for him. Coasting now, we rolled down through the moonlight in a ghostly silence that set me to shivering with an unnerving sense that we had become inhuman company on an unearthly errand.

"We'll be safer in the valley." Even Kyrie's soft whisper startled me. "We can surely start the motor when it's light enough to see. Can't we, Uncle Kim? I hope we reach Skygate tomorrow."

The night was thicker in the canyon, but I knew the road from driving it on winter holidays in that long-ago world, now queerly unreal, when a few of us used to ski on the high Sandia slopes. Suzie had come once, though not exactly with me. I got to thinking of her, wondering what had happened to her since I left Skygate, and whether Thorsen had survived his space infection. With the need for sleep forgotten, I drove on in a kind of waking dream.

Two or three times, where the grade was too flat, we had to wake Tom to help us push again, but the thin cold moon was still half an hour high when we came out of the canyon into view of the mesa and the valley.

Steering by the gray edge of the pavement, searching the dark for washouts or rocks on the road, I wasn't looking far ahead. I felt Kyrie stiffen and shiver, heard her gasp of dismay. Braking to an instinctive stop, I saw the fog.

A flood of luminescent white, nearly as bright as the bitten moon, it drowned the dead city. It filled the wide valley from the mounded ruins just below us to the line of lifeless volcanoes on the horizon. It reached north and south as far as I could see.

Though I could feel no wind, it was stirring strangely,

rising and falling in soundless waves that broke against the rocks and the dark rubble islands, shattering into ghostly plumes of dissipating mist.

"No!" Kyrie sobbed. "No!"

But it was there, too deep for the morning sun to break it up, too wide for anything to bridge, spread too far to leave us a way around it. For a long time we simply sat there in the dead hearse. There was nothing else to do.

I fastened my jacket and shivered in it, as the chill of the desert night followed the heat drain of the snake, but Kyrie seemed to feel no cold. A remote white goddess in the dying light, she gazed sometimes at the useless glow of the tetrahedron in her hands, more often at that wild but silent sea ahead. My throat ached with a dull regret for the failure of our mission and a sharper pity for her.

A breath of wind must have risen, because the odor of the fog rolled over us in a sudden, suffocating wave, rank as a jungle swamp, fetid as a sewer, its muskmelon sweetness blended with an overpowering foulness. Though Kyrie seemed unconscious of it, I felt nauseated.

"Let's get out," I urged her. "I guess we can't move the hearse, but we ought to make camp before the moon goes down. Somewhere higher—we passed a possible spot, back in the canyon. The fog may rise in the dark."

She nodded dully, as if nothing mattered now. I set the brakes and clambered out of the hearse. I was dancing a slow shuffle on the pavement, trying to bring my stiffened limbs to life, when she screamed.

Her outcry was wordless, agonized, desolate. When I called to know what the matter was, her only answer was a thin moan of pain. I struck a match and found her kneeling over Guy in the back of the hearse.

"He's dead," she sobbed then. "Guy's dead!"

Tom groaned and woke. We all crowded into the back of the hearse, trying to examine Guy by the feeble flare of matches. He lay inert and swollen, with no breath or

187

pulse, his paws already cold and stiffening. Kyrie splashed water on him, rubbed and flexed his furry limbs, tried to breathe into his mouth. Nothing revived him. Working over him, I began to catch an odor of dissolution, ranker than his barnyard body scent, stronger than the fetor of the fog.

Retreating from that smell of death, I climbed out of the hearse and saw the fog again. Though the moon had set, it glowed with its own cold light. Rising silently, it had already drowned those black rubble islets. A wide tongue of it had licked into the canyon, lapping at the pavement not a hundred yards below the hearse.

I shouted a warning. Tom scrambled out to join me, but Kyrie refused to leave Guy. He was too heavy for us to carry, but she stayed in the hearse, hauling vainly at him, until Tom assumed our father's thick accent to tell her a peasant tale about a goat boy who was eaten by a wolf because he wouldn't leave his millet porridge.

"I suppose we ought to save our lives," she whispered huskily then. "Though I see no good that we can do alone." We were waiting to help her from the hearse, but she flung herself wildly back upon the corpse. "Oh, Guy! Guy!"

She lay sobbing on his body till a long foul tongue licked into the ditch beside us, drowning us with its nauseous miasma. Silently then, moving in a slow somnambulism, she let us lead her up the canyon road away from the fog.

As we started away from the hearse, my foot struck something that made a jangling clatter. I picked the object up. In the pale glow of the tetrahedron, which Kyrie clutched in both stiff hands, I saw the glint of a hexagonal head and the gleam of wire-like limbs.

It was a dead mechanical ant, one of a swarm that lay in a glittering drift along the edge of the pavement, where they must have fallen when Nick was killed. I held it out toward Kyrie, I suppose with some fantastic hope that she might revive it. She looked at me with a sort of bleak, white-lipped accusation, and I tossed it back into the dark.

Dull with despair, silent as the fog itself, we climbed back into the canyon. The pyramid gave light enough to help us follow the pavement. Tom and I had brought blankets and canteens and our small stock of food. Plodding stolidly, wheezing to breathe, he smoked his last narcorette.

I stopped to look back once. Always higher, that wild white sea was tossing as if an unseen storm raged beneath it. The rocks around the canyon mouth broke it into soundless spray. I shuddered and heard Tom muttering a Yiddish prayer. We stumbled after Kyrie.

We made a cold and cheerless camp a mile from the fog, in a shallow cave above the road that refugees from Albuquerque must have dug. I found a few sticks of wood stacked beside a circle of fire stones, but Kyrie was afraid a fire might draw the snakes. A dull hunger was gnawing at my belly, but she said we should save our food. I washed my bitter mouth with one sip of water and crawled into my blanket.

Tom was soon snoring, but Kyrie didn't sleep. Immune to cold, she sat cross-legged at the mouth of the cave, the luminous pyramid cupped in her hands, her sad eyes watching the way we had come. Her stricken desolation shook me with disturbed emotion.

Bare to the glow of that great stone, her lean body was infinitely inviting, yet it stirred in me only a cold ghost of ardor. In the shattered world around us, desire itself was dying. What I felt was an infinite pity, an almost maternal urge to comfort her, to break her black despair. I remembered all the childhood years when she had been almost a daughter, with a child's frank affection for her fond Uncle Kim. But now, somehow, in this doleful moment, I couldn't even speak to her.

At last I slept, though I had meant to share her vigil. I woke numb with cold. The cave was dark, the glow of the nexode gone. Tom's snores had ceased. I whispered and fumbled and found nobody.

Shaking with terror, I stumbled barefoot out of the cave. Seeing the high blaze of Orion, I knew that midnight was long past. The starlit road looked empty. When I called, the only answer was a whispery echo from a distant cliff.

As I blundered toward the pavement, my toes struck a rock. The flash of pain cooled my first panic. I limped back to the cave for my shoes and then crept down the road to search for Tom and Kyrie.

I failed to find them. The odor of the fog stopped me above the canyon mouth, a wall of unbreathable evil. I climbed a rock to look for the hearse. That insane white tide was breaking over it now, so that it appeared and vanished again beneath the writhing tongues of luminescent mist.

A funeral calm crept over me as I stood there. I gave up my useless shouting, and wandered back at last to the cave. Trembling more from numbing dread than the actual cold, I got back into my blanket and waited aimlessly for day.

In my haunted thoughts, Tom and Kyrie had died in some new effort to rescue Guy's body. I could visualize the fog flooding all the world, squeezing out the last human zone as it rose to meet the high dominion of the snakes. Perhaps I was already the last man alive. Nor could I last long, trapped here against a desert wasteland as deadly as the fog.

Oddly, my own fate didn't matter now. Existence had become an emotionless abstraction. As I looked back into the past from that comfortless cave, my life revealed itself as a meaningless monotony of shabby failure and deadening frustration. I had been a lonely spectator, silently watching the rich feast of being that I could never fully join.

I recalled my old unwilling envy of Tom, who had always seized the good things I somehow could never reach for. My opposite, always the bold actor, never the timid or self-denying or self-righteous onlooker, he had lived what seemed a more rewarding life than mine. Perhaps our father had been right. Perhaps I really was the schlemiel.

Exhausted by such profitless reflections, I fell into a

troubled sleep. I recall a dream in which Tom and I were skiing down the highest Sandia slope. I was stiff and clumsy with the bitter cold. Tom swept far ahead, and I envied his bold skill at the jump. Unsure of myself, I was afraid I couldn't make the turn. I thought I was going over the rim, into the black, pine-fringed canyon below it.

But then a girl's warm voice called my name. At first I thought it was Suzie, but it was Kyrie I saw when I looked back, nude and splendid, somehow flying over the snow with no skis at all. She overtook me and reached to grasp my hand. I knew we could make the turn together.

Something woke me then, and the shock of stark reality shattered the joy of that improbable dream. No voice had called my name. One gray ray of sunlight stabbed into the soot-blackened cave, but it brought no warmth. I was numb with cold and utterly alone.

Too numb at first to stand or think, I crept out into the heatless sun. I sat for a while on a rock outside the cave, kneading my stiff muscles. When I felt able, I drank a careful third of the water left in my canteen and shuffled down the road to look for Tom and Kyrie.

Where the canyon widened, I could see the upper stages of the tachyon terminal, rising out of pink mushroom fields of far-off cumulus into the cloudless stratosphere, still wavering and fading like a high mirage beneath the shadow of the nesting snakes.

The pavement lay empty ahead, with no trace of Tom or Kyrie, until I came out of the canyon on the shore of the fog. Its heaving surface seemed calmer by day, dissolving into crawling bluish tatters as its tiny live balloons exploded in the sun, but its putrid fetor turned me ill.

It had receded enough to uncover our abandoned hearse, though its vanishing tongues still licked around the wheels. Beneath those fading wisps of mist, I saw patches of a wet, blood-colored slime on the pavement and the rocks where the fog had lain.

191

Reeling and retching from that rotten sweetness, I improvised a mask from a handkerchief saturated with the last water in my canteen and plunged through those writhing tendrils to reach the hearse.

Guy's body was gone. For a moment I thought Tom and Kyrie must have come back to carry it away. Then I saw blood puddled on the floor, seeping from a mound of putrefying fur. Glass-black claws gleamed on the fingers of a queer glove peeled from a gray-furred paw. I reached gingerly to move a dark-tipped ear, and spilled loose fangs that clattered like gravel.

Shrinking back, numb with shock, I thought the body had been butchered by the unseen creatures of the fog. I searched the pavement, alert for any other evidence, for any sign of Tom or Kyrie, and found another puzzle.

Wet red gouts had splashed the pavement behind the hearse. At first I thought the receding fog had left them there, but then I saw that the glistening patches of blood-colored slime had not come so high. The gouts were Guy's blood, marking a trail where his flesh had been dragged.

The odd thing was the direction of that darkening trail. It led me off the pavement, across a rocky ditch scattered with the dead metal ants, and up a steep slope away from the road and the slime and the fog.

Scrambling up that slope, I discovered Tom and Kyrie —in a scene that stunned me. The mechanical ants lay dead in glittering windrows of silver and black around the edges of a great disk of white stone. Kyrie sat cross-legged on one side of the stone, her golden nudity splotched with darkening blood. Tom stood at the other, bare to the waist and scarlet as a pirate. Between them lay the red body they themselves must have skinned out of Guy's fur.

I caught my breath to call out, but something stopped me. My wonder and horror were compounded with a sudden sense of almost religious awe. The shining, snow-white stone was like an altar. Kyrie was the mad priestess, Tom the sacrificial priest. The bleeding offering between them must have been Guy's corpse.

Shaken with a horrified idea that Kyrie's mind had

come unhinged from her desolate despair, I crouched behind a shelving stone to watch what went on. The skinned head lay in Kyrie's lap. She held the blazing nexode against its forehead. Standing over the dark-clotted feet, Tom was chanting ritual words I didn't understand. In response to the chant, Kyrie's red fingers flashed about the nexode, touching its bright triangles as if they had been the controls of some mysterious machine.

I lay there a long time. Ants crawled on me—the live desert insects. Afraid they might sting, I was more afraid to move. From Tom's voice and Kyrie's action I began to catch a sense of urgent tension, a grave purpose and a growing fear of failure.

Tom's chant abruptly stopped. Kyrie froze, staring at him across the tetrahedron. In the silence I heard the lazy drone of a big blue fly and saw it settling on that stiff red face. A red hand brushed at it, and I gasped with astonishment.

The body was alive. A stranger discovery—what I saw beneath the blood was not naked muscle and tendon, but intact skin. I realized that this was not the hideous flayed thing that I had been imagining, but somehow a whole man. His hand reached for the nexode. Moving with an easy grace, he sat up on the spattered stone.

"Hi, Ky!"

"Nick!" Her breathless cry was a sob of mingled agony and joy. "Nicky!"

Something close to terror shook me, because the voice was Nick's—perhaps a little deeper than I recalled it. The blood-bathed man was Nick—or at least an excellent copy, perhaps a bit heavier and taller. Frowning a little against the sun, he looked around and saw Tom.

"Hello, Hood."

"Gevalt!" Tom stumbled backward, his red-mottled torso sheened with new sweat. His fat hands flew up defensively. For once in his life, he was ruled by pure emotion, by terror at his own handiwork. "What—what sort of thing are you?" His glazing eyes appealed to Kyrie. "What have we done?"

193

"We've beaten death," Kyrie whispered.

"What is all this?" Nick came to his feet with the agile grace I remembered, peering down at the blood-smeared stone, off at the crawling fog, back at Kyrie. "Where's Uncle Kim?"

I caught my breath, but found that I could not announce myself. I was still too deeply shaken, my voice paralyzed with bewilderment and dread. Besides, I felt a sudden shame for having spied so long. I crouched uneasily down again.

"Asleep in the cave," Kyrie was saying. "Poor little man. I'm afraid he hasn't entirely got over his gamma-form infection. I couldn't bear to disturb him."

"Let him sleep." Nick turned as if to step off the gleaming disk, paused to frown at the glistening piles of lifeless ants around it, came slowly back to Kyrie. "We've problems enough of our own."

"But we're all right, now." Her soft voice was almost too quick and eager, as if she could hardly believe her own words. "We can solve them, Nicky—now that you're alive!"

Unhearing, he stood staring across the tattered sea of fog, toward the far white billows of cumulus and the dim mirage of the terminal tower rippling in the sky above them.

"The most singular thing." He glanced at the bright pyramid in his hands, and back at Kyrie's tense face. "Stranger than all of this." Anxiously, he stepped a little toward her. "I've been dreaming. Dreaming I was Guy. I even thought I'd killed Nick—"

His puzzled voice broke sharply off. He leaned to peer at Kyrie's hands, swung to frown at the dark-stained knife stuck in Tom's belt, suddenly looked down at himself, rubbing in a startled way at his own blood-stiffened skin.

"So I *was* Guy!" Nodding in a dazed way, he looked back at Kyrie. "But I've been—he's been—changing?" Slow at first, his breathless voice came faster and faster as he spoke. "The nexode did it, I suppose. The nexode and the nonhuman side of our own nature. I must be—a metamorph! Like that red bubble of the beta-life in my mother's laboratory bottle. All Guy's illness—that sleepiness and pain we couldn't understand—that must have been the beginning of the process. And now I've been born again. Out of his skin. With you and Hood for midwives."

"Oh, Nicky!" Kyrie was shivering, her voice so low that I could scarcely hear. "It's true Guy killed you back at Fairfax. Last night when the fog stopped us here I thought he—you—were dead. I thought we were done for, our lives wasted and the terminal lost. I can't quite believe—"

"I never expected anything like this." Nick was turning and flexing his clot-caked hand, eyeing it with the dazzled wonder of a child unwrapping some fabulous toy. "I never hoped—" He stopped to nod. "But I suppose our experience here on only one planet was too limited to show us the full capacity of life." He looked at Kyrie. "How did you do it?"

"You did it, Nicky. Though I suppose the nexode helped. Last night in the cave, it showed me that you were alive in Guy's dead skin. It showed me what we had to do, and I woke Tom to help. But with time enough—if there had been no danger from the fog—I think you might have done everything yourself."

"You're too good, Ky." He was fondly teasing for an instant, before his grave eyes lifted back to the shadow-mantled terminal. "But we still have work to do. There's our beacon, dead."

"A roosting place for the snakes."

He frowned at the lifeless ants piled around the white stone. "Our replicators, also dead."

"They stopped when you died."

"Then they ought to start again."

Hesitantly, trembling, she picked up a small still machine and held it before him. He thrust a red forefinger toward its silver head. Though no spark passed, the bright device came alive, stirred in her hands, rose to wheel around Nick's head.

I heard a high mosquito whine, which spread all around me. The dead ants below the stone began rising off the

195

ground, by twos and threes, by scores, by hundreds. They flew to join a circling swarm, which settled toward the end of the stone. I smelled hot sulfur.

"Ai-yi-yi!" Tom cowered back. "All this is too much."

"It's okay, Mr. Hood," Kyrie called to him. "The replicators are no space invaders. They are ours."

The spinning swarm poured down toward the stone. Though I saw no gesture of command, the ants began joining together, limbs interweaving, silver heads joining to form honeycomb panels which flexed and fused into a hollow ten-foot globe, a black gangway rising to its open door.

"Perhaps we weren't born for nothing." Almost gaily, Nick waved Tom and Kyrie toward the ramp. "Let's get the nexode back to the terminal. If the snakes don't object too much, I think we can light the beacon after all."

"Nicky! Nicky!" Kyrie whispered. "If we can!"

She skipped up the ramp with the tetrahedron, but Tom hung back, scowling at its surface of slick black tail balls if he expected them to sting him.

"Will the ants do anything you want?" He squinted shrewdly at Nick, loud and bold again, almost himself. "Could you make them find me a pack of narcorettes?"

"Come along," Nick said. "I want to pick up Uncle Kim."

"My yekl brother?" Tom shrugged. "Why waste time on that poor shmuck? Better leave him where he is. He's no utopian. He'll never be happy in our new world."

Stung with anger, I stood up to challenge Tom. Kyrie was calling from inside the bright globe, I think defending me. Nick took Tom's fat arm, swung him firmly toward the black ramp. None of them saw me. I tried to shout, but something caught my voice.

Something made me giddy. Something brushed me with icy sweat. Something left me drained and swaying. I sank back behind the shelving rock, sick with a puzzled rage at myself.

Though I never knew exactly what had seized me, there was the blackness inside the hollow globe. There was the piercing stridor of the ants that formed it, and their steamy, acrid reek. There was Tom's cautious shrewdness as he tested the black ramp, and his bold swagger when he climbed it.

Then there was Nick, red with alien blood, newborn from Guy's hide, gazing impatiently across the heaving tide of fog toward the bank of far cloud and the snake-veiled stages of the tachyon terminal. Though I had known the children all their lives, Nick was a frightening stranger now.

Sobbing miserably, bewildered at myself, I began to feel a barb of piercing truth in Tom's scornful words. I had known and loved the children as fascinating visitors to my own familiar world, but this was theirs. I felt a sudden sick conviction that it was not for me.

My world had been the narrow ghetto flat where the heat was often off and cockroaches swarmed under the sink and the toilet overflowed. It had been the petty bickering of my parents, my father's ugly business and my mother's ugly death. It had been Tom's scheming climb and my own half-honest career in promotion and publicity. I was what that gray and painful world had made me —a schlemiel, perhaps, as my father used to say. Looking at myself in this cold light, I could see no useful place for me in the new world beyond the fog, in that dazzling future the children were about to usher through the tachyon terminal.

I lay silent, in the grip of a sick paralysis, as Nick followed Tom into the silver globe. The ramp rolled up to seal the dark opening. Sweating and trembling, uncertain what I wanted or what to do, I watched the bright ball sail up the canyon toward the cave. It dropped beyond the cliffs. Nick or Kyrie must have left it to search the cave for me. A few minutes later it rose again, a diminishing moon, gliding high above the fog toward that far tower.

Calmer after it was gone, I began to feel a remote sense of hope and joy. Whatever became of me, Nick and Kyrie were moving toward their cosmic triumph. After sixty million years on the barren moon, the black seed from the messenger missile was about to bear its destined fruit.

Impelled by an aimless curiosity, I climbed to that reddened altar stone. Its top was circular and flat, twenty feet across. White and dense, slick and oddly warm to touch, it was hard enough to break the point of my pocketknife. Before I had solved its riddle, a new swarm of ants funneled down upon me.

Frightened and bewildered, I stumbled out of their way. They rattled on the stone like metal hail and began to knit themselves into a silver shell around it. The sun flickered and my tongue turned bitter. Their shrieking whine drilled into my brain. Staggering back, I watched them rising with the stone.

Its shape astonished me. No disk, it was a cone—the conic capstone, I believe, shaped to complete the onion dome of the tachyon beacon. Dropped by the ants when Nick was killed, it had fallen point down, penetrating to leave its base nearly level with the rock it shattered. Extracted, it left a yawning pit.

Blind to me, the ants soared away with it. Their shriek died, and their brimstone scent dissolved in the stagnant stink of the fog. The sun turned hot and bright again. I tossed a pebble into the pit and wandered back to the road.

I plodded up the canyon through a mist of gray regret, thinking wistfully of Guy's abandoned kingdom and the warm refuge from all the terrors of space I once had found there. My dull wonder about the fate of Billie Fran and Andy Elving and our green-gartered guards became a sudden decision. I would go back to Fairfax.

The short climb had left me already puffing for breath and looking for a place to sit. My impulsive purpose wavered a little when I realized my weakness and remembered the cruel ordeal Clayton Carter had endured in his epic retreat from the ants. Yet now, a fugitive from the terminal and the children's new world, I had nowhere else to go.

The journey might be easier for me, I promised myself, than Carter had found it. After the autumn rains, there should be water enough. With luck, I might find food plants maturing on abandoned farms and game or cattle that I could kill. By afternoon I was almost cheerful, whistling as I cleaned the deer rifle, sunned the blankets, filled the canteens from a spring I had found above the cave, repacked my slim provisions—already finding an emotional haven in the primitive simplicities of a roving hunter's existence.

As I lay that night on my hard bed, waiting to start at dawn, I felt a curious detachment from everything, almost as if my life had already closed. Looking back at myself, with no emotion save a dull desire that things had been different, I found myself weighing all my shabby failures. If I had really been a schlemiel, where was the blame?

My flaw had been a failure to love, it seemed to me, due to a failure to understand. It was, I thought, a family fault. If my mother had ever learned to laugh at my father's Yiddish jokes, if he had ever learned not to laugh at the ways of her Ozark kin, if Tom and I had really known each other—

At last I slept, with dreadful dreams in which the scarlet, skinless monsters of the fog were stalking me to take my hide. I woke before dawn, aching all over, soaked with sweat and shivering. Imagining that the gamma-life was teeming in my blood again, I lay staring drearily at the dark until I saw a blood-red glow on the back of the cave.

At first I thought it must be just another symptom of my space infection, distorting my senses and eroding my reason. I tried to lie still, but a panic terror began to whisper that some new doom had come to consume the world. I crawled out of my wet blankets to find the source of the glow.

The westward sky was turning strangely scarlet, above the black canyon rim, as if a dying sun were rising in the wrong direction. I staggered out in bare feet and went back to get my shoes. That red glare was bright enough to help me find them.

Shaking with cold and dread, I crept down the road to get a better view. The glow in the west grew brighter as I went. Slowly changing color, it had washed the stony cliffs with gold before I came in sight of the tachyon terminal.

A dazed comprehension stopped me there, my terror fading into awe. The light in the sky shone from the onion dome that topped the tallest tower—no doubt completed now with that conic altar stone on which Nick had been reborn. Half-relieved, yet still appalled before all the unknowns of the transgalactic universe, I knew that Nick and Kyrie already had the beacon going, calling across the light-years to their mysterious progenitors.

I stood there a long time, watching the beacon change. The shroud of snakes was gone. Dazzling in the crystal air, the tower looked near enough to touch. The tall cone bathed the barren landscape in an eerie green, which faded slowly through midnight blue into a dying violet dusk. I waited, shivering in the wind, until the red was born again.

The actual tachyon signal was invisible, of course, leaping across its own strange domain beyond the limited velocity of light. This visible signal must have been meant only to guide a decelerating starship through its final homing approach to the landing stage. Even as I thought of that, the changing splendor of the beacon brushed me with a vain regret.

I might have been part of all this. I might have called out to Nick and Kyrie, and followed them into their flying globe. I might have been with them in that wondrous tower now, waiting for their starborn creators. Instead—

Whimpering and miserable, I stumbled back to the cave. As I lay there, shivering through the rest of the night, staring at the changing glow on the smoke-stained rock, I nearly decided to wait, to watch for the tachyon ship to come in.

As the gray dawn came, a cold west wind drowned me in the fetid muskmelon sweetness of the fog, and suddenly I knew I couldn't stay. I had no way of knowing when that tachyon signal might reach the unknown builders of the messenger missiles, or whether it ever would. Even if the signal should bring a starship to earth, I had no way to guess the time a tachyon flight might take. I did know that the handful of dried beef and parched corn left in my pack would keep me going for only a very few days.

Sick with the breath of the fog, I struggled stiffly into my gear and began the long climb out of the valley, toward the snake-haunted summit and the abandoned lands beyond. The rainbow glow of the beacon was still washing the cliffs above me with colors of wonder when I set out, but the gray daylight soon erased it.

Here my recollections blur. Whether from starvation and exhaustion, or from that recurrent gamma-form infection, or from sheer death of hope, my awareness shattered into unconnected fragments. Sun, dust, rocks, frost, hail. Mountain wall and desert mirage. The blinding blaze of thirst, the crazy fever buzz in my head, the black laughter of despair. Days of slugging on when all I wanted was just to lie down. Nights of paralyzing cold in cheerless camps where I was afraid to make a fire because I thought the snakes might come.

Those cruel trials were real. They are tangled in my memory with stranger impressions, in which hard reality seems to blend into fantastic dreams. I recall one moonless night when I lay on flat high ground, with not even a rock or a bush to break the icy wind. I couldn't sleep. I was following the wheeling constellations, wondering dully what sort of creature might come from the stars to answer the tachyon signal, if anything did, when I thought I saw a new star in the east.

Or a planet, perhaps, for it didn't twinkle. Yet, cobalt blue, it was the wrong color for any planet, and it was soon too bright. Its color slowly changed, to an unbelievable green, to ocher and orange, to a redder red than Mars. It went out and winked back again, indigo blue.

Faster than any possible planet, it climbed toward the

zenith. In the green and yellow phases, its unearthly light tinted the dead landscape around me with a frosty, moon-like strangeness, so bright I trembled with an irrational terror that the snakes might see to discover me.

Sailing overhead, it swelled into a visible globe. I put down the mad urge to look for a hiding place and stood to watch it sinking toward the west. The cycle of its changing hues had begun accelerating, and now I began to notice a sort of echo that must have come from the tachyon beacon.

The terminal was below my horizon here, but I could see its remote glow against the sky, a red explosion as the red globe winked out, a race through the spectrum while the globe was dark, a blue dusk dying behind the black mountain ridge as the globe burned blue again. Always alternating, those cycles of light ran faster, faster, until the flicker hurt my eyes. Yet I watch until the globe had set like a flashing moon behind the far peaks and the night was abruptly black again.

I don't remember wondering what that luminous object could have been, or why the terminal had answered its flashes, or where it might have fallen. Rolled in my blanket again, I lay numbly waiting for the snakes. I must have slept, for I remember thinking they had found me. Turned to ribbons of raw red flesh, they stank with the suffocating foulness of the fog and sang to me in Kyrie's voice while they licked my skin away.

Again, in an endless nightmare that must have been at least partly real, I thought I saw the fog. Drenched and shivering from a thin fall rain, I had nerved myself to climb one last hill. In the valley beyond, instead of the firewood and shelter I longed for, I found a flood of heaving whiteness, invisibly stirred from beneath, reaching as far as I could see.

I slept under the road in a concrete pipe, sweating through dreadful dreams in which the fog had risen over me and its flayed creatures had trapped me in the pipe. I lay too weak to move or even breathe as they crept in to seize me. When I crawled out at dawn, that evil sea had somehow drained away, leaving wet red slime to mark the level it had reached. My real dreams are still haunted with the figments of the strange daymare that followed, in which I was struggling to cross that fearful valley where the fog had lain.

Sick with its lingering muskmelon fetor, I slipped and toppled and crept through the blood-colored muck. I saw animal bones coated with it. Once I heard a dreadful mewing sound, and saw a quivering strip of naked redness trying to hide itself in a reddened human skull.

At the bottom of the valley, the highway bridge was missing. I was trying to cross the rocky gorge, splashing and staggering through a shallow river of that clotted slime, when I heard the shrilling of the ants and caught their sulfuric scent and saw a silver-colored ball dropping toward me.

With my red-splashed hat, I tried to wave it away. When it came on, I raised the deer rifle and fired. The only result was a flicker of darkness and a bitter tang on my tongue. The globe dropped to the brink of that red river. A long strip of honeycombed ants folded down to make a black-lined gangway.

Kyrie stepped out upon it. Dream or not, I wasn't certain. Her nude beauty clashed against the horror of that red-walled valley in a way that dazed me. The daylight washed her marble flesh with swift pink and gold, as if she had been a stone Venus touched with instant life. Not quite sane, I brought the rifle up.

"Get away!" I gasped. "I can't endure anything else."

"Uncle Kim!" Pain choked her gentle voice. "Don't you know who I am?"

"You're a space alien." I listened to my own hoarse rasping with a dull astonishment, as if some insane stranger had been speaking. "Like the snakes. Like the things that make the fog. Like the gamma-forms in my blood. Like whatever creatures the beacon will bring from the stars—"

"But the ambassadors are already here, Uncle Kim." Her fast voice and her anxious dark-eyed smile tried hard to comfort me. "They arrived on the tachyon ship, but you don't need to fear them. They've come to bring the transgalactic culture. To help everybody. I think you need help—"

"No!" The rifle rose, almost in spite of me. "I've had enough from space—"

"The snakes are gone." She glanced into the sky. "They never liked it here. Our air has too much water and oxygen for them. They prefer to meet our visitors out in space, in the vicinity of Jupiter, where they feel more at home."

"But there's the fog." I waved the rifle at the red-slimed cliffs above us and the blood-colored river lapping at my knees. "The things from space that make the fog—"

"We asked for them." Distractingly, she tossed back her flowing hair. "When we invaded Venus. You remember the color changes our manned probes observed? They were caused by blights that spread from the garbage we dumped—spread somewhat faster than the gamma infections ever spread on earth. Those blights killed half the aerobic life in the upper air of Venus. Down in the temperate middle levels, the more intelligent flying things found their food supplies depleted. They struck back in self-defense. The fog covers a military expedition, composed of special mutant creatures bred to survive in our biocosm, sent to stop us from polluting their planet. It was a force from Venus, by the way, that trapped our men on Mercury."

"If we—" The simple truth staggered me. "If we had only understood!"

"That's why the snakes were here." Her urgent bell-clear voice came faster, faster, in a way that made me think of Nick. "They're well meaning and more or less intelligent—though I don't think they ever knew what they were doing to our aircraft. They were trying to communicate. The breakthrough came when they were able to explain the situation to our transgalactic friends. You should have seen the happy way they dived around the terminal when the Venusians began pulling back the fog."

"Why bother about the fog?" Bitterness croaked in my throat. "When the human race is dead! Why not just invite our space friends to take the planet over?"

"Uncle Kim!" She made a face at me. "Things aren't that bad. The Venusians were pretty humane, by our old military standards. They concentrated their forces around our space centers, at Skygate and the Sino-Soviet installations in the Gobi. There was no mass slaughter. Though the snakes did stop air travel, and the fog drove men off the sea, we've found most of the human race alive and well, on dry land."

I stared down at my red-caked hands, and blankly back at her.

"So the world didn't end." Her rapid voice had slowed, and she had time for a quizzical smile. "If you can stand the shock! Our big job's done, and we've got a short vacation. The ambassadors are off to call on our neighbor planets. Your enterprising brother has invited my poor mother to try the new snow on the Sandia slopes. Nick is on his way to visit old friends back at Fairfax—enough of Guy is left in him so that he had to see those women again.

"Won't Billie Fran be surprised!"

With a flash of laughter, she shrugged. That careless gesture may have hidden more feeling that she showed, but the liquid flow of her whole golden body nearly stopped my heart.

"And I came out to look for you again, though everybody else had given you up." Halfway down the black gangway, she paused to study me. "About time, too. If you could see yourself—a perfect scarecrow!"

She laughed at me. Wading to meet her, I stopped again, stung by her look of sheer delight.

"Kim!" Concern erased her laughter. "What's wrong with you?"

"I'm just a man, for one thing." My own sardonic voice surprised me. "I'm afraid I don't belong on your bright new superhuman world." I saw her hurt protest, and raised my gritty voice. "For another thing, I believe my old gamma-form infection has come back."

"Our new health service will soon cure that." She left the ramp, and her golden cat-feet picked their way across the slick red rocks to the brink of the blood-colored stream. Pausing there, golden hands on golden hips, she surveyed me with enigmatic eyes.

"There's a quicker treatment." Her warm amusement was mixed with something else I was almost afraid to understand. "You know our bodies can make what Nick calls antibanes to save us from every sort of infection. There's a way I can share them with you—though your doctor might frown at the therapy."

Waiting to discover what she meant, I stood admiring her tawny loveliness. I felt my pulses throbbing, and wondered vaguely if her unearthly power had already begun to lift me out of my long exhaustion. Fond recollections were dancing in my brain like champagne bubbles—images of Kyrie's infant grave-eyed elfin charm, of her tiny hand trustingly in mine, of her secret delight in her own peculiar music, of her strange games with little Nick, of that magical moment when the touch of the nexode made her a woman. As she turned a little now, the sunlight gilded her breasts and thighs anew, and I was shaken with a spasm of unexpected lust. Dismayed, suddenly conscious of my own bold stare, I tried to turn away.

"You needn't feel so damned incestuous!" Her ringing laugh mocked my confusion. "After all, you aren't my actual uncle." Her eyes turned grave and almost sad. "You see, Kim, the nexode showed me long ago how you felt about me. I think I've always understood you better than you understand yourself—and loved you more than you dare love anybody. That's why I've come to find you."

Her impish look faded into a cool directness that took my breath.

"That's the reason for my only reservation now. I don't want to hurt you more than you've been hurt. Whatever—" She paused as if to weigh me. "Whatever we do, I hope you won't let it matter too much."

I waited, in a sort of tingling daze.

"First of all, there's something I must tell you." Her voice fell soberly. "Nick and I will be leaving on the tachyon ship. We're to represent our whole group of planets. I don't know when we'll be back."

Her face reflected my jarring pain.

"I'm sorry, Kim. I don't like leaving you, my mother, or Uncle Yuri and Aunt Carolina. But it's part of the job we were born to do, and we're both excited about it. It's another big mission, helping all our worlds adjust to the culture of the stars."

I nodded bleakly, as that sank in.

"I thought you ought to know," she said. "Because no other creature can follow until certain problems of health and law have been cleared up. We'll have to leave you here."

She came splashing toward me through the clotted mud. I dropped the rifle and mutely turned to show her the foul drying slime that covered me. As if it had not existed, she opened her golden arms. She kissed me—Kyrie kissed me.

I followed her out of the mud. The shrilling of the ants was suddenly a joyous nuptial song. They carried us to an ice-rimmed mountain lake, high in the pines, unsoiled by the fog. She made me discard my mud-caked rags, and we bathed there. The snow-cold water should have numbed me to the bone, but somehow she was sharing her more-than-human talents. The water was just invigorating. Afterwards—

That day and night are special in my memory, too precious for any bare description. Drunk with the wine of her lilaclike scent, wedded to all her golden wonder, for that tiny time I was more than merely mortal. She let me forget that I had ever been a schlemiel.

Kyrie! Giving me that taste of superhuman joy, how could she have asked me not to let it matter? Her last long kiss left a desolate ache in my heart. Blind with tears, all I saw was a blur of blue when she opened the door of the globe.

"The starship is loading on the top stage now." Her

voice was hurried and uneven, as if she felt my own regret. "The air up there is too thin for you. I'll have to leave you here." Her cool arms caught me in a last quick embrace. "Don't forget me, Kim."

As if I could ever forget!

Blinking out into that blank blueness, I saw that the globe had brought me down to the middle of a vast white plain with only blue fog around it. A chill wind bit my shrinking nakedness. A forlorn desolation seized me, when I turned back for a final glimpse of Kyrie.

"You'll be okay, Kim." Her voice had an edge I needed. "After all, you're a big boy now. I know you're well—and strong enough!"

I heard the love beneath her impish malice and suddenly it struck me as a monstrous fault that I had never properly told her how I loved her. I tried to speak, but my throat hurt and anyhow I knew she understood all I felt. I gulped and waved and stumbled down the gangway.

The blue glow had died, and now the cloudy dawn revealed the far loom of the central tower, lifting forever that higher stage where the air was too rare for me. In a moment the beacon was burning through the gray clouds again, a glow of rose, a shower of gold, a floodlight flowing over all the unearthly magnificence around me. I saw Yuri Marko and Carolina riding up a ramp to meet me, undismayed at being left behind, waving and grinning greenly as the beacon changed. With a certain reluctant eagerness, I stepped down into the future I had fled.

9-73